yesterday's news

Book Three of the Woodvale Series

KATIE CAWOOD

Author's Note

Dear reader,

Yesterday's News is the third book in a series of interconnected standalones. While you don't have to read the first two books to follow along, I hope you at least go back to them! It'll help you better understand the dynamics of the couples in the friend group that's beginning to form at this point in the series.

Please be aware that grief is a large theme throughout this book. While it's been a few years since Meghan has experienced loss, those grieving moments can sometimes come out of nowhere. And they cut like a knife.

You should also keep in mind that this is an open door romance, meaning there will be multiple sexually explicit scenes. (It's a slow burn, but they'll get there, I promise!) Other content to be aware of includes body-shaming, a character experiencing homelessness, a brief mention of a violent death that occurred decades ago, and a casual conversation/dark humor about death by fire.

For a full list of potential triggers, please visit **www.authorkatiecawood.com/contentwarnings**.

Much love,
Katie

chapter one

meghan

"They should've bulldozed this monstrosity when they had the chance."

I wanted to tell my colleague and fellow reporter, Xander, he was exaggerating, but as we made our way up the crumbling steps of the once-abandoned Clark Elementary School, I knew he was right. Adjusting the box of office supplies on my hip, I reached for the railing to steady myself. "At least they painted over the graffiti."

"I enjoyed that, actually." Holding a heavy printer against his chest, Xander propped the front door to the school open for me with his foot. We were in the middle of moving all of our supplies, furniture, and every last scrap of paper from our old offices at the dedicated Woodvale Times building to the second floor of this old, dilapidated school. Our new home.

"I think the 'fuck Enzo' on the side of the gymnasium was my favorite," Xander continued. "It raised so many questions. Like, who's Enzo? And what did he do to earn such a declaration?"

"Maybe someone was just giving us a little snippet of their to-do list," I suggested as we made our way down the pea-green painted hallway. "Like, 'What was I supposed to do on Thursday? Oh, right, *fuck Enzo*.'"

This joke didn't quite land with Xander, who just shook his head as his eyes scanned the dusty old trophy case. "I'm surprised they're not sticking us down in the old art room in the basement. It's like a windowless prison, and, if my memory serves me correctly, it smells like a sweaty ballsack."

I didn't know how to respond to that, so I didn't. Adjusting the box in my arms, I turned around to face the open door to my right. You'd never guess this was an ancient school from the looks of the former library now. The room had been completely gutted and remodeled to accommodate WWTV and all their equipment. It looked just like an ordinary newsroom, with a curved anchor desk as its focal point. That was where my best friend, Jillian Taylor, sat every day to deliver Woodvale's most exciting news, like the return of a missing cat, or highlights from the annual corn-shucking contest. And she was sitting there now, sipping a coffee while listening to her producer rattle on about something.

She spotted me at the same time, lifting her hand in a casual wave. I lifted my fingers from the box to awkwardly wave back. The only positive thing about the media merger we were in the middle of was that I'd get to see my best friend at work all the time.

And the worst part?

I'd have to encounter my ex on a daily basis.

"Explain to me how someone like you ever slept with a nerd like that," Xander muttered behind me. We were both looking at Chase Monroe, who was untangling some cords off to the side of Jillian's new desk. He was a TV news reporter, too, although his approach was a little more unconventional. As a field reporter, he preferred working alone, setting up his own stationary camera to report breaking news or human-interest stories. We ran into each other at events a few times a month, and that was already enough for me.

Chase lifted his head and glanced toward us peering at him through the newsroom doors. He adjusted his glasses and, like Jillian, gave us a polite wave before turning around and getting back to untangling the extension cord. His brown hair was unruly, like always, and he was wearing his usual uniform of a gray T-shirt and jeans. He only threw on a navy blazer when he was on camera.

Xander and I turned to make our way up the steps. "Surprised he's not roaming these halls with his little buddy looking for g-g-g-ghooosts," Xander mocked.

I rolled my eyes. Chase and his best friend were ghost hunters with a YouTube channel, and they had grandiose plans of becoming big-name influencers in the paranormal community. "You don't always have to make fun of people, Xander."

"Oh, but I do," he said as we curved around the landing to go up the next set of stairs. "And your ex makes it too easy."

If it weren't for Xander's incessant need to insult people at every given opportunity, he might have fewer enemies in this town. I was probably one of the few people in the community who could tolerate him, but only because I enjoyed commiserating with him sometimes.

In some ways, he was like my twin. We both had pale skin and jet-black hair—though my hair tended to verge more toward a deep brown hue if left to its natural state—and our choice in all-black attire was strikingly similar. We tried going out the previous summer, but we quickly discovered being too alike had its downsides. The chemistry was so lacking we both decided to never speak of it again.

Xander and I made our way to our new workspace, a classroom on the second floor. Unlike the WWTV space downstairs, our area still resembled the interior of a school. There was still a chalkboard along the wall and an old pencil sharpener by the door. Only instead of school desks, there were cubicles. When we walked in, our editor, Graham, was already seated at the head of the small conference table at the front of the room. He looked up from his iPad and raised his eyebrows at Xander, who dropped the heavy printer down onto the shelf along the wall with a loud thud.

"Where the hell have you two been?" Graham asked, tugging on the collar of his brown suede blazer. "And don't say you stopped for coffee, because despite your incessant complaining, the coffee I make here is perfectly adequate."

"Graham," I said, putting the box of office supplies down on the table beside him. "We had to stop and give the old building a tearful good-bye. It was only right. Sorry it took us so long, Xander got especially choked up."

Xander shook his head, but he didn't call me out on my lies. "The difference between the coffee we drink and the coffee you make, Graham, is that I've never once taken a sip of a cold brew from Riverside and thought to myself, 'Hmm, that was *perfectly adequate.*'"

Graham was known for making the weakest coffee on the planet. Some of the other staff members tolerated it, but Xander and I never touched the stuff. "Fine," Graham said with a dramatic swipe up on his iPad. "Go ahead and get your fancy six-dollar drinks. I know how much both of you earn. I would accept the free coffee if I were you."

I made a face at Graham before glancing over at Devonte, who was taping pictures of his family on his cubicle walls. Devonte was our part-time sportswriter who spent half of his time collecting and reselling rare sports memorabilia. He only kept this job for the insurance—a fact he wasn't shy about admitting aloud.

I couldn't see Byron in the cubicle beside Devonte's, but I heard his cough echoing throughout the room. We were all sort of waiting for Byron to retire, but deep down we knew writing baby announcements and classified ads were his entire reason for existing. That and the egg salad sandwiches he brought every day for lunch.

"Now that we're all here, let's have our meeting," Graham announced. Ignoring this, Xander headed toward the door to the hallway. Graham took notice. "Whenever you're ready, of course. Don't let my meeting interrupt your… whatever it is that you're about to do."

"Just gotta get my coffee from the car," Xander said, making his way out the door.

"Oh, grab mine!" I called out before wincing at Graham.

He let out a heavy sigh. "You two are the reason behind my premature grays. You know that, right? I'm only forty, but look at my sideburns." He motioned toward the salt-and-pepper hair above his ears, which I actually thought made him look distinguished—the same as the crow's feet in the corners of his eyes. Jillian once told me she'd love to roll Graham up into a ball and stick him deep in her pocket, but she said weird, horny stuff like that all the time, so I didn't think much of it. "If I had any sense, I'd fire you both."

"Would you?" I asked, putting a hand on my hip. "I could use some time off."

Graham didn't laugh. Ribbing him was one of the few things that made this job enjoyable—I loved teasing him until his jaw clenched and those crow's feet deepened just a little more. The truth was, if I didn't have Xander and Graham to spar with, I probably would've lost my mind a long time ago. I needed to focus on that, and not on the fact my ex-boyfriend was lurking somewhere just beneath my feet.

The thought made me shiver.

chapter two

meghan

After retrieving my planner from my cubicle, the one in the farthest corner of the room where I could tune everyone else out, I pulled up a chair to Graham's right at the conference table. With a sigh, I crossed my legs, yanking down on my black skirt to better cover my thighs as Byron and Devonte made their way to the table, too. I was the only woman on this newspaper staff, and I had been for two years. Xander, who left us to work for the *Chicago Tribune* for a while, came back to replace Jenna after she quit to teach journalism at the high school.

To this day, Xander had not explained why he moved back to Woodvale from Chicago. He said he resigned, but Graham and I suspected he may have been threatened after rubbing some politicians the wrong way up there. He was always pushing things to the limit, testing to see how much he could get away with.

Whatever it was that happened, he refused to talk about it.

"Question," Xander said as he re-entered the room. He placed my iced coffee in front of me before plopping down in the chair across the table. "Silas said the Woodvale Times, WWTV, and WRBO are equally important. That they're the three pillars holding up Woodvale News Network or whatever bullshit that douchebag was peddling the other day. Right?"

Silas Brown was our new CEO. The news conglomerate, now called the Woodvale News Network, included the newspaper, the TV station, and the radio station, all of which, until a few weeks ago, operated separately. When Silas took over WWTV, he bought us out and decided to shove us all into the same building.

Since the merger, words like "synergize" and "cohabitate" were constantly being hurled at us by a clueless man who barely understood how the news operated at all.

He wasn't even from Woodvale.

We were promised everything would improve and all these changes were for the better, but so far, it appeared Silas was only interested in cutting corners to make record profits.

"Yes, the three pillars," Graham said, nodding at Xander. He sang Silas's praises on a regular basis, but Xander and I could see right through him. He hated the guy as much as we did, and one of these days, we'd get him to stop brown-nosing and admit it. "I've heard all about the three pillars. What about them?"

"You don't think one of those pillars is a bit shinier than the other two?" Xander tilted his chair backward as he spoke. "Anyone can see he's prioritizing WWTV."

"It's not just Silas," I said, clicking my pen. "It's everyone. This entire town would rather get their news from them. No one's reading our shit anymore."

"Speak for yourselves," Byron said in his usual gentle tone. He folded his hands atop his trusty yellow legal pad of paper. "People buy three copies of the paper just for their baby announcements or family members' obits. So as long as people keep getting born or dying, we're going to sell papers."

He let out a soft chuckle, but his smile quickly faded once he caught the way Xander was glaring at him. Xander's reason for hating Byron? He was "too nice."

Graham was leaning back in his chair, just listening. The longer he remained quiet, the more it worried me. Something about the apprehensive look in his eyes made me think he was keeping something from us. Swirling the ice in my clear plastic cup, I asked, "Do you have something to share with us, Graham?"

He scratched his eyebrow, staring down at the table in front of him. "You guys aren't wrong. Nobody's reading your articles. And Silas knows it."

Devonte finally spoke up. "What's that mean?"

Graham sighed. "I'm just going to put it bluntly: All our jobs are on the chopping block. There's nothing we can do that the news team at WWTV can't, and-"

"Bullshit," I blurted. "Jillian can deliver the news like nobody's business, but that woman couldn't spell to save her life. You should see her texts."

"With the help of AI tools, they're set. The truth is, they don't need us. Physical paper sales are almost non-existent, and even our online subscriptions are down. And because of the way they've set up the site—where people can view the video segments for free, but they have to pay to read our articles— we're all going to have to step up our game."

"How?" Xander asked. "How do we do that, Graham? Do you want us to put out clickbait-y headlines? Because I'm not doing that."

I shook my head in disgust. "Wouldn't the solution be to stop putting our articles behind a paywall?"

"Or put their videos behind the paywall, too." Xander rolled his eyes.

Graham sighed. "Look, I want you guys to take this seriously, alright?" He cleared his throat. "I cannot stress this enough—we need people clicking on those articles and subscribing. We have to prove to Silas he needs us. Otherwise?" He slid his pointer finger across his neck in a slicing motion. "It's not looking good."

"Exactly how are we supposed to get people to subscribe?" I shook my head. "Nothing happens in this town."

"We need controversy," Graham answered. "Controversy sells papers."

I looked across the table at Xander. Controversy was his middle name. "Got any more school board members you can throw under the bus?" Xander smirked, but the way he lifted his eyebrows and tilted his head to the side clued me in that he probably *did* have something on one of them.

"Here's an idea," Graham said, rubbing his chin, "what about that Owen Gardner guy?"

Xander and I turned to him in unison. "The STEM podcast guy?" I'd interviewed our local celebrity a handful of times. He was married to the principal of Grissom Elementary, and they'd sort of become Woodvale's power couple. "What about him?"

Graham narrowed his eyes. "How does a guy go from being a schoolteacher to running a seven-figure company in just two years? Who did he step on to get there? And has anyone combed through his past tweets to see if he ever-"

"I'm going to stop you right there," Xander said, leaning forward. "Anyone who publishes a single negative word about Owen Gardner will have to answer to me. You couldn't find a more honest guy with a cleaner history. Move on."

He didn't break eye contact with Graham, who let out a slow exhale. I raised my brows, taking a sip of my coffee. "Wow, Xander," I said. "Is this you actually caring about someone?"

Xander shifted his gaze to me. "I have a very short list."

"Is Owen above Abigail on that list?"

He chose to ignore me. Xander never liked being called out on the fact he had deep feelings for his best friend, Abigail. She worked as a librarian at the same school where Owen's wife was the principal. He swore their decades-long relationship was strictly platonic, but his eyes twinkled anytime he mentioned her name.

Turning back to Graham, Xander asked, "Should we expect to have jobs six months from now?"

"I wouldn't expect to have jobs *three* months from now if something doesn't change," Graham admitted.

Beside Xander, Devonte tapped his fingers on the table. "Damn, I hope the high school football team either has a good year or their coach finally gets fired for his little tantrums."

"Like I said," Graham said, scooting his chair back. "Controversy. You all need to go find it."

"Even me?" Byron asked, placing his hand upon his heart with wide, worried eyes.

Xander slowly turned to him and blinked a couple of times, like he couldn't believe the man had the audacity to ask something so stupid. But before he could say anything rude, Graham answered with a gentle, "Not you, Byron. Keep doing what you're doing."

The meeting adjourned, and we all made our way to our cubicles to put our things away. I was too busy finishing up an article about a citywide spring cleaning day to decorate my space. I only pulled one thing from the crate from my old cubicle—a framed photograph of my parents, which I propped up in the corner of my desk. It was a photo from their honeymoon, with them standing in front of Niagara Falls. Technically, I was in the picture, too. My mom's hand rested on her belly, and they both looked blissful.

It's how I liked to remember them—before a heart attack stole my dad from me when I was just ten. Before cancer took my mom sixteen years later, leaving me alone in a world that didn't feel the same without them.

I rubbed the cold obsidian pendant hanging from my neck as I flipped through my notes from my interview with the mayor, wishing I could vent to my mom about the possibility of losing this job. She'd probably tell me worrying about it wouldn't get me anywhere, and that everything happened for a reason. Until four years ago, my mom was a constant beacon of positivity in the midst of my gloom and doom. Now with her gone, there was no one to be that silver lining in the dark cloud above my head. I only had the memory of her.

The scanner we kept in the newsroom caught my attention, jolting me out of my daydream. There was a fire in the kitchen at The Noshery downtown. At first, I tried to ignore it, expecting Xander to head toward the door any second. But there was no sound of movement from his cubicle.

I knocked on the wall dividing us and hollered, "You going to get this one?"

"It's just a kitchen fire," he shouted back.

"Yeah, but-" I sighed, knowing this argument wasn't worth my time.

When I got out to my car on that chilly March morning, I couldn't help but notice Chase was loading up his video equipment in his own trunk. Great. We were probably headed to the same place. I just hoped I could stay far enough away from him that we wouldn't have to interact.

When I turned my key in the ignition, nothing happened other than a few clicking sounds. "Son of a bitch," I muttered. This happened a week ago, and a neighbor had to give my car a jump. I thought it had just been a fluke, but now I could see that wasn't the case.

I tried it a few more times, but still, the engine didn't turn. For a moment, I sat still, contemplating my next move. I could ask one of the guys upstairs to give me a jump, or I could just send Xander out to cover this story and deal with my car later.

Deciding on the latter, I flung my car door open and started to step out, only to realize I'd almost hit Chase, who was standing there with his hands on his hips. I tried to downplay how much he'd startled me, looking up at him with a scowl. "Can I help you?"

He moved closer, returning the scowl. "That's what I came over here to ask you. What's going on with your car?"

"I have no idea."

The only thing I knew was that he was blocking me from getting out, with one hand on the door and the other on the frame of the car above my head. Eyeing my dashboard, he asked, "Are you out of gas?"

"No, I'm not out of gas," I snapped. Did he think I was stupid? As I licked my lips to prepare my next retort, his muscular arm reached past me for the keys in the ignition. He gave it another turn, and again, nothing happened. I shook my head. "Do you think you can somehow turn the key better than I can?"

Still towering over me and blocking me in, he said, "Just wanted to listen to it. Your battery's dead."

"You think?"

Finally, his green eyes met mine. "Heading to the fire?"

"Yes." I swallowed, my mind briefly jumping to a memory of him leaning into my car just like this to kiss me goodbye. It had been over three years since we touched, but suddenly, the memory felt too recent. There was a subtle change in his expression—the inner corners of his brows shifted downward, and his lips slightly parted. Maybe being this close to me was flooding his mind with memories, too.

"Just ride with me," he said.

I clenched my jaw, trying to avert my eyes from his cleft chin—the very first thing I ever noticed about him when we met in college. That little indention on his chin was all I could stare at the day he worked up the courage to ask me to grab coffee after our Media Ethics class. "Absolutely not."

"Figured you'd say that," he said, finally tearing his eyes away. He took a step back. "I'll give you a jump."

"No, I'll get one of the guys upstairs to help me," I said, but he was already walking back to his car, running his hand through his hair the whole way.

I supposed there was no harm in letting him help me, other than feeling like I owed him one, or something. I popped the hood and settled back into the driver's seat, crossing my arms as he parked his car next to mine. He retrieved jumper cables from his trunk and got to work.

As he waited for the jumper cables to do their thing, he walked around to my side of the car with his hands in his pockets. "Did you leave your lights on or something?"

"No. This is the second time this has happened lately."

"Then you might want to get a new battery as soon as you can."

"We'll see."

Chase shook his head, rolling one of his feet over a rock on the asphalt. "That's right," he muttered, "you don't like being told what to do, and instead, you do the opposite of what you're told." He lifted his eyes back to my face. "Let me try this again: don't get it fixed. Let your battery die in the middle of the interstate so a semi plows into you and you die in a fiery crash."

"I wish a semi were plowing into me right now so I could be done with this conversation," I shot back, rolling my eyes. "I'm going to get the battery replaced, Chase."

I thought I caught a hint of a smile on Chase's lips when he looked up and said, "Oh good, reverse psychology still works on you."

"Oh good, you're still an asshole."

Now his grin wasn't so subtle. "An asshole who's jumping your battery for you."

"Only because you've got an unbearable hero complex."

"Oops, you pronounced 'thank you' wrong."

I opened the door a little wider, nearly hitting his legs with it. "Take your fucking jumper cables. I'll get Graham or Xander to do it. I don't need this."

He ignored me, maneuvering around the car door to lean across my lap and turn the key in the ignition again. This time, my engine roared to life. Turning his head toward me with the most infuriating smirk five inches from my face, he said, "Still waiting on that 'thank you', sweetheart."

I held my breath. "Don't call me sweetheart."

He just blinked. Waiting.

"Thank you," I muttered through gritted teeth.

He stepped back, walking back around to the front of my car to disconnect the cables. After slamming both hoods shut, he came toward the side of my car, shaking his head as he coiled up his cables. "I'm never helping you with anything ever again."

"I never asked." I reached for my door to close it, but he placed his hand at the top, preventing me from doing so. "Um, let go?"

"I checked your oil. It's pure sludge. Get that shit changed, too. Or don't. Whatever." And with that, he slammed my car door shut before walking away.

Staring him down in the side mirror, I fantasized about throwing the car in reverse to run him over. Repeatedly. It would make a good headline, at least.

chapter three

chase

The Banyon Manor had been high on the list of places Sean and I most wanted to explore since we started this whole ghost hunting thing. We'd been denied permission to enter it a total of three times, and even though I was perfectly comfortable trespassing at the abandoned mansion, Sean was too fearful of getting arrested.

For someone who spent all of his free time hunting ghosts, he was afraid of everything.

We'd given up hope, attempting to push it far from our minds. And then the goddamn Blakely Brothers descended upon the place, giving their eight million subscribers a complete tour. It made us livid, to know these out-of-state hacks came into our county and got access to the one place we'd been pursuing for years.

As it turned out, the property had switched ownership, which somehow flew under our radar. Once we got over the embarrassment of another YouTube channel beating us to the punch, I contacted the owner, who gave us permission to explore the house and its surrounding grounds for just two hours.

"It's an eerie feeling," I said at the center of the foyer, slowly turning the GoPro on myself, "stepping into the foyer of the Banyon Manor. Echoes of its tragic history almost seem to… reverberate through every creaking floorboard and shred of torn wallpaper. And here we stand, where-"

"What torn wallpaper?" Sean asked, tucking his thumbs beneath the straps of his backpack while eyeing the walls around us. "Everything looks pretty modern in here."

Sighing, I closed my eyes in annoyance. But then again, this was the kind of banter our subscribers liked. I knew it would make the final edit. So, I shook my head before attempting to speak again, describing the historical yet modernized room we stood in. Yet this time, I stumbled over my words.

"Don't call me sweetheart."

So far that night, I wasn't sensing any ghostly presence. The only thing haunting me was the sound of Meghan's voice from earlier that day. That and the way she smelled. It gave me a small sense of pleasure to know she was still using that goddamn Bath & Body Works spray she used to ask for every year for her birthday.

She probably had someone else to buy it for her, now.

Stepping up on the first stair, I turned the GoPro back on, with Sean breathing loudly just behind me. I opened my mouth to speculate about poor Ruth Banyon's last ascent up these very stairs, but the words never came. My mind went blank. And there was Meghan's face again, occupying every square inch of my brain until there was no room for anything else.

"Fuck," I muttered, clenching my eyes shut like that would somehow help.

"What? If it's about the wallpaper comment, I was just fuckin' around."

"It's not you. It's-" I leaned back against the curved wall beside the stairs. "I'm just not feeling it tonight."

"You're not feeling it," he repeated with a doubtful stare. "Tonight, at the Banyon fucking Manor? Bro. Do you know how hard it was to get away for the night? I'm putting in so many hours at the store, and between this and planning Comic Con, Erika's going to kill me. I'm not as flexible as I was before the baby, man."

Sean had an infant at home, which often threw a wrench in our plans. I sort of hated myself for the way I resented that baby. Dimitri was cute, I'd give him that—but Sean and I had less time to shoot now. And when we were together, Sean was usually exhausted and spent half the time talking about the kid's diaper blowouts and acid reflux.

Why did people have babies, anyway?

The Woodvale Comic Con was the other thing occupying most of Sean's time. I halfheartedly agreed to help him with it when he first came up with the idea a year ago, assuming it would resemble something like a small vendor fair in the high school gym, but the thing just kept getting bigger and bigger. Now that he'd somehow roped in a local science podcaster to help us build hype, we'd switched venues to a small convention center, and we still had to turn interested vendors away. We were in way over our heads.

For the past eight months, Sean had been relentlessly attempting to get Ethan Killian to make an appearance. He was a C-list celebrity, but a god among nerds like us because his show *Starlight* had such a devoted fandom, despite getting canceled after one season. Sean got in contact with Ethan's publicist somehow, and he'd been emailing the woman for months, simply trying to get yes or a no. I didn't have the heart to tell him he had a snowball's chance in hell of getting Ethan Killian to come to Woodvale, Indiana.

"What's with you today?" Sean asked, closing the pull-out screen on his camcorder. "Did you go on a Wikipedia spiral again? Is it Mothman? It's Mothman, isn't it."

"No," I said, wishing I hadn't spent an hour rambling to him about cryptids of North America a week ago. It was high time I learned to keep my hyperfixations to myself. "It's not Mothman."

"Then what-" Sean stopped himself short, smacking his lips. "Ah. The *Times* moved into your building today, and Meghan's got you all worked up."

I didn't want to talk about her, so I turned away from Sean, gazing up the stairs into the dark hallway above. "I'm not 'worked up.' Today's just an off day."

"Did you talk to her?"

I drew in a slow breath. "A little bit."

Though I wasn't looking at him, I could feel his eyes on me. Sean was around back in my Meghan days. In fact, he met us at the same time, the day his comic bookstore opened and I dragged Meghan there to see what it was all about. He was there through the break-up, even renting the studio apartment above the comic bookstore to me when I had nowhere else to go. He'd been using the space for storage.

And, as a matter of fact, he still was—but I'd gotten so used to the commercial shelves and spare comic book boxes, I wouldn't know what to do without them. The Venom cardboard cutout no longer made me nearly shit my pants in the middle of the night, either. I lovingly thought of him as my roommate and dressed him up for every holiday.

He was currently wearing Mardi Gras beads.

"Great," Sean continued. Ignoring him, I started to walk up the stairs, knowing I couldn't let my emotions squander what might be our only opportunity to explore this place. Sean followed, his footsteps heavier than mine. "Every time you see that woman, you get so fucked in the head for the next three to five business days." I opened my mouth to argue, but I knew he wasn't wrong. "Guess you're going to have to get used to seeing her, huh?"

I didn't know how I could.

Because I still got this lump in my throat every time I saw her. Despite my best efforts to play it cool when our faces were inches apart earlier that day, I was crumbling on the inside. I could tell she wanted me far, far away from her, but all I could think about was how much I missed being even closer.

"Hopefully we won't encounter each other much more than we already do when we're out on assignments. Just coming and going. It'll be fine." I cleared my throat, stepping up to the landing at the top of the stairs. The hairs on the back of my neck stood up the second my feet reached the hall floor.

Behind me, Sean fell silent, and we both turned on our cameras. He and I were pretty in sync when it came to sensing ghosts, and I knew he was feeling it, too.

I licked my lips and began to speak, my words coming back to me now. "We are definitely not alone here," I whispered, taking a few careful, backward steps down the hallway, where the floorboards creaked beneath my feet. "But the question is— is it Ruth Banyon's soul still lingering within the walls of this house? Or is it her violent husband, Willie, searching for his next victim? And might his next victim be… Sean?"

I turned my camera on Sean, whose eyes were as big as saucers as they darted back and forth. He took a couple of steps away from the stairs. "I'm not about to let some ghost push me down the stairs! No sir, not today."

Laughing, I started to forget all about my encounter with Meghan, remembering just how long I'd waited to be standing in this very spot. But just as I took a few steps toward what I assumed was the bedroom where the Banyons had their final argument, Sean's phone rang loudly behind me, startling us both.

I shut off the GoPro. "Damn it, Sean."

He winced, looking at his phone screen. "It's Erika."

With a sigh, I turned away to hide my annoyance. I had no grounds for irritation. With a baby at home, I should pretty much expect Sean to be an on-call father. And sure enough, that was exactly what this phone call was about. "A hundred and two?" I heard Sean say with a gasp. "What do we do? Did you give him Tylenol?"

And just like that, our Banyon Manor exploration came to an abrupt end, and it wasn't even my fault. Sean needed to get home to help Erika with Dimitri, who was running a fever. I didn't know anything about babies and fevers, so I just nodded my head and said, "We'll figure something out. No worries."

Sean quickly packed up and peeled out of the driveway, leaving me standing alone in front of the old house. I looked up at the balcony, dropping my eyes to the patio below, where Ruth Banyon met her demise. It didn't look like that far of a drop, but she must have hit her head just right on the stone.

All I could think about in that moment was how I'd told Meghan I hoped she got hit by a semi and died in a fiery crash, and how those words couldn't have been farther from the truth. Her malicious response made me smile, though. That eat-shit-and-die look she so loved to give me only made me want to provoke her even more.

I had a personal rule for my interactions with Meghan, though. I would never tease her unless she initiated it. I always started out civil and respectful when we encountered one another, allowing her to be the one to say something mean first. It usually didn't take very long, and once she started in, I gave myself a free pass to let her have it.

She was so hot when she was mean to me.

**

"Did it ever occur to you that all the people within a quarter mile radius don't want to listen to your white boy rap?"

That meanness was off to an early start the next morning outside of Woodvale Middle School, where Meghan and I coincidentally arrived at the same time. We were both there to cover a student's reading of an essay that won them a statewide contest. I joined her on the walkway and said, "You used to know 'Ch-Check It Out' by heart, so don't even pretend you hate my music." I had one specific memory of her rapping that song while curling her hair in the bathroom we used to share.

"Sorry, it got a little played out after three years of heavy rotation in your car," she said, flipping her hair over her shoulder before ringing the buzzer by the door. I kept my eyes fixed on the back of her head so I wouldn't be tempted to keep stealing glances at the back of her black skirt.

"Well," I said, "we can't *all* listen to sad girls who sing like they downed an entire bottle of cough syrup before recording."

"You just don't have the emotional capacity to understand the lyrics, and you know it."

"Maybe I could understand the lyrics if they'd fucking enunciate." I mumble-hummed along to the melody of the only Lana Del Rey song I could remember. "What even is that?"

Meghan twisted her body around and squinted at me, her gray-blue eyes as icy as her soul. "If she repeated 'intergalactic planetary' a billion times in a row, would that help you understand?" she snapped, sporting her infamous go-jump-off-a-bridge look. It made my heart beat a little faster.

"Depends. Will she open her mouth the whole way when she sings it?" I asked with a grin.

"You're so-"

We were interrupted by a buzz from the speaker in front of us, and an "Um… hello?" from the school receptionist. I had a feeling she'd heard most of our argument.

"Hi, Anna," Meghan said, suddenly unable to look at me. "It's Meghan from the Woodvale Times and Chase from WWTV. Here for Jordyn's speech."

"Oh, yes! Stop at the front office for your visitor passes." The door in front of us clicked, and I held it open for Meghan, noticing the pink tint in her cheeks. I could tell she wanted to kill me, but she held it together while we got our passes from the front office, even politely signing my name for me on the visitor log.

We were then ushered toward the center aisle of the auditorium, where I quickly set up my video camera on its tripod, and Meghan pulled out her Nikon camera. The newspaper let its photographers go a couple years ago, and Meghan had been doing a pretty decent job of filling their shoes, as far as I could tell. At the very least, I'd noticed she'd been getting better.

We stood shoulder-to-shoulder as twelve-year-old Jordyn Ellis took the stage, wowing the audience with their speech about the bullying they'd endured as a non-binary middle-schooler. They didn't appear to be reading from a paper, either—did this kid actually have their speech memorized? The auditorium around us was silent, save for a couple of knuckleheads in the very back, whose teacher couldn't get them to stop giggling. Sarah Gardner, the principal of Grissom Elementary, was sitting near us in the crowd. At first it didn't make sense that she was there, but Jordyn mentioned her by name as the first teacher who made them feel like they mattered. Meghan and I watched Sarah pull a tissue from her purse and dab her eyes.

"I can't imagine what it's like to be a non-binary kid in a town like this," Meghan whispered close to my ear so the mic wouldn't pick it up. It sent goosebumps down the right side of my body.

I swallowed. "No, I'm sure it hasn't been easy for them. Woodvale doesn't seem like a very progressive place to grow up."

"It's not," Meghan confirmed. She would know—she grew up in Woodvale, and I didn't. She never liked to talk about her youth much, but I knew she was bullied in high school for being a little on the weird side. If those assholes could only see her now.

Just as I opened my mouth to share that sentiment, Meghan seemed to come to the realization she'd accidentally been a little too nice to me and took an enormous side-step away, as though my closeness was causing her physical pain.

We didn't talk for the rest of the assembly, in which two other students read their runner-up speeches. It was clear to see why Jordyn's essay won the contest, because the other two nearly bored me to death.

Finally, the principal took to the stage to wrap everything up, and Meghan and I made our way to the nearby choir room where we were told we could interview Jordyn. With my camera bag draped over my shoulder, I opened the classroom door for Meghan, who nodded a thank you. For a second, our eyes met in the doorway, and then she took me by surprise when she said, "Hold on, Chase. C'mere." She yanked my arm back through the doorway until we were standing alone in the narrow hallway between the stage and the choir room. I waited, confused, as she dropped her own bag to the floor and reached up to adjust my collar. "Do you even look at yourself in the mirror before you leave in the morning? Jesus."

I was too stunned by her sudden touch to respond, too distracted by the tiniest hint of a smile on her lips as she ran her fingers down both sides of my collar to straighten it just right. I would have loved to have answered with some snappy comment, but she stole the breath from my lungs with this gesture.

"But I'm guessing you grabbed this blazer from your backseat five seconds before we walked in, didn't you?"

She still knew me a little too well. "Maybe," I answered, smiling from one side of my mouth.

As she slid her fingers around the back of my neck to lay my collar perfectly, I swallowed, wishing for the hundred-thousandth time I'd never let her go.

"Not exactly fresh… attire," Meghan said, her gaze meeting mine for a split second before she stooped to pick up her bag. The Beastie Boys reference nearly brought me to my knees, and she knew it, too, judging from the smirk tugging at the corners of her plum-tinted lips.

So. Goddamn. Mean.

chapter four

meghan

When I got to my car in the parking lot at the middle school, Chase lingered next to his, staring at me like he was waiting for something. What did he want from me, a fucking hug? I almost rolled down my window to ask him why he was watching me like a weirdo, but that was when I turned my key in the ignition—and nothing happened.

Oh.

That's what he was waiting on.

A moment later, he was pulling his car into the empty space facing mine. This time, I decided to be a little more grateful. I opened my car door to holler at him. "Thank you!"

"Yeah, you're welcome," he said, making his way over to my car. "I'm going to have to start charging you after this one." His boyish smile as he lifted my hood almost made me forget all the reasons I hated him. In fact, I could almost remember why I liked him in the first place. But then, I quickly remembered how much he hurt me, and the happy memories dissipated.

Yet he was coming to my rescue for the second day in a row, so I kept my mouth shut and let him do his thing. I even bit my tongue when he reminded me, again, that I needed to get a new battery and have my oil changed. "Your tires are looking a little bald, too. You're driving a death trap."

"Good."

Chase just shook his head as he coiled up his jumper cables, and I heard my phone buzz in the seat beside me.

Xander: Graham wants to know your ETA. About to have an impromptu meeting. He just got done talking to Silas and now he's pacing.

Meghan: omw

Xander: Grab me a coffee

Meghan: No

When I glanced up, Chase was looking at his own phone with a scowl. "Hmmm," he said. "Marco wants to 'chat.'" Marco was the head producer at WWTV—his supervisor.

"Weird. So does Graham."

Chase and I exchanged prolonged stares. Though we'd run into each other a handful of times since the Silas Brown takeover, we'd never had a conversation about him. I could only guess how Chase felt about the guy. "What's Silas fucking up now?"

And I was right. "I almost don't want to know. He's such a moron." It was a little bit of a relief to know that whatever it was affected WWTV, too. At least that meant the newspaper wasn't shutting down.

Chase tucked the jumper cables beneath one of his arms. "I guess there's one thing we can agree on."

I couldn't imagine Silas's presence affected Chase's day-to-day all that much. I knew from my conversations with Jillian the WWTV staff wasn't all that happy about having to relocate, but what difference did it make to Chase? He spent half his time driving around town and the other half slumped over his computer to edit his videos. Jillian said he didn't really socialize with the rest of the team much. He didn't need to.

"Why do *you* hate Silas?" My fingers hovered over the window button. "You guys are getting the star treatment."

"Silas Brown stands for everything I hate," he answered with a scowl, "and he's trying to get me to wear a suit."

I couldn't control the laughter that burst from my mouth. "I can't even picture that."

"If that asshat wants me to wear a suit, he can buy me a new wardrobe himself."

"Are you still sinking all your money into those little toys? What were they called… Pop-Its?"

Chase's eyes met mine, and I wondered if he could tell I was being obtuse on purpose. I knew exactly what those 'little toys' were called because they took up half our bedroom years ago. He kept them all in their boxes, organizing them first by fandom and then alphabetically—he had a whole system. I wasn't allowed to touch them. "Funko Pops," he muttered, his voice small and monotone. "I sold them all for some… ghost-hunting equipment for me and Sean."

He seemed so embarrassed to admit this to me, I almost felt bad for teasing him. I swallowed, trying to come up with a way to walk it back. "Oh. Smart." Clearing my throat, I buckled my seatbelt and said, "Well, we should probably head back to work to discover our fate."

"Yeah. Good luck." Just as I started to roll up my window, he turned toward me to say one more thing. "Get a new battery."

"Yeah, yeah."

**

Graham was pacing and scratching the bridge of his nose with his thumb when I arrived, which wasn't a good sign. We were all quiet as we took our seats at the conference table, and I exchanged a worried glance with Xander. Were we about to lose our jobs?

I didn't even wait for Byron to find his seat before breaking the silence. "What's going on, Graham? You're stressing us out."

"Ha, that's a nice change of pace," he said, standing behind his chair at the head of the table. This was news worth standing for, apparently—it was clear he wouldn't be sitting for this. "Now you guys know how it feels."

"I don't stress you out, do I?" Byron asked as he pulled out his chair, smiling because he already knew the answer.

"No, I was talking about these two a-holes," Graham answered, nodding from me to Xander. "They're the ones-"

"Enough with the small talk, get to the point," Xander urged. "Are they shutting us down?"

"No, we're not getting shut down," Graham said, gripping the back of the chair in front of him. "But you know what, guys? That's not out of the realm of possibility in the future. I'm going to be straight with you—all of our jobs are on the line. People aren't reading the paper anymore, and Silas and his board members know it. But don't worry, he's got a solution."

"Here we go," I mumbled.

"Let's hear it." Xander crossed his arms.

Graham took in a deep breath, and with an exhale, he said, "We're going to create hybrid content with WWTV. The newspaper, at least the online version, will no longer be a separate entity. You'll collaborate with their reporters for your stories. Your written content will match their reports, and vice versa."

I was too dumbfounded to speak, and from the looks of it, so was Xander. He normally had plenty to say, but we both stared up at Graham in stunned silence, waiting for him to reveal this was an early April Fools' joke.

But it wasn't.

"How the fuck does this work?" I asked

"Well," Graham said, clearing his throat, "you'll team up with your counterparts at WWTV to craft this integrated content. I understand it's a bit unconventional, but it's where journalism is heading. We all need to adapt if we want the Woodvale Times to thrive."

There was something suspiciously optimistic about his tone. I squinted at him. "And you're actually on board with this?"

"Well, yeah," Graham said, glancing down at the table as he scratched the back of his neck. "They've made me the Hybrid Content Director, so of course I'm on board with it."

I glanced across the table to assess Xander's reaction to this new tidbit of info. He was still quiet, his expression unchanged. I, on the other hand, couldn't keep my mouth shut. "You're one of them now."

"No, I'm still one of you."

"Bullshit."

"Meghan," Graham said with a sigh. "I'm still your editor."

"Did you get a raise with this promotion?" Xander asked, keeping his eyes locked on Graham's face.

It took Graham a moment to speak up, and his hesitation told us everything we needed to know. He was a corporate shill now, and his lips were permanently attached to Silas Brown's ass. Returning Xander's stare, he asked him, "Want me to lie to you, Xander?"

"I want you to tell me you advocated for us and shot this idea down," Xander said. I nodded in agreement.

"Okay, look." Graham looked over his shoulder into the hallway as though Silas Brown himself might be sneaking up on him. When he accepted the coast was clear, he turned back to us, loosening his tie. "I know it's bullshit. You think I don't know exactly how I sound right now? Like I'm selling out? I have no choice but to go along with it. It's this, or we're all thrown out on our butts. But you know what I said? I said, 'My guys might be a little reluctant to try this, but they'll make it work.' And that's exactly what we're going to do."

Was he considering me one of his "guys"? I wasn't sure whether to feel honored or disgusted. I was more appalled at the way he kept saying "we" as though any of these new policies applied to him.

"What if I refuse?" Xander asked.

"Then I have to fire you," Graham said, holding Xander's gaze. "I would have no choice. You're partnering with WWTV or you're outta here."

Across from me, Xander was completely still. I half-expected him to retort with some outrageous insult, but instead, he turned to me and declared, "I call Jillian."

"Um, I think the fuck not?" I laughed. "She's *my* friend, not yours."

"I'm not working with your goofy ex-boyfriend."

"You think I want to?"

"Actually," Graham interjected, wincing at me. "It's… already been decided for you. Meghan, I'm sorry."

"No." I already knew what he was about to say.

"Look, you guys already report the same content. As do Xander and Jillian. It only makes sense."

"No. Nope. Fuck this. Fuck all of this."

He let out a heavy sigh before pulling out his chair and finally taking a seat. "Do you want to know what other idea was tossed around in our meeting this morning? They suggested replacing you all with AI." Graham paused for a second, allowing that last point to sink in. I chewed my bottom lip, waiting for him to continue. "They're not fully convinced they need you guys, despite my best efforts to prove otherwise. This hybrid thing is the best possible outcome. I would advise you guys to just play along. Don't give them a single reason to shut down the Woodvale Times for good."

The mere thought of having to work alongside Chase— and not only that, but *collaborate* with him on my stories—made my blood boil. The compulsion to storm out of the newsroom and never look back was getting stronger by the second. Did I really need this job?

I pictured 14-year-old me, the girl who spoke in front of the entire auditorium full of people as the eighth-grade valedictorian, who said she dreamed of being a reporter for the Woodvale Times when she grew up. And here I was, doing just that. This was always the plan. First, I wanted to be the editor of the school paper, and I did that. Then, I wanted to major in journalism at IU. Did that, too. And I came right back to Woodvale to check off the last item on my dream career list.

This was all I ever wanted. To live and work in the town I grew up in, spending my days interviewing locals and telling their stories. The thing I loved most about it? Working independently. Making my own schedule. Doing exactly what the fuck I wanted.

And now that was being stripped from me.

For a while, I buried my head in my hands, half-listening to Xander and Graham argue about our new predicament. Xander seemed more annoyed about having to wake up earlier to keep up with Jillian's schedule than anything.

"Tell you what," Graham boomed, cutting Xander off. He removed his tie completely, dropping it on the table in front of him. "If the prospect of losing your jobs isn't high stakes enough for ya, let's raise them. How about a healthy competition?"

"Between us and WWTV?" I pulled my hands away from my face to raise an eyebrow at Graham. "We've already lost."

"No, between the two of you," he answered, nodding from me to Xander. "I can see all our metrics on the site, right down to the article that made someone decide to buy a subscription. Let's see which one of you—with your respective partners—can garner the most subscriptions in the next couple of months."

"What's our prize?" Xander asked, stealing the words from my mouth.

"The winner," Graham said, folding his hands, "gets to come with me to NYC, all expenses paid, to the ECJ conference this summer. Silas gifted me two tickets."

The East Coast Journalism Conference had been on my bucket list for years. Xander had attended himself a couple of times when he was working for the Tribune, and he often spoke dreamily about it; bragging about rubbing elbows with famous journalists and drinking cocktails in the same room as Anderson Cooper. I whined about wanting to go so much last summer, Graham half-jokingly banned me from mentioning it.

"Your old Tribune buddies will be there, won't they?" Graham rubbed the stubble on his chin as he stared down Xander, whose ever-present scowl slowly faded. Could he want this as badly as me?

Graham didn't wait for a response from either of us. Instead, he rose to his feet and made his way over to the chalkboard at the front of the room. He found a stubby piece of chalk and wrote our names on the board like this was still a school and we were his students.

"Wow," Xander muttered. "Flashbacks. Not the first time my name's been written on that board."

I was too busy processing all of this new information to respond to him. "When's our deadline, Graham?"

"Let's give it… six weeks?" Graham drew a vertical line between our names, extending it toward the bottom of the chalkboard. "Let's go until the eighth of May. I'll keep track of your subscriber numbers up here."

The concept of a healthy competition with Xander, I had to admit, already had my mind racing with feature ideas. Maybe this wasn't such a bad idea. And I'd do just about anything to get into that conference.

"Well, good luck," Graham said. "Get out there and create some viral content. Do some damn good writing. And quit fucking complaining, you big babies." And with that, he snatched his tie off the table and walked out.

chapter five

meghan

"Have they talked to you about this whole 'hybrid' thing?"

Jillian leaned against my cubicle wall that afternoon wearing a Poppy's Bar & Grill T-shirt and a pair of ripped jeans. Her hair was pulled into a messy half-bun, which was all she could manage with her blonde bob. Afternoon Jill was so casual—almost unrecognizable from the woman on the news.

Still a total knockout, though.

"Ugh," I said, sipping my second iced coffee of the day. "Don't remind me. I don't ever want to hear the word 'hybrid' again."

"I tried to twist Marco's arm into letting me and you partner up, but it's a no-go. Beyond his control, he said."

"We can thank Silas Brown for this," I said, spinning my desk chair toward her. "I want to send that man a glitter bomb."

Jillian shook her head. "Send him one from me, too. I'm not really sure how working with Xander is going to go down. Although he's been surprisingly professional in our email exchanges so far. Have you talked to Ghost Boy yet? Because he definitely looked like a ghost when they were giving us this news."

I sighed. "No. I'm trying to pretend like this isn't really happening."

"Good luck with that, sweetie." She giggled, stretching her arms high above her head with a yawn as she glanced up at the window. "God, this sunny weather makes me wish I were getting railed in a sundress right now."

Seconds later, Xander wheeled himself from his cubicle to mine on his desk chair, propping his elbows on his knees and his chin on his closed fists like he was part of this conversation. "What are we talking about over here?"

"Nothing that concerns you," Jillian said, placing both hands on the back of his chair and wheeling him right back to his own area. I covered my mouth, trying not to laugh. "Please," she scoffed once Xander was back at his own desk. "If I were to get railed by anyone in this building, it would be Graham. No contest. Just imagining his hands..." She stopped herself short and shivered with a grin, which almost made me want to vomit. She continued before I could make fake retching sounds. "Maybe Devonte. And I bet Byron could get it back in the day, too."

My eyes nearly bulged out of my head. "Fucking hell, Jill."

"I can still hear you. These cubicle walls are very thin," Xander shouted from the other side.

Jillian smiled, shaking her head, before mouthing the words, "Him, too."

I covered my ears. "Oh my god. Please get a vibrator so I don't have to listen to you talk about my coworkers that way."

"Girl, I just got a new one. It thrusts, too. Want me to send you the link?"

"No, I'm good," I said, speaking low so Xander wouldn't overhear. "Penetration doesn't always do it for me."

"Then you've gotta get you one of those rose toys."

"Way ahead of you there."

My mind wandered to Chase, who not only knew about my toys but had used them on me in the past. He never saw toys as competitors—he understood they were his teammates. He didn't let the fact I couldn't get off from penetration alone discourage him. He simply adjusted his approach, and between the toys, his fingers, and his tongue, he made it happen. Every single time.

My last few partners left a lot to be desired. I'd come to accept the fact I would only finish half the time, especially with someone new who didn't know how I operated. My most recent situationship, Nolan, could work magic with his hands, but he had more red flags than Daytona Beach after a shark sighting. The guy literally smacked his phone out of my hand when I picked it up to look at the time. That was the last time I went to his house—and the last time I had an orgasm with another person.

Jillian hung out in my cubicle while I packed up all of my stuff for the day, absentmindedly scrolling through her phone and blowing bubbles with her gum until Graham's head appeared around the corner. His mouth was open to tell me something, but no words came after the inhale once he saw Jillian. She was equally speechless, only a foot away from him. She swallowed hard, and though I couldn't be sure, it looked like she'd just accidentally swallowed her gum.

"I don't even want to know what you have to tell me, Graham," I said, tossing my empty coffee cup in the trash can.

He tore his eyes off Jillian to turn to me, shoving his hands in his pockets. "Well, there's a small protest gathering downtown about the new crystal shop opening. Some lady is out there screaming about devil-worshipping and-"

"I'm on it," Xander hollered from his cubicle. We heard his laptop slam shut, and a second later, he was flying past Graham, unwilling to give me a chance to have this story. But he quickly reappeared, taking a few backward steps to peer around the corner to look at Jillian. "Shit, I forgot. You comin' or what?"

"I'm not-" She stopped abruptly, glancing down at her casual clothes. "I'm not sure if this necessitates television reporting, does it? How is this supposed to work?"

Graham, who stood in the middle of them, slowly turned from Xander to Jillian, shifting uncomfortably on his feet. How was he going to handle this as the Hybrid Content Coordinator, or whatever the hell he was called now? He cleared his throat and said, "It's more about the web content, Jillian. Could you and your cameraman just, uh, put together a thirty-second clip? Maybe… do a voiceover?"

It was adorable how he didn't like telling Jillian what to do, because he sure as hell didn't mind bossing Xander and me around. Who was this guy?

Jillian licked her lips, "Okay, boss," she said, maintaining eye contact with him as she handed him her gum wrapper. He slowly accepted it, blinking as Jillian followed Xander out of the newsroom.

Graham lingered in my cubicle for a moment, staring at the floor as he rubbed the back of his neck. "Fuck, that was hot. I could really get used to her calling me 'boss.'"

I threw my bag over my shoulder and rolled my eyes, trying to push aside the memory of Jill shivering when she imagined Graham's hands on her. God, if he only knew.

**

The Bradford pear trees around the edge of the Woodvale Cemetery were in full bloom, making it rain white petals onto the pavement below. It appeared the city was still ignoring the local gardeners' club's request for the removal of the invasive trees. I knew that if I opened the Facebook app to the Concerned Citizens of Woodvale group right now, there would be a post with a hundred comments about these trees.

Those people would argue about anything.

Maybe that's why I preferred the company of the dead. In the quiet cemetery on the edge of town, with only my pen and notebook in my hand, I pushed aside every distraction, making my way down the winding footpath between the headstones. I stopped at my parents' grave first, like I always did, just placing my hand atop the headstone. My usual greeting.

Sometimes I had something to tell them. Other times, I had something to ask. But on that evening, like most evenings, I just gave them a quick hello before moving on.

I wasn't sure who I was there to visit yet, but I would know them when I saw them. Once a month, I came to the cemetery like this and made my way to the very back, where some of the earliest families of Woodvale were buried. An old wrought iron fence bordered this section of the graveyard, making it a popular spot for esthetic Halloween photoshoots.

I would know.

The gravestones there were crumbling and covered with moss, some of them toppled over completely. There were even a few headstones leaning against a dead, old tree. Not a single person was coming back here to place flowers on these graves while shedding a tear. The people buried here had been long gone for over a century, and if it weren't for me, they would've been forgotten, too.

Once a month, in the Sunday edition of the Woodvale Times, I wrote a column about one of the people buried there. I chose a grave—or, rather, the grave chose me–and I spent a few days diving into the historical archives at the library to uncover everything I could about the person. Oftentimes, I found little more than census records, which gave me creative freedom to invent a story. I frequently imagined lives for these people, describing what their day-to-day might have been like back in the early 1800s. I'd become pretty friendly with the historians at the public library, who shared so much about life in old Woodvale that, when I closed my eyes, I could almost see it.

Years ago, I put this all online in a blog I shared with Chase. On *Woodvale Whispers,* I gave our readers a snapshot of the person's life—a mix of factual info and my own hypotheses—and then he'd talk about the places they likely haunted. We'd go scope out the spots together, and sometimes he would claim to hear or see something. Interestingly, his "ghost sightings" always aligned with my narrative.

For three years, that was how I spent my weekends: Indulging in Chase's ghost obsession because I was fascinated by the history. I was just happy for an excuse to trespass in an old barn or tour the now-defunct theater downtown. Our blog granted us special access to a lot of places, and when it didn't, we helped ourselves anyway. I could recall saying, "*If we get caught, I'm telling them you dragged me here to kill me.*"

And he'd just go along with it.

But that was then, and this was now. Our blog was dead, and we were each doing our own thing now. I could do my writing and researching without his interference. And on that particular evening, I was drawn to a small, moss-covered grave near the fence. The headstone was difficult to read, the inscription faded from years of weathering and neglect. I knelt down, gently brushing away the moss and dirt, tracing the letters with my fingers until they formed a name: Fannie Decker. She died just a few weeks short of her thirtieth birthday, and it looked like she never married.

"Well, fuck," I muttered under my breath, opening my notebook. I was finding Fannie a bit too relatable. I noted the time period she lived in and likely places she may have spent her days. Where in Woodvale might she have resided? What did she do for fun? She didn't have a husband, but did she have any lovers at all? Who mourned her when she passed away?

I wrote about Fannie for maybe fifteen or twenty minutes, oblivious to the sun sinking behind the hill at the far end of the cemetery. When I finally looked up from my notebook, I was taken aback by the darkness enveloping me. The streetlamps had turned on since I'd arrived, illuminating two male figures walking down the pavement in my direction. One was tall and white, with a GoPro camera strapped around his neck, while the other guy, shorter with dark skin, carried some kind of electronic contraption.

Wonderful.

Chase spotted me long before his friend did. As Sean rambled, motioning with his hands, Chase stared straight ahead at me, a smirk forming on his lips. Sean stopped talking, following his gaze. And then he saw me, too. "Oh, great."

I straightened my posture. "Nice to see you again, too, Sean."

They stopped at the edge of the pavement, a few gravestones over. Chase stood with his hands on his hips and looked around at the old graves before his eyes settled on me again. "Performing a ritual?"

"Yeah, a ritual to banish unwanted company. Fuck, it didn't work."

Sean made a face, but my snarkiness only made Chase's smile grow. "Thought you might be out here trying to banish Silas Brown."

"Oh, I've got a voodoo doll of him."

"Stick an extra needle in there from me, will you?"

We locked eyes for a few seconds, both of us silently acknowledging our displeasure at our new partnership. Xander and Jillian were already off covering their first story together like the professionals they were, and here I was wishing I had a real voodoo doll of Chase. So I could rip its head off.

"You boys out here looking for poltergeists?"

"Something like that," Chase said.

"There's been some ghost sightings by the mausoleum up there," Sean interrupted. "Usually around this time in the evening. If you stay here any longer, you might see one yourself."

"Don't ghosts usually haunt the spot where they die? Not where they're buried?"

"Funny you should mention that," Chase said, clearing his throat. He put his hands in his pockets. "Back in the seventies, a young woman came here to–"

"Save it for your YouTube channel," I interrupted.

"Right. Sorry." As Chase glanced down at the ground, I felt a pang of guilt for cutting him off like that. It's just that once Chase got started on one of his spiels, it was difficult to get him to stop, and I didn't have all night. He exhaled and turned to Sean. "Hey," he said, lifting his GoPro strap from his neck and handing it to Sean. "Will you go get us set up? I'll catch up in a few."

"Yeah. Just don't take too long," Sean said, glancing over his shoulder as he started down the path toward the mausoleum.

Chase strolled toward me and squinted at the gravestone with his hands on his hips. "What the hell kind of name is Fannie?" he asked, lowering himself to the ground beside me. He didn't notice the way I slammed my notebook shut.

"It was actually a popular name around that time, and–"

"Probably not in England," he muttered.

"–you should know better than to disrespect the dead."

"How'd she die?"

I pulled the cap off the bottom of my pen with my teeth and snapped it back on. "I don't know yet."

Chase leaned back into a stretch, making his shirt rise on his abdomen. I tried to avert my eyes from the once-familiar hairs below his belly button as he said, "Probably offed herself because her parents named her Fannie."

"Do you need something, Chase? Why are you here right now?"

He paused for a moment, his eyes briefly catching mine before he glanced down at the ground. "What'd you say when they told you that you had to work with me?"

He didn't actually want the truth, so I watered it down for him. "I asked to work with Jill instead."

"Figured." He ran his fingers along the lichen growing on the side of Fannie's grave. "Guess we'll just have to endure it. Maybe it won't be so bad, considering we're always reporting on the same bullshit, anyway. Might as well share notes."

"You really think we can do this?"

"I'm not sure we have a choice."

I fiddled with my pen, twisting it around the spiral of my notebook. I'd have to hold back all of the insulting words on the tip of my tongue. I wasn't about to let myself be the unprofessional one in this situation—he'd have a lot to say about that. Instead, I said, "I'll start a shared calendar for us. Do you still have the same email?" He nodded in response. "I'll set that up, then. And we can keep all of our content and resources in a shared folder."

"Okay."

"We should probably touch base every Monday morning to sync up our plans for the week."

"Okay."

I was momentarily distracted by his attentiveness. His eyes were fixed on my face like he was hanging onto every word I said. "And I need us to be strategic about the stories we cover. I'm in this contest with Xander, and I don't want to fuck around."

"What contest?"

"To see who can get the most online newspaper subscriptions. Graham's tracking our analytics, and he's going to take the winner to the ECJ conference in New York."

Chase's eyes widened. "You've always wanted to go to that."

"Yeah, that's why I'm going to win this contest. We need some high-impact stories. Nothing clickbait-y. Just… articles people actually want to read."

"Need me to pay off a local arsonist?" He gave me a little half-smile as he adjusted his glasses, and something about that expression took me right back to the days he used to win me over with that exact smirk. That twinkle in his eyes used to make me *swoon*.

I shook my head, willing myself not to grin at his little joke. He might misunderstand it as flirtation, which was something I'd like to avoid. Sighing, I flipped open my notebook and glanced at what I'd written about Fannie, double-checking I'd correctly copied the details from her headstone so I could do some research. The breeze picked up, making it rain white petals around us again. I brushed a couple of them off my notebook before looking up at Chase, who was watching my left hand absentmindedly rub the pendant hanging from my neck. It was a nervous habit; something I didn't even notice I did until Jillian pointed it out a couple years ago.

"Do you think a hundred years from now," Chase started, folding his hands on his crossed legs, "someone will come here and sit beside your headstone, making up stories about your life?"

He'd spoken it so quietly, as though he feared the dead might overhear. The sudden shift in tone made my breath catch in my throat. "Oh, I don't know. I hope so."

The thought of nobody remembering me a hundred years from now made my heart ache. Would I fade into obscurity, or would I make a name for myself? Would anyone read my newspaper articles a century from now? I turned to Chase to express these thoughts aloud when Sean's voice cut through the quiet cemetery.

"Dude, are you coming, or what?" It wasn't until I saw the flashlight on Sean's phone that I realized it was completely dark outside now. "I swear I heard some moaning up by the mausoleum."

"Yeah, I'm comin'." Chase turned to me. "Uh… I'm covering the library's unveiling of their new STEAM room tomorrow at nine. You should probably join."

My mouth dropped open. "At the library?" I scoffed. "Why didn't I know about this?"

He shrugged with one shoulder. "I don't know. They called me up and asked me to be there, so…"

"What the hell? They know me there—why didn't I know about this?" I yelled. He melodramatically cowered as though my disappointment was aimed at him. "I volunteer in the archives department there all the time. Why didn't they ask me to cover it?"

"Because print media is dead," Chase said with a grunt as he stood up.

"Yes, Chase, our local librarians must believe print media is dead." I rolled my eyes. "That's the most ridiculous thing I've ever heard. They're the ones trying to preserve it."

"You're right," he said, brushing dirt off his jeans. "I guess they just don't like you."

"But they like you?" I couldn't help but laugh.

"I mean, I'm the one they called. So… yeah." He shrugged at me before glancing over at Sean, who looked like he was growing more impatient by the second. Chase started walking toward him, but he stuck his hands in his pockets and turned around to say, "See you, Wednesday."

"What? I thought you said it was tomorrow?"

"I was calling *you* Wednesday."

I blinked. "As in… Addams? Why?"

He didn't answer with words. Instead, he motioned toward me with one arm, looking me up and down before widening the gesture to include my surroundings. The headstones. The wrought iron fence. The dim streetlamp. "Gee, I don't know."

I rolled my eyes, further proving his point, as he walked off to join Sean on the pavement. Just before they disappeared over the hill, however, Chase peered over his shoulder for one last glance. And amazingly, I resisted the urge to flip him off.

chapter six

chase

Meghan was going to be late.

Unless she'd changed a lot in the past few years, this wasn't like her. It was eight minutes from the official unveiling of the STEAM room, a space dedicated to science, technology, engineering, arts, and math activities. A small crowd was already gathering in the youth department, where the library staff members had formed a half-circle around Owen Gardner and his business partner. They were the guys who created and funded the entire project.

With my equipment already set up and ready to go, I made my way over to the window facing the parking lot—and there was Meghan's car. Empty.

And I knew exactly where to find her.

The archives department was in the basement of the library. Along with old, official records and photos, it was where they kept the microfilm readers and bound volumes of the *Woodvale Times*. For the past few years, Meghan had been working on helping the librarians digitize old newspapers. For fun. If I had to guess, this was one of her favorite places to be, second only to the creepy graveyards she frequented.

And sure enough, there she was, standing at a mahogany table with one of the old volumes of bound newspapers spread open in front of her. Frowning, she ran a finger along one of the yellowed pages. Without looking up at me, she said, "She froze to death."

"Who?"

"Fannie. She was feeding her chickens during a blizzard, fell down in a snow drift, and died of hypothermia."

"Oh. Bummer."

Meghan glared at me from beneath her bangs. As she closed the worn leather book and added it to the stack at the edge of the table, the light from the green desk lamp caught the tears glistening in her eyes. "She lived alone," she said with the slightest quiver in her voice. She shook her head, sticking her pen inside the spiral coils of her notebook. "I can't stop thinking about how long she was lying there like that before someone found her."

Aw, jeez. Not this right now. Willing myself not to roll my eyes, I said, "I'm sure she led a very happy, fulfilling life before she froze to death. Anyway, let's–"

"She was twenty-nine."

"That was well past middle-aged back then. Look, our interview's upstairs in a couple of minutes. Wanna maybe push the morbs aside for a little bit?"

The corners of her brows pushed inward. "The morbs?"

"It's Victorian slang for being all melancholy and emo, basically." I stood in front of her with my hands on my hips, trying not to grin at the way she scowled. "And that fits you to a T, doesn't it, Wednesday?"

"Stop calling me that," she said, lifting her laptop bag from the chair beside her. Meghan's irritation only fueled my desire to double-down on the nickname. I made a mental note to change her name to Wednesday in my contacts on my phone as we made our way up the stairs together. That would help me remember to call her that as often as possible.

When we neared the top of the stairs, Meghan stopped dead in her tracks, whispered "shit," and began frantically arranging her bangs.

"What's the matter?"

She ignored me, pulling her phone from her bag to look at her face with the selfie camera. She was using my body to hide herself, I noticed. But from who? I looked over my shoulder to scan the room and spotted Owen close-by, deep in conversation with the library director.

Oh, for the love of…

I shook my head at her. "You know he's married, right?"

"Who?" she asked, pushing her eyelashes upward with her curved pointer finger.

"Don't play dumb. You're trying to look good for Owen Gardner."

"That's ridiculous." She dropped her phone back into her bag and watched him closely, her eyes shifting to the side. "Who's the guy with him?"

She was staring at Owen's business partner, whose long hair was pulled back into the most pretentious-looking man-bun. He looked like he was trying too hard to emulate Kurt Cobain. "He works for Owen. I don't remember his name. Want me to ask him for you?"

"I'll ask him myself, thankyouverymuch," she said, finally walking again. She didn't have to ask him his name, however, because Owen introduced him as Mason Reed, his "right-hand man" during his little spiel before opening the door to reveal the new room. They gave us a little tour of the space, showing us all the STEAM toys they'd funded or even built themselves. The focal point of the room was a large table with an interactive touch screen top, where Mason opened a digital sketch app and effortlessly drew Mickey Mouse. The librarians all giggled and complimented him, but none of them were as impressed as Meghan, who scooted right up beside him as she said, "Oh my gosh, you make it look so easy. How did you learn to draw like this?"

Mason, shooting a quick side-glance at Owen, shrugged. "Years of practice."

And Meghan's flirtation didn't stop there. As the guys continued showing off all the new STEM tools, she remained hyper-focused on Mason. Her forwardness may have gone undetected by everyone else, but I could see right through her. She never took her eyes off of him, and she smiled more in those ten minutes than I'd seen from her in years. Unlike the pseudo-smile she often plastered on her face to seem professional, this was genuine.

When she bit her bottom lip as Mason spoke about their launch of STEAM Saturdays for local middle schoolers, I'd had enough. I rolled my eyes as I touched her elbow, whispering, "I'm going to try to get a wide shot of just the two of them. Will you scoot back a little?"

And just like that, her smile faded, or rather, it jumped from her face to mine. Oh, how I enjoyed making her move out of my way. She listened, taking a few steps back, so I could capture a wider shot. I let the camera roll and stood to the side of it, listening to the library director outline all the STEAM programming they'd be able to offer now. And it was all thanks to Owen's company, *STEM for the Win.*

Owen stared down at his feet as the director bragged about him, nodding a polite thank you. Something I'd noticed about Owen Gardner in the handful of times I'd interviewed him over the years was that he was always quick to credit other people—all while downplaying his own success. He was still humble, despite having all that money and a huge following. Anyone else would've let it get to their head.

A few months ago, when Sean and I asked him to participate in the Comic Con, he stayed on the Zoom call with us for an hour, sharing a bunch of ideas for the event. He came up with the idea to record a live podcast during the convention, interviewing Sean and me about the science behind paranormal investigating. He'd been promoting the whole event a little on his own platform, too, which had to have been the reason for the boost in ticket sales.

With all of this in mind, I approached him after the presentation as the rest of the attendees broke into smaller groups to interact with all the new STEM toys. Meghan was seemingly distracted by Mason's artwork on the table, so I saw this as a good opportunity to ask Owen something that had been on my mind since the first time we spoke. "Hey, can I pick your brain for a second?"

Owen crossed his arms. "Sure, but you might not find much there."

I chuckled as I zipped my camera bag. "No, I think you've got exactly the information I need. See, Sean and I have been working on building a YouTube following for a couple of years now, and I feel like we could be growing so much faster. You started your channel after we did and yours has obviously exploded. How'd you do it? What advice do you have?"

He inhaled, absentmindedly looking ahead at Mason, who had pulled out his phone to show Meghan some more of his art. "I think luck has a lot to do with it," he said, turning to me. "And the fact that I had the podcast first. Sort of a built-in audience there."

"That grew really fast too, though, right? Why do you think that is?" I swallowed, realizing I was starting to sound a little desperate. "Is there a particular strategy that you think really contributed to your success?"

He thought for a minute. "Honestly, I saw the feedback I was getting, saw what people liked, and leaned into that. People like my self-deprecating humor, I guess. For you and Sean, I'd say it's the dynamic between the two of you, the way you're complete opposites. You're calm and collected, while Sean's—"

I couldn't help but interrupt. "Wait. You actually watch our stuff?"

"Yeah, sometimes," Owen said with a little laugh. "My wife and I have watched a lot of your videos. We liked the one where you guys took a boat out to that haunted pond and Sean dropped the paddle."

Trying not to smile like a dork, I cursed Sean under my breath. "I didn't think we'd ever make it out. I almost killed him for that."

"That's what I'm talking about. You're entertaining people with that kind of banter, so keep it up."

We were both distracted by a loud "aww!" coming from Meghan, who had scooted even closer to Mason to look at his phone. I stopped talking to Owen to listen in on their conversation. "That's your daughter?"

Meghan stared at Mason's face as he said, "Yeah, she begged me to draw her as a mermaid surrounded by jellyfish, and, well, she's my boss, so…" He glanced over at Owen, and I thought I caught his eyes widen slightly, like there was a silent exchange of words between them. At first, I took it to mean he was attracted to Meghan. Because, I mean, why wouldn't he be? But then, shoving his phone in his back pocket, he took a small step away from her and said, "I'm working on a canvas of her and my girlfriend right now with both of them as mermaids. I'm not sure which one of them's going to love it more."

There was a slight downturn in the corners of Meghan's lips, almost as imperceivable as Mason's look of desperation seconds ago. I thoroughly enjoyed it, though. The guy had to work in that he had a girlfriend because it was obvious to all four of us standing there that she was attempting to flirt with him.

Meghan noticed my grin as we walked out of the youth department moments later. "What are you so happy about?"

"Nothin'."

We descended the stairs to the main floor of the library, where the faint smell of old books was almost overpowered by the scent of the coffee from the cart by the circulation desk. I stopped by the cart on my way out to pour myself a little paper cup of coffee and creamer.

"Want some?"

Meghan made a face. "I have better coffee in my car."

"You're a coffee snob," I said, taking a careful sip of the hot beverage as I made my way to the door, opening it for her. This tiny, chivalrous gesture seemed to annoy her, and she took the heavy door from me with a sigh. "You're the one who waited for me," I pointed out. "Did you forget how to open a door?"

"No, I wanted to make sure I got the chance to tell you how amusing it was to watch you fanboy over Owen Gardner," she said as we made our way down the sidewalk toward our cars.

I almost choked. "Oh, really? It was just as entertaining to watch you throw yourself at his business partner. How's it feel to be rejected by a guy with a man-bun?"

"Excuse me?" She turned on her heel to look me in the eyes. "What are you even talking about?"

"C'mon. You were flirting with the guy as he inched farther and farther away from you. Hands-down the highlight of my day." I smirked at her over my coffee cup. "Maybe my whole week."

She rolled her eyes. I totally had her; she couldn't deny it, and we both knew it. "At least I'm putting myself out there. Haven't seen you date anyone new in a while."

"You don't know my life."

"Yeah? Are you seeing someone?" Meghan put one hand on her hip. We'd both come to a complete stop on the sidewalk between the stone building and the row of cars in the parking lot. This library was one of the oldest buildings in the county, with a half-wall made of stone and wrought iron enclosing a small courtyard between two wings of the building. It was honestly a little creepy—no wonder Meghan felt so at home here.

I adjusted my backpack and shot her a casual grin, deciding to turn her inquiry into a joke. "Wow. I'm flattered, but I'm sorry, I'm not interested."

"Oh, fuck all the way off," she muttered, turning back around.

"I was going to just fuck halfway off, so thanks for clar—"

"Sounds like you. Always doing things half-assed."

I laughed as I followed her down the sidewalk. "Oh really? Like what?"

Meghan came to such an abrupt stop, I nearly bumped into her, spilling some of my coffee between us on the pavement. Her eyes dropped from my face to my shirt. "Getting dressed, for starters. Could there be any more wrinkles on that shirt?"

I smirked. This was fun. "Gotta get the girlfriend first if I want to have neatly pressed clothes," I joked, rubbing my hand down the front of my cotton t-shirt which looked fine to me when I pulled it off the chair this morning–the spot where I kept all of my not-quite-clean, not-quite-dirty clothes.

She knew the misogynistic comment was a joke, but she dropped her mouth open anyway, pretending to be offended. "Wow. Is that what your Tinder bio says? No wonder you can't get a date."

Damn, she didn't miss a beat. "Something like that. 'You iron my clothes, I help you iron out your problems.'"

Meghan let out a cold laugh, her eyes locking onto mine. The sound pierced right through me, shifting the mood from playful to something else entirely. Even the air around us felt cooler as she mumbled, "Because you're sooo good at that."

I struggled to form a reply. It was easier to argue with her when we were just playing around, but when it started to get personal, that was usually when I took a step back. I never liked hashing out the problems we had in our relationship. It would only waste our time. I knew when to tuck my tail between my legs and retreat.

Thankfully, we were interrupted by the sound of a sniffly nose coming from a nearby bike rack. We both turned toward a blond preteen boy balancing on his bike, eating from a bag of Doritos and staring at us like we were primetime entertainment

"Um. Shouldn't you be in school right now?" Meghan asked.

With a bratty scowl, the kid said, "None of your business, lady."

Her mouth dropped open, but the kid's reply made me snicker. "Yeah," I said. "Mind your business, lady." The delinquent-looking kid in the black zip-up hoodie and I exchanged a nod, which made Meghan roll her eyes and stomp off toward her car.

"What's her problem?" the kid asked, his mouth full of chips.

I sighed and took a long sip of my coffee, listening to the sound of Meghan's engine struggling to turn over. Shaking my head, I said, "She never listens to me. That's her problem."

chapter seven

meghan

"I know you're dying to say 'I told you so', so go ahead. Get it out of your system," I told Chase as we watched a tow truck pull my car from the library parking lot.

But he kept his mouth shut, bending down to throw all the junk from his passenger seat into the back of his car. I wanted to point out his messiness probably wasn't a good look for WWTV, considering he was driving around with their logo on the side of his car. But if he could keep his comments to himself, so could I. For now, anyway.

Inside the car, I put my watery iced coffee in the cup holder and dropped my bag between my feet. "Ugh. I really hope it's just my battery and not my starter or something."

"Could be your transmission," Chase said, turning his keys in the ignition. "That'll cost ya."

I glared at him. "I'm trying to be positive here."

"That's a first," he mumbled, glancing down at a Spotify playlist on his phone. Oh boy—what kind of music was he going to subject me to this morning?

Before I could brace myself, he hit play, and the unmistakable opening riff of "Sabotage" blasted through his speakers. A smug grin spread across his face as he shifted into reverse, perfectly syncing his movement with the drums in the song.

"You're ridiculous," I muttered, reaching to turn the volume down, but he gently pushed my hand away without even looking at me, smirking the entire time. Suddenly, I was taken right back to all the moments we had just like this one when we were dating. Always arguing about our music. There were a few bands we could always agree on, like Pixies, The Cure, and Joy Division—but I found myself listening to them all a lot less now. Chase liked to think he "educated" me about New Wave music. I couldn't hear "Just Like Heaven" without remembering Chase rambling on about Robert Smith's decades-long love story with his wife.

As he drove, I renamed the voice memos on my phone OWEN & MASON 1 and OWEN & MASON 2 while drafting my article out in my head. And then it hit me: I couldn't remember packing my laptop charger that morning. I quickly rummaged through my bag at my feet, hoping I was wrong, but it wasn't there.

"Shit."

"What's the matter?" Chase asked, turning down the music.

"I don't have my laptop charger."

"Oh. Do you need it?" What an idiot. I just blinked at him a couple of times until he got the clue. "Sorry, dumb question. Need me to swing by your place so you can grab it?"

I hated asking him to do another favor for me. God, how many times was he going to have to help me this week? Sighing, I pulled a cat hair off my knee and said, "Yes. If you don't mind."

"Not at all. Where you living now?"

I directed Chase toward my apartment complex, a cluster of modern buildings near the river with French Quarter-style architecture. They were meant to pay homage to the early French settlers of Woodvale, which I thought was appealing when I applied to live there a couple years ago.

But the building I was assigned was Pepto-Bismol pink, and I hated it.

That's probably what Chase was chuckling about when we pulled into the lot. I just rolled my eyes as I rummaged for my keys in my bag. "I'll just take a second."

He put the car in park. "Do you still have Wanda?"

I paused, glancing at him. Wanda had been ours, once upon a time. That scraggly, underfed orange kitten showed up on our porch while we were watching Infinity War, and I let Chase name her Wanda after Scarlet Witch. I didn't mind, because let's be honest, Scarlet Witch is a badass. When Chase and I split up years ago, I sort of decided I was taking Wanda with me, and he didn't protest. He knew I needed her more.

"Yeah, I still have her," I said.

Chase looked down at his hand on the gear shifter and smiled. "Does she still sit on your chest and make biscuits when you try to sleep?"

"Every night," I answered, and I almost felt my lips pull upward in a smile, too. *Oops. Can't let that happen.* Though Chase let out a quiet chuckle, I saw a hint of sadness on his face. He missed Wanda, didn't he? I closed my eyes for a second and inhaled before asking, "Do you want to see her, Chase?"

He glanced up. "Could I?"

"I guess."

"Do you think she'll remember me?"

I unbuckled. "Let's find out."

Chase trailed behind me as we walked past the daffodils lining the stoop that stretched along the front of the building. My apartment was on the first floor, and while I was a little bummed I didn't have a balcony like my upstairs neighbors, I appreciated the easy access. "I'm going to guess the inside doesn't match the outside," Chase said with his hands in his pockets, nodding toward the pink siding.

Without answering, I swung open my apartment door to reveal just how right he was. I'd been sort of going for that whole "moody maximalist" look. I wasn't allowed to paint, so the walls were an awful shade of millennial gray, but I did my best to make up for them with my decor. My tall, wooden bookshelves displaying all my books and curios took up an entire wall, which helped. A large tapestry depicting the phases of the moon stretched along the opposite wall above my forest-green velvet couch. I'd spent the past two years curating this space to look exactly the way I wanted, but I still wasn't finished. It was an ongoing project, and the reason I always went broke around Halloween.

In here, it was Halloween 24/7/365.

"Wow," Chase muttered as he walked through my doorway. He paused to take it all in, zeroing in on the philodendron plant hanging from a skull pot in front of my window. "You've become completely unhinged."

"Thank you."

"Wasn't a compliment."

I ignored him, clicking my tongue for Wanda. Normally, she'd emerge from her hiding spot to greet me, but she must have sensed I had a guest. "Here, kitty, kitty. Where are you, baby girl?"

As I made my way around the apartment, I eyed Chase, who was standing before my living room shelves with his hands in his pockets as he took it all in. I wanted to tell him he was here for Wanda, not to nose around my things, but it wasn't worth the argument.

Wanda wasn't on my bed, and she wasn't hiding behind the hamper in the bathroom, either. I continued to flit around the apartment, clicking my tongue every few steps. "I don't know where she's hiding."

"She's right here," Chase said, and I whirled around, following his gaze to the bottom shelf, where Wanda was sitting atop a stack of botany books, staring up at him with her enormous pupils. He took a couple steps forward, warily holding his hand toward her. I could tell she wanted to dart away, but there wasn't really anywhere for her to go. And then, after giving him a good sniff, she sat up, bowing her head down so she could rub against his hand.

Chase looked over at me and beamed. "She remembers."

I wished I could deny it, but she began to purr as Chase scratched her ears. I watched him pet her, sticking his fingers beneath his glasses to wipe the corner of his eye. Was he about to tear up over this? It almost made me feel guilty about taking her from him all those years ago. "I guess she missed you," I said, walking over to join him in front of the bookshelf. I stood back with my arms folded against my chest, letting him take his time to pet her. When he finally stopped, he turned and nodded toward the record player on a little table nearby.

"So, you still listen to music on vinyl, huh," Chase asked, adjusting his glasses to get a closer look at the records on the bottom shelf. I could almost feel the judgment rolling off him as he silently sized up my album choices.

In that moment, I was struck by the memory of our last big fight, the one before I left. I had been sitting on the floor in front of this very record player in our old apartment, listening to one of my mom's old records. It had become my nightly routine, letting the music wash over me until the tears came. The intro to "Don't Stop" by Fleetwood Mac did it every time. I couldn't hear that song without seeing my parents dancing in the kitchen, singing it to each other like they didn't have a care in the world.

On that particular night, Chase approached me slowly and quietly, walking over to lift the needle from the record. He squatted before me with a sympathetic look on his face—an expression I'd grown to perceive as more condescending than anything else—and said, "Don't you think it's time to move on?"

Those words crushed me. They took all the sadness I'd been carrying and twisted it into something ugly. With a sudden surge of anger flowing through my veins, I sprang up, grabbed the Rumours album off the record player, and smashed it against the corner of the table. Chase held up his hands to shield himself from the shards of plastic flying everywhere.

"There, I'm over it. Are you happy?" I spat the words at him, my voice trembling with rage and pain. I had never done anything like that before, and the look of horror on Chase's face mirrored my own shock. That was my parents' record. What had I just done?

But underneath the anger, I could feel my heart breaking. Six months of grieving, and he decided that was enough. He'd been making those little comments for weeks, like knocking on the bathroom door and asking if I was done crying yet, or putting his head in his hands when we had to pull over on the way to Sean and Erika's because some flowers reminded me of my mom.

He was over my grief, and he wanted me to be over it, too.

That night, I dropped to the floor, tears streaming down my face as I tried to pick up the broken pieces of the record, but my hands were shaking too much. I was hysterical, sobbing so hard I could barely breathe. I couldn't even see. And then Chase was there, wrapping his arms around me from behind, holding me tight. His hands slid just beneath my breasts, pulling me into him. But instead of encouraging me to let it out, he shushed me. Even after all of that, he was still trying to get the crying to stop. He didn't get it. He never would.

I jerked away from him, something inside me snapping. "You're right, it's time to move on. From you."

In a daze, I packed up all of my things—and Wanda—and he just watched me go.

He didn't grovel.

He didn't fight for me.

That night, Chase just let me go.

And now, the two of us were staring at that same record player in silence. Suddenly, it dawned on me he'd asked a question. "Oh. Uh, yeah. I still use the record player sometimes, especially when the Wi-Fi is down."

"Ah."

Chase was staring into my eyes with an intensity that made my heart speed up. Why did this feel awkward all of a sudden? I was the first to break the connection, turning away from him to unplug my laptop charger from the outlet by the couch. "Ready to go?"

Chase nodded. He gave Wanda a few more ear-scritches before following me toward the door. And as he started the car, scrolling through his playlist for another song to torture me, I wondered if the memory of that night haunted him as much as it did me.

chapter eight

chase

When I was little, my mom was at her wits end with me after I ruined one shirt after another, chewing and sucking on all of my collars until they were soggy, stretched-out, and sometimes even torn. As an anxious kid with sensory issues, that was my only way of coping with separation anxiety after she dropped me off at school.

And then she made me go to this therapist who suggested I start wearing a chewy necklace. Instead of ruining all my shirts, I could chew on this lime green silicone dinosaur hanging from my neck. And that was just fantastic—until I was eventually teased for it and went back to chewing on my shirt collars.

At twenty-nine, I still caught myself pulling my collar up to my mouth every once in a while. Never to chew on them or anything like that, but just to feel the texture against my bottom lip. It helped me focus. Made me less anxious. Meghan noticed it years ago. When she heard about the dinosaur necklace, she squealed and told me it made her fall in love with me even more. "Aw. I wouldn't have teased you for it if I knew you back then," she swore, and she joked she was going to get me a new one.

I was thinking about all of this as I watched her fiddle with the obsidian pendant holding her parents' ashes, drawing it up to rub the smooth crystal against her lips as she stared at the record player. I'd seen her do it before—she always did it when she was anxious or just lost in thought.

I had a feeling I knew what was on her mind, too.

In the car, she sighed as she flipped through her notes from the interview. And she was still rubbing that pendant. I turned the New Order song down. "Something wrong?"

Another, louder sigh. "Just thinking this article is probably going to be a little boring. Nobody's going to be clicking to buy a subscription for this one."

"Hey, they might," I said, glancing over my shoulder before changing lanes. "I mean, it's Owen Gardner. People love the guy."

She slowly turned her head toward me. "Uh huh."

I rolled my eyes. "I'm not talking about me. He'll probably share the link, right?" I gripped the steering wheel, thinking back to how we used to always do this. Her fearing the worst possible outcome, me assuring her things aren't always as gloomy as she made them out to be. "What's Xander reporting on?"

"I don't know. Probably some epic town scandal. We need to find a good story, Chase."

I recalled my schedule of upcoming features, fully aware this interview with Owen was the pinnacle of my entire week. Ribbon cuttings, road closures–it was all downhill from here. "Well," I said, tapping my fingers against my leg. "What about the old orphanage?"

Sean and I went out to the abandoned orphanage when our YouTube channel was brand new. It was one of the first haunted sites we visited. There was a fire there in the 1930s, and some people claimed they could still hear the sound of children crying or screaming in the middle of the night. Sean and I didn't hear anything, but we saw a shadowy figure moving in one of the halls. It was enough to make both of us nearly piss our pants as we packed up our stuff and got the hell out of there.

It didn't dawn on either of us until the next day that the shadowy figure we spotted was probably just the homeless man who often hung around that place.

"What about it?" Meghan asked, scrunching up her face in confusion. "Are they tearing it down?"

"No. Why not report on the lore surrounding it?"

She smacked her forehead with her notebook. "I knew you were going to say that. And the answer's no."

"Oh, come on," I said with a little chuckle. "Is it because you're afraid you're going to see the ghost of a little orphan?"

"No. I'm not afraid. And do you know why?" She paused to inhale. "There weren't any children in the building when it burned. Every single one made it out safely. There's even a picture of all the kids smiling with one of the firefighters. The story that kids burned alive up there is just a rumor perpetuated by people like you."

Oh. Oops. I hadn't known that. And knowing Meghan, she was absolutely correct about this piece of historical information. She'd spent hours poring over old newspapers, and the woman knew her shit when it came to Woodvale history. "Well. Maybe they forgot one," I joked. "Poor little Billy... he was never going to get adopted, anyway."

"Chase! They didn't forget one," she yelled, shaking her head with a laugh. She actually *laughed*. "You should be ashamed of yourself."

"Never," I said with a grin. "Okay, but maybe we could make that part of the story. Give them the facts but highlight how everyone in town has a story about going out there. You did when you were a teen, right?" I recalled her mentioning something about it before.

Meghan stared down at her shiny, blood-red fingernails. "I may have had a small, unsuccessful seance with my friends there when I was sixteen."

"See what I mean?"

"But I'm not reporting on this, and nothing you can say will change my mind."

"Okay, fine," I said, deciding to take the long way through town to get back to the studio and hoping she wouldn't notice. "Then speaking of seances, what about all the witchcraft activity in this town?" I turned to her with one eyebrow raised.

"What about it? Plenty of people practice witchcraft, Chase. Pagans, Wiccans—it's perfectly normal and getting more popular, actually." She was rubbing her pendant again.

"I'm talking about really dark witchcraft. Culty shit."

"You're starting to sound like that paranoid evangelical who was screaming in front of the crystal shop the other day."

"Wait, I got it." I snapped my fingers like I was suddenly hit with inspiration, my eyes widening with mock seriousness. "The alien abductions."

Meghan covered her face with her notebook again. "Got any normal story ideas you want to share? Nobody cares about your paranormal and occult stuff."

"My six hundred and twenty-two subscribers indicate otherwise."

Her eyebrows lifted in disbelief. "Yeah? How many does Owen Gardner have?"

Okay, rude. "How many does your little newspaper have, Wednesday?"

"Fuck you," she snapped. I could only laugh, knowing I'd won this round. As I drove us the rest of the way to the newsroom, I caught the way she was pressing her lips together tight, fighting hard to keep her smile hidden.

I couldn't help but relish in this tiny victory, a warmth spreading through me at the thought that I could still make her smile. It used to happen all the time—I used to be the reason for those genuine, carefree grins that lit up her entire face.

And then, at some point, everything I said just seemed to be the wrong thing. I read articles and listened to podcasts about how to help your partner through grief. When she started therapy, I did, too. And I stuck it out even longer than she did. When I encouraged her to keep going, to give it a chance to have an effect, I was wrong.

When I told her to stop self-sabotaging by driving past her childhood home just to make herself cry, I was wrong.

When I suggested we go on a weekend getaway during Mother's Day to keep her distracted, I was wrong.

When I tried giving her space, thinking she needed time alone to process, I was wrong.

And when I stupidly blurted, "Don't you think it's time to move on?"—the words that made her walk away from me and never look back—I was so, so wrong. For her, that was the last straw.

I just couldn't stand to watch her self-destruct. There had to be healthier ways of handling her grief, but she hated me for suggesting them. I could sense her pushing me away, so on that fateful night when she told me she was ready to move on from *me*, I knew I had to give her what she needed and just let her go.

But for the first time in three years—or maybe more—I'd not only made her smile, but I had made her laugh, too.

It felt good.

**

The energy in the newsroom when I returned was nervous. At first, I wasn't sure why everyone seemed like they were trying hard to look busy, talking in quieter tones than normal. And then I noticed Silas Brown pacing aimlessly with a takeaway coffee cup in his hand, looming over everyone as they tried to work. Jillian was doing her best to make small talk as she reviewed her notes, but I could see her discomfort from a mile away. Silas was completely unaware his presence was more of a disruption than anything.

I sat at my desk in our open office and began uploading my files until, to my disappointment, Silas strolled toward me.

"I'm curious about something," he said before he even reached my desk.

No greeting. Just diving right into whatever bullshit was on his mind.

I cleared my throat and looked up from my monitor. "What's that?"

"Who's your cameraman?" He glanced over at Jillian before turning back to me. "She's got a whole crew. Am I correct in assuming that you don't?"

"Uh… yes." I tapped my fingers on my desk, wondering where this could be going as I tried to work out a way to explain that would neither make me look like a moron or undermine Jill for her own methods. As I formed a better answer, Silas walked even farther around the side of my desk so he could see my screen. It made the hairs on the back of my neck stand up.

"Do you edit your own videos, too?"

I blinked a couple of times. "I, uh, just do a basic edit before submitting them. Sometimes I upload a quick clip for our social media, but Ryan still edits anything that ends up on air."

Like a predator circling its prey, Silas walked all the way around my desk until he was in front of me again. I fiddled with the corner of my mousepad, which was already coming apart from years of nervous picking. This scrutiny could end any time now. But he wasn't done yet. With one hand clutching the coffee cup and the other in his pocket, he stood at the front of my desk and said, "No suit and tie, no cameraman. Just you and your jeans against the world, huh?"

What a condescending prick. "I guess you could say that."

He nodded and took a sip of his coffee. "I'd like to see you in action sometime, out on the field. Email me your schedule so I know where you're headed, alright?"

"Yeah, sure."

With a nod, he finally walked away, deciding to pester Marco for a little bit.

Great. Just great. The last thing I needed was our douchebag CEO breathing down my neck, scrutinizing everything I did while I tried to work.

Meghan was going to hate this even more.

chapter nine

meghan

Could someone just rob a bank or something?

As much as I personally enjoyed talking to Owen and Mason that morning, writing their article almost put me to sleep. I could usually knock out a piece like that in thirty minutes, but I found myself staring at a blinking cursor a lot that day. I wasn't finding it very easy to make interactive snap circuits sound exciting.

Then again, maybe it wasn't the content of the story slowing me down. Maybe it was my own distracted mind. I kept thinking about Chase and his infuriating ability to make me smile without even trying. His charm actually irritated me—mostly because I hated that it still worked on me.

Shaking off every thought of him, I forced myself to focus on the STEAM article until it was finally finished. I normally bypassed Graham's proofreading when it came to web content, so after integrating the video Chase uploaded, the article was officially out into the world. "Let the subscriptions come flooding in," I mumbled to myself.

Over in the next cubicle, Xander was hammering away at his keyboard, likely transcribing something, judging from the speed in which he typed and the absence of pauses.

Graham held a typing contest for us once, and I'd beaten him by just a hair.

As much as I tried to concentrate on my own transcriptions and the phone calls I needed to make, my curiosity kept pulling my attention toward Xander. What was he working on over there? Was his article going to outperform mine? He had a knack for stirring the pot with his stories, which usually resulted in Graham having a total meltdown. But that controversial edge would probably give him the upper hand in our competition.

I had to know.

I stood up, grabbed my desk chair, and wheeled it into his cubicle, pulling up right beside him. Xander, sensing my presence, pulled his earbuds out and paused the voice memo he'd been listening to. With a slightly annoyed glance, he closed his laptop as if he were guarding some top-secret information. He blinked at me. "Can I help you?"

I couldn't let him know I was scoping out the competition. "I was just wondering if you ever did that DNA kit I got you," I said, propping my elbows up on his desk. Last Christmas, I gifted just about everyone I knew an ancestry kit, which—selfishly—might have been more of a present for me than it was for them. So far, Graham and Jillian had let me pore over their info with them. Graham connected with an uncle he never knew he had, which may have been even more exciting for me than it was for him.

Xander sighed, pulling his dark hair away from his eyes with his palm. "I haven't gotten around to it yet."

I crossed my arms. "Xander! Don't you want to know where you came from? I bet you've got some Italian in you."

He inhaled, putting his earbuds back in their case. "You're right, I do. I had Moretti's for lunch." As he spoke, I attempted to casually glance at the title of the voice memo on his phone, but he caught me. Tilting his head to the side, he swiped up on his screen to close out of the app. "You want to know what Jillian and I were up to this morning, don't you?"

"No, I don't care. Because Chase and I covered something really… exciting." My mind flashed back to Owen and Mason playing a competitive game of Checkers on the big tablet at the library to demonstrate its features.

Maybe "exciting" wasn't the right word.

Xander leaned back, mimicking my pose with his arms crossed. "Is it more exciting than a sweet little old lady with a parrot that can quote *Forrest Gump* by heart?"

I scowled at him. "Oh come on, that is *not* what you're writing about." Xander was above fluff pieces like that, always passing them on to me, Graham, or even Byron. If it was in any way heartwarming or uplifting, he considered it beneath him.

He just shrugged, examining his fingernails. "Cute pets sell subscriptions, Meghan. And Jillian and I just interviewed an African grey parrot named Reginald. Or Reggie, for short."

"Shut the fuck up." He wouldn't really sell himself out just to win this competition, would he?

Xander lifted one hand, keeping the rest of his body still as he tapped his phone and pushed PLAY on his voice memo. I was not at all prepared for the immediate squawk, followed by a screeching, "Run, Forrest!"

No fucking way. "How did you keep a straight face?"

Xander paused the voice memo. "I just pictured myself at that conference in NYC."

God, I hated him more than Chase at that moment. I shook my head, trying not to smile. He was taking this competition pretty seriously, which meant Chase and I would have to come up with something really special to blow him out of the water. Owen Gardner was cool, but not *Forrest-Gump-*

quoting-parrot cool. "Keep picturing it, Xan," I said, standing up to wheel my chair back to my own cubicle, "because that's as close as you're going to get."

**

One of the most important things on my calendar each week was a standing appointment with Jillian. Location? Poppy's Bar and Grill. Purpose? To bitch about our lives and indulge in whatever seasonal Thirsty Thursday special the place was currently offering. We rarely canceled, both of us understanding this ritual was our version of therapy.

"Whoever decided lavender should become a trendy drink flavor needs their head examined," I said, wincing after taking a sip of my lavender lemon drop martini. "I'm glad I only paid four dollars for this."

Jill, who had almost reached the bottom of her own glass, giggled as she flipped over the drink menu. "And I'm thinking of ordering a second one. But I wonder how many calories are in these things?"

Over the years, I'd watched Jill cycle through different diets and workout programs, feeling pressure from the constant scrutiny that came with being a newscaster. A viewer once told her they loved how she wasn't "stick-skinny like other reporters," and Jillian didn't take it well.

That person had managed to both insult other women and ruin Jillian's body image with that back-handed compliment, and I hated them for it.

"They're totally zero calories," I said, scooting my drink across the table to her. "Finish mine for me. Please."

"Maybe I would if I hadn't driven us here," she said.

As it turned out, I was dealing with more than just a dead battery—it was a bad alternator caused by a wiring issue. Basically, my car was completely fucked, and they told me it would be several days before they could get to it. "So is Chase going to be your personal chauffeur for a while?"

Jillian, the little masochist, enjoyed seeing my discomfort over the mention of Chase. She giggled, swirling the ice around in her empty glass. "Keep laughing, Jill. I'm not the one who interviewed a parrot today."

"Xander told you, huh?" She hid her face with her hands, laughing even harder. "You should've seen the way he dry-heaved when we stepped out of that lady's house. It smelled like a zoo in there."

"Funny, he left that part out." I shook my head. "I'm anxious to see our stats in the morning. He's going to be so cocky if he pulls more subscriptions than me."

"You interviewed Owen Gardner, right? That should catch people's attention."

"I hope so," I said, pausing our conversation when the server brought us our food; a burger for me, and a Caesar salad for her. I shook my head, pouring ketchup onto my plate. "What else do you guys have scheduled? I want to know what Chase and I are up against."

Jill shot me a sheepish grin. "You'll just have to see."

I laughed. "Whatever. Just tell me."

But she shook her head, pretending to zip her lips. "I can't spill our secrets. Xander would have my throat. On second thought…" She slowly brought her hand to her neck, likely imagining Xander choking her.

"Oh my God. First of all, why are you like this? Second, are you my friend, or his?"

"Only one of you is promising me an interview with the elusive Pearl Town biker gang if we win, so…" With a nonchalant shrug, she popped a crouton into her mouth and smiled. "I have been trying to get an in with them for years. He's got connections."

"That dirty, manipulative, little snake," I said. Of course he had connections with Pearl Town. It was one of those places you heard about but never really saw for yourself. Tucked away near the river on the south side of town, the community was practically a world of its own, run by a biker gang who was known for roughing up anyone who came into their territory. You'd have to be crazy to enter that neighborhood uninvited, which was why it didn't surprise me Xander somehow had a connection there. "Should've known he'd get you to conspire against me."

All Jill could do was laugh. "I'm sorry. He and I are just going to have fun with this. You and Chase could, too, you know." She raised one eyebrow at me. "I mean, you used to with *Woodvale Whispers?*"

I was surprised she remembered the name of the blog Chase and I shared. Of course we had fun together back then, sometimes spending an entire day scouting locations and committing mild acts of vandalism. Our initials were etched into more abandoned houses than I could count, usually inside a jagged heart Chase carved with his pocketknife. "Yeah, well, that was ages ago," I said. "He still does his ghost thing, and I still do my gravestone thing. Just, you know, separately."

"I still think you should revive it, but okay," she said, not really conceding. "So what dead person are you writing about this month?"

I washed down a bite of my burger with a sip of water, and I began to tell her all about Fannie Decker, including what I'd learned that afternoon: Fannie was a vocal opponent of the town's temperance movement. When they were trying to cut down on alcohol consumption in Woodvale, she was quoted in the Times saying, *"The Temperance Society seems a bit overwrought; perhaps a sip of apple brandy would do wonders to calm their nerves."*

Jillian's mouth dropped when I shared that little tidbit with her.

"If your nerdy ex-boyfriend ever invents time travel," she said, "we are *so* going back to the eighteen hundreds and befriending this bad bitch."

"Agreed."

We toasted Fannie and wrapped up our meal, deciding to call it a night. Jillian waited until my door unlocked before driving off, the same I would for her. I clicked my tongue for Wanda, who was sitting just inside the kitchen next to her empty food dish, glaring at me like I'd just committed a heinous crime against her. "I don't think you're going to starve anytime soon," I said, slipping my shoes off. She meowed when she saw me reaching for the plastic cereal container I kept her food in. But before I could pour it into her dish, my phone buzzed in my pocket.

Chase: Get that voodoo doll of Silas ready

Meghan: Why?

Chase: He's shadowing me (us) tomorrow at that ribbon-cutting

Meghan: Whyyyyyyyy?

Chase: He wants to see me in action, he said. I think he's doubting my professionalism

Meghan: As he should.

Chase: Says the woman who giggled like a schoolgirl during her interview today.

Meghan: I never giggle.

Chase: You're right, sinister cackling is more your style. I'm starting to think you're a descendant of the Woodvale Witch.

Meghan: I fucking wish.

Deciding she was done waiting on me, Wanda headbutted my phone, knocking it out of my hand. "If I were a witch, would that make you my familiar?"

She let out a chirpy meow in response—but that probably had more to do with her impending death by starvation than my ridiculous question. But I took it as a yes, anyway. After filling her dish, I scratched her butt as she ate, and my phone lit up with another notification.

Chase: You'd probably put a curse on me

Meghan: Bold of you to assume I haven't already.

chapter ten

chase

"This town doesn't deserve her," Meghan whispered to me in front of the barber shop, where Mayor Angela Michaels had just arrived for the ribbon-cutting on Main Street. Wearing tennis shoes with her navy pantsuit, she'd walked the four blocks from city hall, saying the weather was too beautiful not to enjoy the fresh air. She greeted everyone by name as she came down the sidewalk, including both of us. A few years ago, Angela was simultaneously Woodvale's first Black mayor and first female mayor—proof that even in this small, conservative town, people couldn't deny her capability and charm.

"If she doesn't get re-elected, I'm moving," I mumbled to Meghan as I set up my camera, framing my shot to include the red, white, and black balloon arch around the door to the new barber shop. I hit record just in time to catch the mayor shaking hands with the owner, which would make for some good b-roll content.

"In that case, I just might start campaigning against her," Meghan said. We exchanged antagonistic glances before I turned back to my camera. We still had a few minutes to go, and a small crowd was beginning to gather on the sidewalk. I liked ribbon-cuttings, because they were usually low-key, predictable events. Occasionally someone would hire a DJ or have a local baker cater the event, but besides that, they were pretty straightforward. A couple of speeches, a comically oversized pair of scissors, and a photo op. Short and sweet.

I'd been to dozens of these, and so had Meghan. Part of the reason I always looked forward to covering ribbon-cuttings was because I knew it meant I'd probably have some interaction with her. Even if it was just a glare in my direction.

But this time, we rode together. And she even complimented me on my appearance—if "Wow, you look more put-together than normal" could be considered a compliment, that is. She took it back when I showed her the retro elbow patches on my new tan blazer that I purchased weeks ago but never worn because I didn't like trying new things. That, and the tag was itchy on the back of my neck.

I also preferred my worn-in Vans over these loafers, which I normally reserved for formal events. My youngest sister, Madi, whom I'd Facetimed the night before, assured me the shoes looked fine with my dark jeans. It appeared Meghan approved of the look, too. I caught her looking me up and down a couple of times while we waited on this thing to get started.

Just as I was ready to call her out on it, a loud rumble down the block caught everyone's attention. We all watched a metallic gray Porsche creep by before parking up on the corner. Its front end blocked a portion of the blue curb reserved for handicapped parking, and it was no surprise at all when Silas Brown stepped out of the car.

He strutted over to the sidewalk, pushing his sunglasses up off his eyes as he approached the crowd. "Nice wheels," the barber shop owner, a guy with a neatly trimmed beard and an obnoxious fade, said. "How fast does that thing go?"

Silas responded with a grin, satisfied with the attention. "At least one-fifty. Ask me how I know." Meghan and I exchanged a look of mutual disdain as this quickly shifted to the Silas show. The ribbon-cutting was scheduled to start three minutes ago, but everyone was so surprised by Silas's unannounced arrival, preparations for the event seemed to come to a halt. It took the mayor clapping her hands together, like a teacher trying to control her pupils, to get everyone back on track. "All right, are we all here? Shall we get started?"

Silas spotted me and made his way down the sidewalk toward us. "Morning," he said, giving us both a little head nod. Then, he took in my equipment—the camera, the tripod, the WWTV microphone on a boom stand—before eyeing Meghan, who was standing beside me with her notebook out and her phone ready to record. His gaze lingered on her tattoos, which were hard to miss that day thanks to the short-sleeved black blouse she had on. Her top button was undone, which was likely an intentional move to reveal the *"this too shall pass"* tattoo on her collarbone.

And she wasn't smiling. I clenched my jaw at the audacity of staring your CEO in the face and not even bothering to fake a polite grin. I was both nervous for her and a little turned on. Thankfully for both of them, the festivities began, and the three of us diverted our attention to a speech given by the barber shop owner. He introduced himself as Troy Hatfield before he started rambling on about how this day was a dream come true.

The mayor said a few words, too, followed by the president of the Chamber of Commerce. After the actual ribbon-cutting, Troy's wife invited everyone to come inside and have some cookies made by a local baker. And that was that. Meghan pulled out her Nikon and asked the whole group to pose for a picture. She had her notebook ready for interview questions for Troy, but before she could say a word, Silas planted himself between the two of them with his back to

Meghan. "How long have you been cutting hair?" he asked, his tone casual but commanding.

"About twelve years," Troy answered. "I started out as an apprentice at a small shop uptown, learning the trade from an old-timer who'd been cutting hair in Woodvale since the '70s."

What followed this exchange was a rapid-fire series of questions from Silas, as though he were conducting his own interview, completely unprompted. All Meghan could do was step aside and let these men talk. She gave me a look of confusion and whispered, "He's asking all the questions I was going to ask."

"Start recording, I guess." I already was, keeping the camera locked on the barber's face with the balloon arch behind him. With a little creativity, I could edit Silas out completely. I'd make it work. Meghan was growing more anxious by the second, though, and I could tell she was debating whether she should interrupt. Finally, Silas seemed to notice her in his peripheral vision, and he stepped aside.

"I apologize—I guess you're waiting to do your job, huh?"

Meghan tilted her head and shot him a tiny smile, but it was the same look she frequently gave me before telling me to go jump off a bridge. I was pretty familiar with that disdainful, sarcastic grin. Luckily for her, Silas wasn't.

I panned the camera to include Meghan and stood back with my hands in my pockets. "So, tell us again how long you've been cutting hair, and where you did your training?" Her voice lacked its usual confidence.

And to make matters worse, Troy gave her a cocky smirk, glancing over at Silas before answering. "As I *just* said,

I've been doing it for about twelve years." He repeated more of what he'd just told Silas.

"What made you decide it was time to open your own place?"

"Again," he began, jerking his head toward Silas, "I had built up a loyal clientele and decided it was time." This was a shorter answer than he'd given Silas. The interview carried on just like that, with this asshole treating Meghan like she was preventing him from doing something more important. The difference in how he spoke to Silas and how he answered Meghan's questions made my blood boil.

If Silas hadn't been standing right there, I might have something to say. I'd remind this guy Meghan was doing him a favor by giving his business some media attention, so if he could stop being a jerk to her, that'd be fucking great. The words were on the tip of my tongue, getting closer and closer to spilling out with every cocky response.

But as it turned out, I wouldn't need to defend Meghan at all.

After another rude, dismissive answer out of Troy, Meghan paused her voice memo and said, "If I'm wasting your time, Mr. Hatfield, just say that. I can go."

Oh, shit—I should've known she didn't need any help from me. I kept the camera rolling. Immediately, Silas swooped back in, holding his arm out between the two of them in an attempt to diffuse the situation. He directed his attention toward the barber. "I apologize for her, Mr. Hatfield—that's probably enough questions anyway, huh?" He glanced at Meghan, but he didn't wait for her to speak up before opening his mouth again. "Why don't you show us the inside of your shop?"

He clapped a hand against Troy's shoulder and followed him beneath the balloon arch through the open door of the shop, leaving Meghan standing on the sidewalk with her mouth gaping open. "What the actual fuck?"

Without hesitation, I pulled the microphone from its stand and maneuvered in front of the camera beside Meghan. "This just in: Misogyny on Main Street," I said in my newscaster voice. "A local barber and hotshot CEO demonstrate the latest in condescending behavior toward women, leaving one local reporter *stunned*. Meghan, do you have anything to say?"

I held out the mic toward her, but she only glared at me in response.

Turning back to the camera, I said, "Folks, she's utterly speechless. Back to you in the studio, Jillian."

"You're stupid," Meghan muttered. I knew she wanted to appear angry, but that dimple on her cheek made it obvious she was struggling to keep herself from smiling. Mission *almost* accomplished.

Grinning as I packed up my equipment, I said, "You know you love me."

"I absolutely do not."

"Come on, you have to admit, that–" Before I could pester her any more, Silas burst from the barber shop, his face red with anger, shaking a pointed finger at Meghan.

"You work for me, correct?"

Meghan glanced down at her notebook. "I'm not doing this for my own enjoyment." *Jesus fuck, Meghan.*

"What's your name?"

"Meghan. Meghan Dobson."

"All right, Meghan—let's be a little more polite to the people we're interviewing, yeah? Especially when they're one of our sponsors?"

"Will do." She was shooting daggers at him with her eyes, despite the fake smile on her lips.

"And you." He turned to me, making me swallow. After looking me up and down, he said, "Keep doing what you're doing. I like it."

Damn it, I really didn't want to accept a compliment at the moment. "Uhh. Yes, sir," I answered, adjusting my glasses. Silas gave Meghan one more long-lasting stare before strolling back to his Porsche. I half-expected her to flip him off as he climbed inside, but she resisted.

"I'm going to quit," she muttered the second his engine roared.

"No, you're not."

"I'm going to burn down his fucking house."

"C'mon," I said, throwing my camera bag over my shoulder. I was tempted to rest my hand on the back of her arm as we started down the sidewalk, but I feared she might bite it off. "Let's go get you an iced coffee."

**

In the car, Meghan's disgust turned into worry. "I probably shouldn't have been such a bitch to our CEO."

I couldn't exactly disagree, so I just kept my mouth shut.

She swirled her iced coffee around—which she refused to let me buy for her in the Riverside drive-thru—and shook her head. "I'm going to single-handedly get the paper shut down with my big mouth. At the very least, I'm probably going to get sacked."

"For what it's worth, that barber was being an ass. I almost said something to him myself."

She let out a little laugh as she swallowed her coffee. "Yeah, right."

"I mean it, Meg," I said. The nickname slipped out–I hadn't called her that since we dated. It felt too intimate, and deep inside, I knew I no longer had the privilege to call her by that name. I quickly spoke again, hoping she wouldn't notice. "You beat me to the punch."

Meghan slowly inhaled and exhaled, either a reaction to the old nickname or mere frustration with me. Maybe both. "You're the most non-confrontational person in the world, Chase."

"When it comes to my own matters, sure. But when someone's being a dick to a person I-" I stopped abruptly, deciding at the last second I didn't want to reveal I cared about her. She'd never let me hear the end of it.

I could feel her staring at me as I drove. "What? Someone you what?"

"Work with. When someone's mistreating a colleague of mine, I can be confrontational if need be. Even if it's you." *Especially if it's you.* "But you didn't need me, did ya?" I smiled, just remembering the look on the guy's face when she snapped at him.

Meghan drew a hand to her forehead. "God. This newspaper's already a sinking ship, and I just lit it on fire."

"Why don't we focus on our next story, huh? Something good enough to make the man realize he can't fire you." I knew from experience distraction was one of the best ways to turn Meghan's mood around. "How are you going to beat Xander?"

"I don't know," she said with a sigh. "He's even got Jill scheming against me now, so we're going to have to come up with something good. Why don't we both spend this weekend brainstorming and meet Monday morning to hash out some ideas?"

"Okay. I have one now, though." The night before, some kid left a comment on our YouTube channel about some weird symbols etched into stones he found in the woods that the Woodvale Witch supposedly haunted, and I was dying to talk to him about it.

"It better not be about ghosts," Meghan warned, and I promptly closed my mouth. "That's what I thought. I want a list of non-paranormal story ideas from you on Monday, please."

"You're not my boss." I glanced over at her, and she responded by blinking at me a couple of times. "I mean, yes ma'am."

And Meghan laughed. It wasn't a cruel, cold laugh, either—it was a genuine chuckle, followed by a smile that wouldn't go away. She even turned toward the passenger window, as if trying to hide it from me. But I'd already seen enough.

I was getting really good at this.

**

"When's the last time you had a home-cooked meal, Chase?" Erika asked me as she placed a bowl of mashed potatoes on the center of the kitchen table. Sean was bouncing

Dimitri on his knee beside me to soothe his crying, but it wasn't working. Between that and the sound of their running dishwasher behind me, it was all so distracting that it took a few seconds longer than it should have for my brain to register Erika's question.

"If you don't count the pizza rolls I microwaved last night, then the last home-cooked meal I had was probably… the last one you cooked for me."

Erika laughed. "Pizza rolls don't count. You either need to learn how to cook or get yourself a wife, sir."

"Hey, I know how to cook," I said, reaching for the green beans. And it was true–give me a recipe, and I could make almost anything. Nobody could beat my barbecue ribs. "But I live alone, so what's the point? I'm not doing all that for myself."

"Then you need to get you a lady friend to cook for," Erika said, taking the seat across from me. The three of us—or four of us, if you counted the screaming infant—were crowded at one end of the table because our Comic Con plans were spread out at the other end.

Now that we were just a few weeks away from the event, Sean and I decided it was time to start meeting weekly to make sure it was all coming together. Sean revealed he finally received an email from Ethan Killian's assistant, who wanted to know more about our security arrangements and local accommodations. He was all set to sign autographs at the convention, as long as we could prove our professionalism.

That's what we were working on that Friday night, ensuring we had everything in place to back up the promises we made to Ethan's assistant. I had started to gather my things to leave when Erika came into the kitchen to cook, but she insisted I stay.

I was glad I did, too—her porkchops were amazing.

Swallowing a bite, I shook my head at the "lady friend" remark. "I don't see that happening anytime soon."

"How's working with Meghan going?" Sean asked, having finally gotten Dimitri to quiet down by holding his pacifier in his mouth.

Erika's head shot my direction. "You're working with Meghan?"

I spooned a heap of mashed potatoes onto my plate. "Yeah, we just started collaborating on some online hybrid stuff this week. And it's going okay, I guess. Neither of us want to be working together, but we're making the best of it."

"Tell her I said hello, will you?" Erika asked. "We keep in touch online, but our interactions don't really extend past her liking photos of Dimitri, and me doing the same for her cat."

"Oh yeah, Wanda," I said, staring down at my plate with a smile. "Got to see her the other day."

"You went to Meghan's place?" Sean looked up with wide eyes.

With a casual shrug, I said, "We had to swing by her apartment to pick something up, and I just wanted to pop in to see if the cat remembered me." I looked up from my food, catching Erika and Sean giving each other a quick, knowing glance. My eyes darted back and forth between them. "She does," I added a bit too quickly while the two of them stared at me like they knew something I didn't.

"Just be careful," Erika said, picking up a knife to butter her roll. "Don't go falling back in love with her. You know how much she hurt you the first time around."

I swallowed, thinking back to the way I often vilified Meghan when I came here to vent to them after our break-up, claiming she left me out of the blue "for no reason." I probably shouldn't have omitted my own fuckups. "I'm the one who hurt her," I corrected, though I was about three years too late.

"That might be true, but I seem to recall you crying on our couch the night she left, drowning your sorrows in a bottle of–"

"He probably doesn't want to relive all that, hon," Sean interrupted, attempting to eat while balancing the baby in one arm. I bowed my head in subtle gratitude. "Let the poor man eat."

He was correct, I didn't want to relive that night for the millionth time, but it seemed no matter how much time passed, the memories crept up on me anyway. With or without Erika's reminders, I could still see Meghan's taillights as she peeled out of our driveway. I still recalled the look on her face when she showed up the next morning to retrieve her things—not to make up, like I'd assumed. I could still feel the shame deep in the pit of my stomach at how I just sat on the couch, barely able to speak, and let her pack up her stuff. All I could manage to say was her name.

"Meg…"

"Don't. It's too late."

And she was gone.

I tried not to think about her while we ate, half-listening to Sean and Erika plan their couples' costume for the cosplay dance party we had scheduled to close out the Comic Con. But my mind kept drifting back to Meghan and how she looked that time we dressed like Mulder and Scully at Jill's Halloween party, and the way she made me say *"I want to believe"* when we hooked up in her bathroom. How it made her laugh so hard she hit her head on the medicine cabinet. Those were the moments I ached for, when we could be completely silly together. Before she hated my guts. Before I let her down.

Erika's warning echoed in my mind. *"Don't go falling back in love with her."*

Well, you can't fall back in love with someone you never stopped loving in the first place.

chapter eleven

meghan

I should have expected Graham would turn the daily adding-of-the-tallies on the chalkboard into a gameshow-like production. He couldn't have made it more cheesy, from the dramatic way he paused between each tally mark to gauge our reactions, to his exaggerated announcement of the daily winner.

"Personally, I love this contest," Xander said, interlocking his fingers behind his head. Of course he loved it—he was leading me by six subscriptions. "You should make it *more* theatrical, Graham. I mean, no drumroll? No entrance music? It's like you're not even trying to motivate us."

Graham scratched his chin. "You're right…"

"God, don't encourage him," I scoffed. It was just the two of us seated at the conference table in the newsroom, since Byron and Devonte were preoccupied.

"If you were winning, you'd want a little more pomp and circumstance," Xander said. "Maybe a confetti cannon."

Graham snapped his fingers. "I'm writing that idea down."

I crossed my arms, ignoring Graham to tease Xander. "Don't you have a talking animal you should be interviewing?"

With a proud smirk, he said, "Don't you have another boring ribbon cutting to attend?"

"Don't you have another one of my friends to bribe?" I watched in satisfaction as Xander's eyes widened. "Yeah, she told me. If you think–"

"Children," Graham interrupted, standing before us at the front of the room like he was our teacher and we were his unruly pupils. When Xander continued to talk, explaining how he and Jillian were easily going to win this thing, Graham turned around and dragged the flat end of the chalk along the chalkboard. The deafening squeak made my hands shoot to my ears, and Xander muttered a stream of expletives. When Graham finally had our full attention, he sighed and put his hands on his hips. "I'm sorry I had to resort to that. Now get out there and make me proud. Or at least less disappointed."

After erasing the streak of chalk from the board, he turned back to us with a dismissive wave and left the room. The alarm on my phone went off, reminding me it was time to meet with Chase. He'd had all weekend to come up with some normal, non-ghostly stories to cover, and I hoped he wouldn't let me down. "Ugh. I have to go meet with Chase."

"I'm surprised you two haven't killed each other yet," Xander said. He was still slouching in his wooden chair at the conference table, yawning like he might fall back to sleep instantly if he laid his head down. "Has it been weird with him?"

Every now and then, Xander showed a morsel of genuine concern, and though I was now running late to meet with Chase, I decided to stay and continue this conversation with Xander. There weren't many people in my life I could open up to—this opportunity was rare. I decided to take advantage. "It's been interesting," I said, "but not as horrible as I thought. I think we've pushed past the awkwardness and we're both just trying to do our jobs. He even tried to buy me a coffee yesterday."

"Does he still want you?"

I squinted. "Um, I seriously doubt that. I'm kind of mean to him."

Xander rubbed one eye with his fist, a small grin appearing on his face. "You'd be surprised how that doesn't deter a man. At all."

"Is Abigail mean to you, Xan?"

He casually rested on his arms on the table. "Abigail…" He stopped to sigh. "Abigail is mean in a nurturing way. Like in a 'why the hell haven't you been to the doctor in five years' kind of way."

"Have you not been to the doctor in five years?"

"She made me go. She even went with me to make sure I didn't skip it."

I shook my head at him. "Xander," I said, the word dripping with shame. How could he be so blind?

"What?"

"Friends don't just go to the doctor together."

"I'm sure they do all the time," he said with the utmost confidence.

"Have you and Abigail ever had, you know, a conversation about your feelings?"

I peered into his unblinking blue-gray eyes, waiting for him to respond. He held my stare for a few seconds before finally lowering his gaze to the table, tracing the wooden pattern with his pointer finger. "Abigail doesn't have feelings for me."

"Have you asked?"

"Don't need to. Anyway, I thought we were talking about you and Chase."

Not wanting to discuss my work relationship with Chase any longer, I started gathering my things, sliding my pen into the spiral of my notebook. "You haven't shared how working with Jillian is going."

"That's enough chit-chat," he said, knocking twice on the table. "Good luck at your meeting," And with a tight-lipped smile, he rose to his feet and retreated to his cubicle without even a glance in my direction. My head was filled with follow-up questions about his abrupt dismissal, but I suspected the repetitive notifications on my phone were from Chase. I was several minutes late now.

He'd asked me to meet him in an empty classroom on the third floor. I didn't have to question how he'd discovered it—he'd been up there searching for ghosts, no doubt. He was sitting on the old teacher's desk when I arrived, his dangling feet partially concealing a hand drawn sign that read *WE LOVE YOU, MRS. BARKER.*

Chase picked up his phone to glance at the time. "Look who finally decided to show up."

I ignored him, looking around the room. Half a dozen student desks were haphazardly stacked in the corner, looking like they might topple any second. Along the wall, there were a few posters featuring notable U.S. presidents. Washington was hanging upside down by a single piece of rolled-up tape, and Eisenhower's photo was so faded, you could barely make out his features. I could almost feel the energy of the students who once sat in those desks and stared at these posters. "Any ghosts up here?" I asked.

Chase hesitated before answering, twiddling his thumbs between his knees like he didn't want to admit he'd been up here with his equipment. "I didn't pick up any readings." He cleared his throat. "But it's a good place to have a quiet lunch if you don't want to be bothered."

"I'll keep that in mind."

"Find your own abandoned classroom. This is my spot," he said, but his lopsided smile indicated he didn't really mean it. I just shook my head at him as I walked over to the stack of desks, carefully lifting one. Chase jumped up to help me, but I'd already managed to get it down without his assistance by the time he even took two steps. He retreated back to the teacher's desk with a, "Hmmm," as he pulled himself up.

"What? Are you surprised to see I can handle this myself?" I pushed the little desk toward the front of the room.

Chase's devious smile irked me. "No. Just remembering… something."

I slid onto the shiny blue chair attached to the desk, opening my notebook to the list of article ideas I'd spent all weekend compiling. "Something about me?"

When I looked up, I was surprised to see Chase's ears were a little red–a surefire sign he was embarrassed about something. "Never mind."

"No, what is it, Chase?" I asked, resting my chin on my fist. I wanted to make him squirm. "Tell me."

"Nah. It's not appropriate."

"Well, now you *have* to tell me."

Chase shook his head, but I can tell from the way he sighed I'd broken him. It was so easy to get him to concede. With his eyes fixed on the floor between my desk and his, he said, "I was just remembering how you had that… schoolgirl fantasy."

I felt my own ears getting hot as he met my eyes. I couldn't believe he was bringing that up right now. I internally cringed, picturing the schoolgirl outfit I still had in a tote in the back of my closet.

He'd said imagining me as a Catholic schoolgirl creeped him out, so we turned it into this whole sorority girl/professor thing—I wore the plaid skirt the entire time, and I insisted he keep his tie and glasses on.

Fuck, was he thinking about all of that right now, too?

"Sorority girl," I corrected, pressing my palms flat against the laminate desktop. Chase was suddenly unable to look me in the eye, which I found oddly endearing. I could feel myself blushing harder when I remembered the way he growled, *"You're going to earn that A,"* before sucking on his pinkie finger to lubricate it.

Chase always played into my little fantasies. Every last one. You might even say he ended up enjoying them more than me.

Sitting before me now, he gripped the edge of the teacher's desk until his knuckles turned slightly white. How many times had those same, sturdy hands grasped my waist, slapped my ass, and brought me to completion? And why was all of that on my mind right now?

His Adam's apple bobbed before he said, "Right. So… I made you a list." He reached for his phone on the desk beside him, his hands trembling. Wow, talking about our past really rattled him. It was hard to focus on his words as he scrolled through his apps—I could only stare at his fingers. "Do you just want to look at it yourself?"

"What?" I realized he was leaning forward to give me his phone. "Oh, sure." I laid his phone atop my notebook and read the list in his notes app.

Skate park dev news

Feral cats

Candy shop turning 75 (Meg likes their buckeyes)

Evil bradford pear trees

Homeless pop. of Woodvale

Local music scene?

I put his phone down and covered my mouth to hide my smile. "What?" Chase asked. "Are they bad ideas? Is it the evil trees?"

"Look at my list, Chase," I said, picking up my notebook and thrusting it outward. He took it from me, and before long, he was smiling, too, because our lists were strikingly similar. The invasive Bradford pears, the anticipated skate park, and the growing feral cat population—they were all on mine, too. And like him, I'd included a mention of my love for the buckeyes at Colemans' Candies.

He lowered my notebook to look at me. "You forgot 'local music scene, *question mark?*'"

"Do we have one?" I raised an eyebrow.

"That's the question."

I let out a tiny chuckle and crossed my arms. "Well, that's a good list. I'm actually impressed you did your homework."

He opened his mouth to say something only to bring his lips back together a second later. Whatever he had been about to say, he'd decided against it. I watched as he licked his lips, reconsidering his words. "Yeah… and I refrained from adding any ghost sightings or witchy cults."

"I'm sure that was very hard for you," I said, scribbling something down in my notebook. "What was that part about the Woodvale homeless population? Do you know something?"

"I hoped you'd favor that one. And no, I don't know anything that's necessarily newsworthy, but I've talked to Lenny a lot, and I know there's a story there."

I knew who he was talking about—Lenny was a Woodvale icon. He rode his bicycle from one end of the town to the other day after day, collecting aluminum cans and talking to anyone who would stop for a chat. And he lived in the–

My face fell. "You just want to go to the abandoned orphanage."

"What? No," Chase said, but he sounded guilty as sin. "Why, is that where he lives these days?"

"Everyone knows that's where he's been staying. Don't pretend you didn't know."

"I forgot."

I shot a stubborn smile in his direction. "Well, regardless, there might be a story there. Everyone in town has a Lenny story, but nobody really *knows* him. We could talk about his life while shining a light on homelessness in Woodvale."

"That's more or less what I was thinking."

"Good. I'm going to do some research and prepare some questions." I flipped to a blank page in my notebook. "Let's make sure to approach this in a respectful, non-exploitative way."

"Agreed. Let him keep his dignity." He looked down at his phone as he typed something with his thumb. "Maybe I'll ask him if he has any ghostly roommates."

I sighed. "Chase."

He looked down at me with a grin. "Relax, Wednesday. I'm only kidding."

"When are you going to stop calling me that?"

"How about… never?"

"That's fine, I'll just give you an annoying nickname, too." I thought for a minute. "What are the Ghostbusters' names?"

"Uh… Peter, Ray, Egon, and Winston?"

Of course he knew. "Which one's the worst?"

Chase raised an eyebrow at me. "In what context?"

"You know what, never mind. I'm just going to call you Egon because his name sounds the dumbest."

We locked eyes, and for a few seconds, neither of us said anything. His ever-present smirk was still there, but I was more distracted by his tousled hair, which looked like it might have a little bit of product in it to give it that perfect, deliberately messy look.

I taught him how to do that.

He licked his lips. "Look at that, I've gone from 'professor' to 'doctor' with you," he said, his voice dipping lower to that teasing, husky tone he used to use with me. He knew exactly what that tone did to me back in the day.

"On second thought," I said, flipping my notebook shut, "I'll stick to calling you 'dumbass.'"

Chase just tilted his head to the side, giving me the usual smug, subtle grin, like he knew I didn't really mean it. His charm was getting through to me, and he could tell.

chapter twelve

chase

By that afternoon, Meghan had more homework for me to do. She spent the rest of her morning researching homeless people, and she wanted me to read all these articles and watch a bunch of videos about how to talk to them. How to talk *about* them.

Meghan: He's unhoused, not homeless. He has a home. It just doesn't look like yours or mine.

Chase: probably more like mine though

Meghan: Probably.

She suggested I talk to Lenny sans-camera first to gauge how he felt about being interviewed. That evening, before sunset, I drove around town scoping out his usual spots, hoping to find him riding his bike rather than having to encroach on his personal space at the old orphanage. Thankfully, I spotted him just down the road from the scrapyard where he sold his cans. He was glad to have someone to talk to, and even more happy to see the ham sandwich from the deli I had for him. I bought one for myself, too, and I ate with him in the parking lot of a Dollar General to make him feel less like a charity case. "Listen, Lenny. There's something I need your help with."

"Me?" He blinked at me in surprise, raising his graying, bushy eyebrows. He was wearing a sock cap even though it was a relatively warm day. "How can I help you, son?"

"Well," I said, tossing a piece of crust toward one of the geese waddling nearby in a ditch. "It's actually for my friend, Meghan. She's a writer for the newspaper, but people just aren't reading it that much anymore. She needs–"

"I read it all the time!" he expressed with a little chuckle. "Every issue. Circle-K gives me all their leftover papers. Kroger, too. Stacks and stacks of newspapers that don't sell. You wouldn't believe how many." Actually, I could believe it, and I was glad Meghan wasn't around to hear that comment. "Anyway, I bet you're talking about Meghan Dobson."

I smiled. "I am. You've read her articles, huh?"

"She writes about dead people a lot." Lenny's eyes widened.

"That she does." I clicked my tongue. "Well, Lenny, you know how you said there's a lot of leftover papers? That's the problem. Other people aren't reading the Woodvale Times that much anymore, and it's bumming her out. She thought—she and I thought—maybe people would like to read about you."

He contorted his face into a doubtful grimace. "Me? What would they want to read about me for?"

"Everyone knows who you are, but I bet you've got some interesting stories to tell. Would you be comfortable talking about how you came to be—I mean, live up at the old orphanage?"

Lenny's brows furrowed, and he gave this some thought for a while. I stared at his hands, rough and weathered, holding what was left of his sandwich. "Well," he said, his voice sounding like his throat might be full of phlegm. "People don't really want to hear what I have to say. She might want to write about someone better."

I looked at Lenny's face, wondering what this man might look like if he'd been dealt a better hand in life. There was an almost youthful spark in his eyes, but years of exposure to the elements made his face look worn and tired. With a sigh, I put my half-eaten sandwich back in its clamshell box and said, "Well, the truth is, interviewing you was my idea. Meghan and I are sort of partnering to do the news together, and I was really hoping you'd talk to me, too. We both want to hear what you have to say—and I know the people of Woodvale do, too."

He looked me in the eyes. "You'll be there, too?"

I nodded. "Yeah, the whole time."

Lenny stared at his hands for a moment. "You're easy to talk to, so that might be okay." I couldn't recall my first interaction with Lenny, but we'd spoken more times than I could count. Anytime he saw me with my camera set up somewhere, he'd stand beside me to watch my screen. Sometimes he rode his bike back and forth behind the people I interviewed, making me wonder if he had a place to watch the evening news to spot himself on it.

"You'll do it?"

Lenny gave a small nod after a moment of contemplation "Alright," he said, "I'll talk to you both. I'll be up at my place on the hill all afternoon tomorrow. You can come by then." I assumed his place up on the hill meant the orphanage. He stared at the ground for a second longer before adding, "But I don't want you showing where I sleep, where I live. I don't need people seeing that. It might seem… strange."

"Gotcha," I said. "We can talk outside, then."

A flicker of relief flashed across his face. He thanked me for the sandwich and got on his bike, stopping at the edge of the lot to pick up a discarded can. And then he was on his way.

**

"Let me preface what I'm about to ask you by saying I'm not trying to stereotype, and I hope it doesn't make you think less of me," Meghan said as she buckled her seatbelt in my passenger seat the next day. Her car was back from the shop, but she suggested we continue riding together for our assignments—it made more sense that way.

"I already think you're the spawn of Satan, so I couldn't possibly think less of you." I tilted my head to the side and gave her the most obnoxiously smug grin I could muster.

And I was lying through my teeth.

"Whatever," she said with a dismissive roll of her eyes. "I was just going to ask... do you think Lenny might get, you know, defensive or aggressive when we start asking him about his past? I mean, statistically, a lot of unhoused people have been through some serious trauma, and I don't want to push him into a bad place or make him mad. And for what it's worth, this is more about him being a strange man than an unhoused person. This is just something women have to think about, you know?"

"Right," I said. I glanced at her, catching a flicker of apprehension in her eyes. "You're worried he's going to get aggressive?"

"I'm saying we don't know anything about this man. I mean, I don't even know Lenny's real name, so that limited my research on him. I'm just a little concerned he might be dangerous."

"Dangerous? No," I said, pausing for a deep inhale because I knew I was about to impress her. Like her, I'd spent the previous day gathering all the info I could. My contact at the police department opened up about her various run-ins with

Lenny over the years, and once I had his last name, most of what I found was public record. "Leonard Eugene Carr, age sixty-four, robbed a gas station in Indianapolis in 2005. Had a couple of DUIs before that. And, more recently, he was picked up for loitering here in Woodvale. Does he have a criminal record? Yes. But he's not dangerous."

"Oh." She reached up to adjust her bangs, perhaps a little embarrassed she wasn't able to obtain this information herself. "Okay, I guess none of those crimes make him unsafe to be around."

I shook my head. "Lenny's a character, maybe a little rough around the edges. But you don't need to be afraid of him. Besides, I'll keep you safe."

Shit. I'd just said the quiet part out loud, and I was too terrified of her reaction to even turn my head. I could feel the heat rising in my neck. Why did I have to say that last part? I gripped the steering wheel tight, bracing myself for her inevitable remark about my supposed "hero complex." She loved throwing that in my face.

But instead of a snarky comment, she simply said, "Thank you."

I glanced over, my heart beating faster when I saw her looking right back at me. Was she actually being… sincere? Our eyes locked a couple seconds longer than they should have, and her gaze slowly softened into an expression I hadn't seen from her in a long, long time—like she might not hate me very much. My eyes flitted down to her slowly opening mouth, the soft peaks of her berry-tinted upper lip reminding me of the way I'd sometimes trace them with my thumb before kissing her.

It wasn't until the car drifted into the gravel at the side of the road that we tore our eyes off of each other. I swerved back toward the center with an overcorrecting jerk, steering to the right just in time to avoid an oncoming FedEx truck. It blared its horn at us as we passed, just missing it by inches. "Fuck!"

Meghan gripped the edges of her seat, her breaths fast and shallow. "You're really off to a great start at keeping me safe," she muttered.

Well. That moment was fun while it lasted.

chapter thirteen

meghan

Everything I assumed about Leonard Carr was wrong.

Interestingly enough, I felt safer talking to him than I did with that asshole barber shop owner on Main Street. Lenny had the kindest eyes, and the most genuine belly laugh I'd ever heard.

Sure, he rambled and went off on tangents, but it became obvious early on that he was just lonely. It wasn't hard to see that he didn't get many opportunities to have someone truly listen to him. We just let him talk. The pauses between his stories were longer than they needed to be, as if he were waiting for me or Chase to interrupt, but we didn't. I wanted him to feel like he had someone's attention, and I knew Chase felt the same.

Every now and then, I'd try to steer the conversation toward his past. Just gentle nudges—nothing too invasive. "Lenny, when did you first come to Woodvale?" I asked, recalling what Chase had said about the incident at the gas station in Indy. I was working up to asking him *how* he got here.

He shifted with his back against the brick wall of the orphanage behind him, his eyes flicking to the ground. He'd met us here on the gravel outside the building as soon as we pulled up, and that's where we remained. "I can't remember exactly. I mean, I've been here a really long time." He chuckled awkwardly, scratching at his beard. "I've been down every street in this town. I bet you I could draw you a map of it from memory."

I smiled, not wanting to push him into answering the original question. Something about the way he changed the subject told me it wasn't worth it. Instead, I just nodded, deciding to let him talk about what he wanted.

The public didn't need to know how he got here to have compassion for him, anyway.

Chase had questions, too, standing in front of his camera wearing that new blazer and holding the WWTV microphone in front of Lenny's face. He transformed into a different person when the camera was on him, and it wasn't just the newscaster voice or his confident posture. He was so calm and composed, and he spoke to Lenny like he was the only person in the world who mattered. I caught the careful way he used the verbiage from the articles I'd sent him the day before, never once calling Lenny "homeless."

And he didn't ask a single question about ghosts.

"Lenny, what's something you wish people understood about folks who are unhoused? About what it's really like for someone living in your shoes, day-to-day?

Lenny rubbed the back of his neck, staring down at the ground while he thought about his answer. Finally, he looked at Chase and said, "People tell me sometimes to just get a job, but what they don't understand is that you have to have an address to get a job. And you have to have a job to get a home with an address. It's impossible. People like me, we're just… stuck."

Chase's eyes flitted over to mine, and in that brief glance, I could see he was struggling to keep his composure. We both felt the weight of Lenny's words. I knew from the way Chase swallowed that he, too, had a lump forming in his throat. It took him a few seconds to ask his next question.

Someone at WWTV was going to have to do some creative editing if they wanted to hide Chase's emotions.

As he continued his segment of the interview, I thought about a phone call I'd made that morning in my research. I'd reached out to a local church that tried to help the few unhoused people in Woodvale get back on their feet. They knew Lenny well, but they said he refused help, insisting he told them he was happy where he was. But they still kept a close eye on him, just in case. It wasn't much, but they couldn't force him to accept help. And really, there was only so much they could do with limited resources in our small town.

Chase was quiet when he wrapped up the interview and shut his camera off. I stuck my pen in the spiral of my notebook, watching him bend over to pack his microphone and cords, when Lenny put his hands on his hips and asked, "Did you know this place is haunted?"

Oh, geez. Chase's head shot my direction, and I just knew he was waiting for me to grunt and sigh to display my annoyance. But something about his boyish grin and the excitement in his eyes made me smile, too. With a playful roll of my eyes, I said, "I'm going to walk around while you guys talk about that." Before I turned to walk away, I gave him a subtle look of approval.

I wandered around to the side of the building, running my hand along the crumbling brick wall. The year 1902 was etched into the stone near the corner—faint, but still visible. I'd read about this place plenty of times, and I knew more than I probably needed to. The orphanage had closed decades ago, long before I was born.

There wasn't a door anymore, just an open doorway. Dead leaves and scraps of trash were piled up in one corner by the entrance. I stood just at the doorway without stepping inside. Beams of sunlight filtered through a tall, broken window, casting dusty streams of light that made the whole place feel eerie, even in the middle of the afternoon. No wonder everyone said this place was haunted.

Just inside the door, there were newspapers scattered around the floor. I spotted my own name printed on a page near my foot. I assumed it would've been an old issue of the Times, but there was my Fannie Decker piece from just a few days ago. It looked like there were several copies of that same edition strewn on the floor nearby. How the hell did they end up here?

I glanced up to see stacks of old papers stuffed in gaps between the broken boards, the stories I'd poured my heart into now being used to insulate walls and patch up holes in the windows. A sigh escaped my lips. *At least the paper's good for something.*

For a few minutes, I leaned against the outside wall and began dictating into my phone, drafting the article. Sometimes that was the fastest way to get my thoughts out, especially when I had a hundred of them at once. "Within these quiet walls, Lenny has crafted a life that's entirely his own… finding comfort and familiarity in a place most have long forgotten." I swallowed, thinking to myself, *a lot like him.*

After making my way around the perimeter of the building, I made my way back to Lenny and Chase. Their voices echoed from around the corner. I paused once I realized they weren't discussing ghosts anymore—Lenny was talking about a woman.

"She's awfully pretty, and she seems sharp as a tack, too."

Chase let out a hesitant chuckle. "Ha, yeah, agreed on both counts. She's a hell of a lot smarter than me, that's for sure, and she's so beautiful it's almost intimidating."

My first assumption was that they might be talking about Mayor Michaels. She fit the description, and she was the only woman who came to mind when I considered whom both of these men knew.

But then Chase added, "Just don't tell Meghan I said that, alright? I've got a reputation to maintain, and I like to keep her on her toes."

Oh, shit. That was about me?

I couldn't move. It was like my feet were glued to the pavement. The warmth settling in the pit of my stomach matched the heat spreading across my face, making it feel like I was blushing throughout my entire body. I couldn't decide which compliment was more difficult to process—the fact he believed I was smarter than him or the thought that I was so beautiful it intimidated him.

I tried to feel annoyed at him for having the audacity to speak favorably of me behind my back while being a menace to my face, but I couldn't deny the way it made my breath catch in my throat. I could handle all of his teasing and insults all day long, but him complimenting me was far more damaging to my psyche.

This after his declaration he'd keep me safe in the car had me completely fucked up in the most confusing way.

Though I said nothing to allude to my overhearing him and Lenny talk, Chase could tell something was bothering me when we got back into the car. "You're quiet."

"Just thinking about Lenny," I lied, holding my breath as he put his hand on my headrest, looking over his shoulder as he backed up. I could smell his deodorant, the same amber and sandalwood scent I used to practically inhale to soothe myself when he held me close. *Fucking hell, Meghan, get it together.*

"You missed all the good stuff. He told me about all his ghost sightings."

I channeled the weird, annoying emotions bubbling inside of me to anger. Chase didn't really deserve my rage at the moment, considering he'd just complimented me, but I found the whole thing displeasing. Most of all, I was angry at myself for the way I allowed him to make my head spin. I clenched my jaw, trying to push down this ridiculous swirl of emotions I never consented to. "I'm sure it was very riveting."

He didn't deserve the attitude. I knew that. And when he bit his bottom lip before saying, "It was, at least to me," something squeezed at my heart.

She's so beautiful, it's almost intimidating.

I'll keep you safe.

Letting him talk about his passion was the least I could do, wasn't it? Reluctantly, I asked him to describe what Lenny shared with him, and he rambled about their conversation the entire way back to the newsroom. I listened to every word, withholding the judgmental remarks on the tip of my tongue.

"You should ask him if the ghost's name is Billy," I said once we pulled into the parking lot at the old school.

"Billy?" Chase's brows furrowed.

Did he really forget? "Little Billy, the orphan you said got left behind in the fire, remember?"

Chase smiled as he shifted into park, giving me a slow nod. "Oh yeah, I forgot about that. Actually, you were right. Lenny said the ghost resembled a tall and slender man. He's never heard kids laughing, either. That might have been made up."

As I reached up to tuck my hair behind my ears, I said, "You should know by now, I'm always right."

Neither of us made a move to gather our things and get out of the car. Chase's thumb traced the seam on the side of his fabric seat while he stared at me, his eyes concentrating on mine. When he lowered his gaze, his face softened, and I got the impression he changed his mind about what he wanted to say. A bigger smile stretched across his face before he said, "I was right about your battery."

I rolled my eyes and unbuckled. "Oh, shut up. So you were right about one thing."

With a satisfied smirk, he watched me scramble to get out of the car. As I tossed my bag over my shoulder on the sidewalk, Chase rolled down the passenger window and said, "I'm right about a lot of things, you'll just never admit it because you're so goddamn stubborn."

I bent over so I could see his face. "So stubborn it's intimidating?" I quipped.

Chase's smile slowly faded. I could practically see the gears turning in his head as he pondered whether or not it was a coincidence that I'd chosen that specific phrasing. I did my best to smirk at him in a way that told him what he feared–that I'd overheard him talking to Lenny. He swallowed. "Something like that, yeah."

God, fucking with him was too easy. However, I was the one feeling embarrassed all of a sudden—because I was smiling so big my cheeks started to hurt. Nothing I could do would make it stop. Not biting my cheeks, not imagining all his nerdy FunkoPops lining the walls of the bedroom we once shared.

Not even his stupid, wrinkly shirt could wipe the grin from my lips.

What's the matter with me?

My smile didn't fade until I made it to my cubicle where a musty, leather journal sat on the middle of my desk, its cover half-torn, revealing the first yellowed page with faded writing. "What the hell is this?" I hollered out, dropping my bag on the floor. I carefully picked it up, flipping it over to see the back cover was completely missing.

"Some lady dropped that off for you," Xander yelled back.

"Why?"

"She's a fan of your column. I don't know." He kept typing, clearly bothered by my questioning.

"Okay," I said, lifting one eyebrow as I opened the journal to the middle. The thing was falling apart in my hands, its loose pages almost slipping out from the bottom. The writing was so faded, it was barely legible. "Xander, would you mind giving me, like, a crumb of context here? Where did it come from?"

With a heavy sigh, he stood up and walked around the corner into my cubicle. "I don't know. They found it in an old barn or something. I almost threw it in the trash because it's stinking up the whole newsroom."

He wasn't wrong—it smelled like it had gotten wet at some point, and the black blotches on one of the corners resembled mold. "Why did they think I'd want it?"

Xander put his hands in his pockets. "It belonged to one of those old dead broads you wrote about."

I looked up with a confused scowl. "Which one?"

"I didn't write down what the lady said. But it's probably in the journal, right?" he asked with a shrug. "You know, 'This journal belongs to 'Jane Smith' or whatever?"

I ran through the names from my recent columns in my mind, narrowing them down based on who might have a journal in this condition. I blurted the first woman who came to mind. "Was it Fannie Decker?"

Xander nodded. "Yeah, I think that might be what she said."

Oh my God—I was holding Fannie's journal.

To anyone else, Fannie Decker was just another name lost to history—a nobody who died almost two centuries ago. But her life, as short as it was, left an imprint on me. It felt like I was holding a piece of her soul in my hands.

I lowered myself to my desk chair, carefully thumbing through the journal to find a scrap of writing I could decipher. The middle pages were less weathered, which made them a little easier to read. A couple of sentences caught my eye, darker than most of her other writing, as though she might have been pressing her pen harder against the paper.

That damn fox has outwitted me again. He lives to taunt me. Next time I see him, I'll shoot straighter.

Well, Jillian was right. Fannie was a bad bitch.

chapter fourteen

chase

Meghan was in an infectious good mood the following Monday. Not only was she on a high from the publication of our Lenny story in the Sunday edition, which was shooting her subscription number through the roof, but this whole Fannie thing was giving her life.

It was refreshing to sit back and watch *her* be the one to hyperfixate on something as I often did. "And listen to this," she said, slowly turning a page in the journal that sat in front of her on the little school desk, "She skinned the fox that ate some of her chickens and used its pelt to make a scarf."

"Gross. Maybe that's why nobody married her." I only made the remark to make Meghan shoot a playful glare in my direction—and I got exactly the reaction I'd hoped for. "How many pages have you transcribed so far?"

Over the past few days, Meghan had gone from carrying a single notebook to wielding three of them at all times. One was for official newspaper business, and another for copying Fannie's words. The third one was the tattered old journal itself. "Still just a few partial pages," she said, eyeing her new notebook. "And it's all about chickens. It's no surprise, I guess, that she froze to death while she was on her way to feed them."

"You might even say she died doing what she loved."

Two weeks ago, Meghan would have scoffed and tossed some hateful comment my way. Hell, she might have even thrown one of her notebooks at my head. But now there was a twinkle in her eyes as she rolled them at me, running her hand through her hair. She wasn't sporting the usual updo that day. Her dark, shiny strands loosely framed her face as she looked down at the open notebooks spread out in front of her.

What caught my attention even more than her hair, however, was the way she smiled a lot more these days. I could tell she was finding me more tolerable, and it was almost like it annoyed her—like she couldn't control the way her hatred of me was tapering off.

I watched as she leaned forward, completely absorbed in Fannie's journal, her brows furrowed in concentration. We'd come up to this abandoned classroom to plan our week, but Meghan was entirely focused on Fannie.

Kind of like I was entirely focused on the subtle way her lips moved as she mouthed the words of the journal entry to herself.

I cleared my throat, forcing myself to snap out of it. "Where do you think Fannie's ghost hangs around?"

Meghan lifted her chin to look at me. "Judging from what she wrote here, I'd say she's still guarding her chicken coop in the afterlife."

"Do you think we could track down where she lived and scope it out?" I crossed my arms against my chest, worried this might be a little forward. After all, this wasn't official news business I was suggesting, and she knew it. I regretted my inclusion of the word "we" more with every passing second, wishing I hadn't inserted myself into her hobby.

But Meghan glanced from me to the window before returning her gaze to the old journal, saying, "Maybe. I know she lived on Persimmon Road."

I tried not to let my surprise show, but damn, I was relishing in her not immediately shutting me down. She didn't laugh it off, didn't scoff, didn't hit me with some sarcastic quip about how this wasn't my business. "Isn't that the road that runs behind the high school?" I asked, trying to keep my tone casual. "That's right by Ackerman Woods."

Meghan blinked a couple of times. "You mean the woods the witch supposedly haunts? Do you have ulterior motives for wanting to come along with me, Chase?"

"I wasn't even thinking about that," I answered with a laugh. And it was true. "If you want to go explore Fannie's old stomping grounds together sometime, I'll take you out there. And I won't bring any of my equipment, I promise."

Meghan tapped her pen on the desk, thinking this over. "Then what's in it for you?"

I slowly brought my lips together, reconsidering my declaration that she was smarter than me. Because if that were true, she'd realize the only reason I wanted to tag along was to have the opportunity to spend time with her. Couldn't she figure that out? "If we encounter anything supernatural, I can always go back with Sean."

She considered this for a moment, finally saying, "Let me think about it," carefully closing Fannie's journal. And then, with a whimsical smile, she said, "We went out to the metal bridge on that road before, remember?"

Of course I did. I'd carved our initials into the rusty supports with my pocketknife. I wondered if they were still visible, or had years of weathering worn the rust away? "Yep. That's where we saw that fat groundhog."

"No," she said, tucking her hair behind her ears. "That was that other bridge, the old wooden one."

I knew better than to argue with her, but I was pretty sure she was remembering this wrong. I merely muttered a doubtful, "Hmm."

"You don't believe me?" she questioned, pulling out her phone. "Let's just fact-check it, then, shall we?"

"Fact-check it? How?" I asked with a laugh.

"There's a picture of it on the blog. Just let me find it."

I lifted one eyebrow in confusion. "You're on our blog right now? How in the hell is that site still up?"

Meghan stopped scrolling to gaze up at me, and her cheeks turned the slightest shade of pink. "Because... because I'm still paying for it," she admitted.

This was news to me. "All of it? The domain, the hosting?"

She nodded. "I mean, yeah? We put a lot of work into it, Chase. I didn't want it to just disappear. I still get emails from people every now and then."

She was even paying for the custom email? I swallowed, struggling to process the reasoning behind all of this. I'd assumed the website died when our relationship died. I almost opened my mouth to point out she could have downloaded the archives rather than pay a monthly fee to keep it open, but Meghan had to have known that. She was no idiot. Maybe there was a part of her, perhaps some small part, that couldn't let go of everything we built together.

Before I could dwell on it any longer, Meghan put her phone away and said she'd look up the groundhog detail later, mentioning we needed to get to work. As we planned out the week's interviews and events, I found it nearly impossible to focus on anything but the delicate way she had one leg crossed over the other, pointing her knees toward me as she spoke.

She is so falling back in love with me.

**

"Meghan's been paying for *Woodvale Whispers* all this time." Those were the first words out of my mouth when I entered The Comics Vault. The stairs from my apartment led into a little hallway at the back of the store. It was five minutes after closing, and Sean was locking the door behind a couple of his regulars, some RPG players who paid Sean a monthly fee to host their games at a table at the back of the store. My bed was just above their meeting area, so it wasn't uncommon for me to be jolted awake from a nap by someone screaming, *"Critical hit! I decapitated the orc!"*

Honestly, I took comfort in the fact there were bigger nerds in Woodvale than Sean and me.

"And?" Sean asked, walking over to his cash register while I grabbed a broom to sweep up the Dorito crumbs on the floor around the RPG table. I often chipped in to help him close up, so we could head out for our ghost stakeouts faster. "What are you implying?"

"It makes me feel like some part of her still cares," I said, bending over to pick up a crumpled character sheet.

"Right," Sean said, popping open the cash register. "About the website."

"Yes. And," I said, pausing for emphasis, "maybe this is a little delusional of me to assume, but… it could mean she cares about me, too."

Sean tilted his head back and groaned, holding a stack of cash in his hand. "I knew you were still in love with her."

"I never said that."

"Are you still in love with her?"

I turned around, still clutching the broom, and scanned the shelf of trade paperbacks behind me. My eyes landed on the newest volume of *Saga*. "Hey, look, I still haven't gotten around to reading this," I said, holding the book up to Sean in an attempt to deflect his question. "You should let me borrow it."

"First of all, this isn't a library, dude," Sean said, slamming the cash register drawer. "And second, you need to move on. For the sake of your mental health. And mine. And probably hers."

"Hey, if I can listen to you describe the color, consistency, and smell of Dimitri's diaper blowouts in great detail, you can listen to me whine about Meghan." I scooped the dirt and crumbs into the dustpan and dumped them in the bin by the counter before grabbing my backpack and GoPro from the table. "Anyway, are you ready to head out?"

Sean nodded. "We should probably hurry. I only have an hour and a half before I need to get home. Let's stay focused. I won't talk about baby stuff if you don't wax poetic about how much you miss Meghan."

"Deal," I said, rolling my eyes. I missed the days when Sean and I could go ghost hunting into the late hours of the night, before he had more responsibilities at home. I understood, but it didn't make it any less annoying. And lately, it seemed like his sense of humor was buried beneath all his stress. The lighthearted jokes I often relied on him for, the very thing Owen said was the reason people watched our videos, were practically a thing of the past. I never thought I'd have to ask Sean to be less serious, but I'd almost reached that point.

I had to hand it to him, though. He was pulling most of the weight when it came to promoting and planning the comic book convention. And amazingly, he finally got a solid "yes" out of Ethan Killian's assistant. The actor's name was officially on all of our flyers, bumping Owen Gardner's name down to the next line. We were rolling with the big-time celebs now.

Well, sort of.

Just as Sean was re-locking the door of the shop behind us, my phone buzzed in my back pocket. I pulled it out, expecting a breaking news alert—it wouldn't be the first time I'd have to ditch our plans to go cover a fire or an accident. But much to my relief, it was a text from Meghan.

Meghan: Is it weird that I kind of hope we run into Fannie's ghost? There's so much I'd like to ask her.

A grin tugged at my lips as I reread the message, pausing on the sidewalk in front of The Comics Vault. Meghan was initiating a text conversation with me, and it sounded like she was down to scout out the woods around Persimmon Road with me, too.

I wanted to show the message to Sean, just to prove Meghan was reciprocating my feelings, but he might start detailing the time Dimitri spit up into his mouth. So, I kept it to myself, typing a quick response as I followed Sean to his car.

Chase: You're not worried she'll come after you for reading her diary?

Meghan: I can take a Victorian ghost.

Chase: Famous last words. Better hope you can run faster than the fox she gunned down.

chapter fifteen

meghan

I would have been beating Xander by a much wider margin if it weren't for Poppy, the bar owner, announcing her retirement after decades of service in Woodvale. She wanted to sell the place to new owners who would promise to keep things the same. But if she couldn't find someone who felt like the right fit, her family was going to shutter the place for good.

Jillian and Xander snatched up the story the second they caught wind of it. It ran the Monday after my Lenny article, and Xander was only trailing me by two subscriptions the following morning.

On the plus side, my count kept growing. Over the past two days, Graham had been entering the newsroom every few hours to add a couple of tallies below my name.

"And that, my friend, is how you create viral content," I said to Xander, who was staring at the chalkboard with his hands on his hips.

"Bask in it while you can, because you're going to be eating my dust in a few weeks."

"Yeah? What are you cooking up?"

With a brief glance at the ceiling, Xander said, "It's confidential. But it's going to send this town into a frenzy."

"Xander, the new bike lane on Hartwell Street sent this town into a frenzy, so that's not really saying much." I picked up my ever-growing stack of notebooks from the conference table, dropping them into my bag. Something about the confident look in Xander's eyes told me not to doubt him—and it reminded me not to let my guard down. "Just stay out of trouble, alright?"

"Never."

I gave him the stern look of an ashamed mother, or at least a disappointed older sister, before I left the newsroom. Chase and I were heading out to interview a tattoo artist who'd just appeared on a few episodes of a tattoo competition show on TLC. Now that the episode in which she got voted out had aired, she could give us the scoop about what really happened behind the scenes.

Mae just happened to be my go-to tattoo artist, so naturally, the story was my idea. Her woman-run, cottagecore-themed shop went against the norm in the best way. Entering it was like inhaling a breath of fresh air.

Fresh, weed-scented air.

"Hey," Mae called out from the back of the shop, elongating the word in a casual, sleepy way. Her pink and orange pigtails reminded me of the sherbet I ate when I was a kid. She looked past me at Chase, who was spinning in a slow circle at the center of the shop, probably assessing the lighting situation and planning where to set up. "Do you sense any paranormal activity in here?"

Chase whipped around to face her, casting a quick glance in my direction before asking, "Why, have you seen something?"

"I wish," Mae answered with a laugh. She grinned at him from the other side of the jewelry display case, resting her hands on the glass. "No, I just recognize you from your vlog. You and Sean are hilarious."

Oh, brother. Chase shifted the backpack on his shoulder with a nervous laugh. I withheld the teasing comment on the tip of my tongue, realizing this might have been the first time he encountered a real, live fan of his vlog. "Tell that to the guy who's been leaving us all the hate comments," Chase said, taking a few steps toward her.

Mae laughed, lifting a hand to play with the end of one of her pigtails. "Hey, you know you've made it when you've got haters, right?"

Were they flirting? Mae and I had only known each other for a couple of years, so she had no way of knowing Chase was my ex. They kept talking about Chase's YouTube channel, and their exchange was innocuous enough.

Mae turned to me with raised eyebrows. "Did you see the one where they got stranded in the pond?"

"Yeah," I said, reaching up to adjust my bangs. "That's why you don't trust Sean with a paddle."

Mae laughed, but I turned my attention toward Chase, whose eyes were locked on me with a look of awe. I tilted my head to the side in subtle confusion, until I realized I'd just accidentally revealed I'd watched one of his videos.

The boat video was their most popular upload, and I simply watched it out of curiosity a couple nights ago with Wanda curled up on my lap. It didn't mean anything. Judging from Chase's wide-eyed expression, however, it meant a lot.

I glanced down at the notebook in my hands. "Well, Chase, do you want to get set up and interview Mae on camera first?"

He blinked, as if coming back to reality. "Right, yeah. Let's get started."

Chase began his segment of the interview with his usual casual charm, and Mae seemed to eat it right up. She laughed a lot, getting more relaxed as the questions went on. Her tone was light and playful as she leaned against the jewelry display case, completely at ease.

Mae spilled some secrets about what it was like working with the TLC crew, choosing her words carefully so she wouldn't break the terms of her non-disclosure agreement. Chase covered almost everything I needed for my write-up, so besides just a few clarifying questions from me, the entire interview was short and sweet. I photographed Mae in front of the ivy wall near the windows, and I had a pretty good feeling about this story drawing people in.

Eat it, Xander.

"Hey, when am I going to get you in here to do a full sleeve, girl?" she asked, eyeing my bare forearms, which probably looked like blank canvases to her. I was the one who'd been hemming and hawing about expanding my sleeves at my last three appointments with her, but I had yet to make the commitment. Mae, resting her elbows on the counter and her chin on her hands, watched Chase pack up his equipment as she waited for my response.

"Oh, one of these days," I answered with a half-smile. Like her, I watched Chase fold up the legs of his tripod, oblivious to the two women staring at him as he whistled the *Avengers* theme song to himself. Having removed his blazer, his muscular biceps were peeking out from the sleeves of his gray t-shirt. I knew he owned a set of dumbbells that probably still collected dust, so the muscles must have come from schlepping around all this camera equipment day after day.

Mae turned to me and whispered, "He looks a little bit like Clark Kent, doesn't he?"

I rolled my eyes, feeling the urge to vehemently agree, but I held myself back. "Oh God, don't say that too loud. He'll let it get to his head."

When Mae let out a soft giggle, Chase finally looked up from zipping his bag, glancing from me to her in confusion. "Am I missing something?"

"Just girl talk," I said on my way to the door. I pushed the bar with my hip. "Ready to go, Clark?"

"What?" I took pleasure in the nervous way he tugged at the bottom of his t-shirt, glancing at Mae like she might offer an explanation. But she just shrugged with a grin.

"Let me know when you're ready for more ink, Meghan, and I'll get you on my books," she said. "Thanks for coming by. Both of you."

Chase gave her a nod. "Thanks for your time."

"Yeah, no problem. I'll try to take care of the haters in your comments for you, alright?" She was fidgeting with the ends of her pigtails again.

"Appreciate it," Chase answered with an awkward laugh, barely looking at her. He had no clue. None. It was all I could do not to give him a shove as we made our way to his car—he absolutely had a chance with that woman, but he squandered it.

"What is wrong with you?" I asked him from the opposite side of the car, waiting for him to find his keys in his pocket to unlock it.

"What? What do you mean?" He looked over the roof of the car at me in a full-blown panic. "Did I say something stupid?"

"You could've gotten her number."

"Who, Mae's?" He glanced past me at the facade of the tattoo parlor, where the window was decorated with painted mushrooms that matched Mae's artistic style. "I don't think so."

"Uh, I think so," I said, pulling the passenger door open after I heard it unlock. "She was flirting with you."

"She was being polite."

"No, she's attracted to you. Trust me, okay? I can tell."

He shook his head. "No." That was it. Just… *no*. Neither of us got in the car, just staring at each other over the top of it instead. Some small part of me was disappointed for Chase's sake, knowing he probably could have asked Mae to come along on his next ghost hunt. She would've said "yes" in a heartbeat.

But another, smaller part of me—a minuscule, microscopic part—was glad he didn't have enough game to notice the attention she was giving him. "You're probably right. She's not your type anyway. You couldn't pull a girl like that," I muttered, finally getting into my seat. I dropped my bag between my feet on the floorboard and checked my bangs in the mirror, not at all surprised at the X-men comic that fell from his visor when I opened it.

Chase leaned through his open driver door. "'Not my type'?" he scoffed. "She's, like, the pastel version of you. And I pulled you once upon a time, didn't I?"

I slowly turned my head toward him. "That was before my frontal lobe was fully developed."

After a slow inhale, Chase asked, "Has Mae's frontal lobe fully developed?"

"She's twenty-six, so I would say so, yes." I stared into his eyes, daring him to do something about it. But he wouldn't. "It's not like you're going to ask her out."

"Wanna bet?" His nostrils flared.

"If you do, it just might be the first time you've ever taken a risk in your life. I'd be shocked." I was calling his bluff, and he was calling mine. For a few seconds, he kept his eyes locked on my face, still just leaning his upper body into the car. And then, giving the metal frame a couple taps with his key, he dropped his things into the driver seat and slammed the door, walking back to the tattoo parlor empty-handed.

Oh my God. Was he really going to do it? I angled my body to see him better, wishing the woodland scene on the windows wasn't blocking my view of what was happening inside. I couldn't see them.

What was taking so long?

I pulled out Fannie's journal to distract myself, but I couldn't focus. What if Mae and Chase started dating for real? Would she feel differently about him if she knew he was my ex? *Should I warn her about his tendency to leave his dirty socks in every room?*

When the door of the tattoo shop opened, I tried to act as casual as possible so as not to seem like I'd been watching for him to return. Chase opened the door and tossed his stuff in the backseat, letting out a heavy sigh as he sat down. In his hand, there was a little white card. I followed it with my eyes as he tucked it into the visor with the comic book.

Like I wasn't going to check? Without hesitation, I pulled out the card and flipped it over. "Wait," I said, turning it over again. "There's no phone number on this. It's an appointment card."

"I know. I made an appointment."

"You went in there and… made an appointment?" I stared down at the card in disbelief. Sure enough, there was a date on it in Mae's loopy, cursive handwriting, the 'i' in April dotted with a heart.

"Yup," Chase answered, pulling his seatbelt over his chest.

"Chase. You've never gotten a tattoo before."

"Nope."

I expelled air from my mouth in a quiet chuckle. "Why the hell are you doing this?"

He shrugged with one shoulder as he started the car, and I couldn't help but notice the way he wouldn't look at me at all as we pulled away from the curb. "I guess I chickened out."

I threw my head back and laughed at the insanity of being so afraid to ask a woman for her number that you book a tattoo appointment with her instead. Only Chase. It was actually kind of cute, in a way. "Are you going to go through with it?"

"I might," he said, shaking his head at himself. "Maybe I'll get a little ghost or something."

"You're ridiculous." My cheeks hurt from smiling.

"Maybe a sick haunted house."

I only giggled in response, shaking my head.

"Maybe…" Chase paused, licking his lips. "Maybe I'll get a luna moth on my chest to match yours."

He glanced at my chest for a fraction of a second, probably remembering every detail of the moth tattoo just under my breasts, having been one of the few people to have the privilege of laying eyes on it. My face suddenly felt warm.

"Sorry," he rushed out, as though he shouldn't have mentioned it. Chase could probably see he'd made me blush. He swallowed, wiping his palm on his jeans. "Will you go with me when I do it?"

"But you won't be able to flirt with Mae if I'm there."

"I don't want to."

I chewed on my bottom lip, rubbing my thumbs together on my lap. "Are you sure you wouldn't rather have your buddy Sean there to hold your hand?"

He shot me a dirty look.

"Okay, I'll go," I laughed out. I wanted to question why he wanted me, of all people, to go with him. I could only assume it was because of my connection with Mae and my experience getting inked up. However, this was the second time in the past week he'd asked me to do something outside of our work responsibilities with him. Were we actually mature enough now to be friends? I stared at his face as he drove—that indention on his chin, his unfairly long eyelashes, and the lips that used to feel like home to me. "But I'm going to be mean to you the whole time," I added.

A grin stretched across Chase's face, making the corners of his eyes crinkle behind his glasses. "Good. I wouldn't expect anything less."

Chase was so cute at that moment, I had to force myself to look away. It was really annoying, the way he kept making me feel so damn attracted to him against my will. Before I could even begin to grapple with these new emotions, my phone buzzed in my lap.

> **Graham:** Hey, come back to the newsroom ASAP. We need to talk about the fallout from your Lenny article.

"What the hell does that mean?" I whispered aloud, angling my phone toward Chase so he could read the text himself.

"Fallout?" He lifted his eyebrows, looking me in the eyes. "What fallout?"

We didn't have to wonder for long, because another message from Graham popped up.

Graham: And for the sake of your mental health, stay off of the Concerned Citizens of Woodvale group.

chapter sixteen

chase

Maybe I'd read too many comic books, but I was beginning to suspect Meghan's moods controlled the weather. Dark storm clouds rolled in above the animal shelter, where an all-day adoption event was in full swing. Meghan wore a subtle scowl the entire time, taking the backseat while I did most of the interviewing.

I wished she would've listened to Graham when he warned her not to read what people said about her article on that cesspool of a Facebook group. What started as a single post by a local woman lacking reading comprehension skills led to a record-breaking number of unsubscriptions from the paper. Everyone had their reasons—some of them saying Meghan's article exploited Lenny, while others claimed her writing was "too progressive."

> We can't even say HOMELESS anymore? The Times has become too WOKE for me! I don't need a lesson on POLITICAL CORRECTNESS every time I open my paper!!

Lenny himself was delighted with the story—the cashier at Circle-K told me he stopped everyone he saw and pointed at his picture on the front page of the Lifestyles section. That temporarily cheered Meghan up, until Graham told her Silas wanted to see more feel-good stories out of us. Our CEO claimed the Lenny article was "bumming the town out." He was inserting himself where he didn't belong, as usual, and Meghan was *not* taking it in stride.

"There's your fucking feel-good story," she mumbled to me at the edge of the dogs' play enclosure as a middle-aged woman let her new black labrador retriever lick the happy tears off her face.

I covered my forehead with my hand and stared down at the ground. "Meghan," I groaned with a grin, nodding at the camera on my tripod. "I'm recording." The shot would still be usable as voiceover footage, but our editor was going to have some fun reviewing my videos.

Meghan didn't apologize, but she was quiet as I got some more footage. I kept rolling until it started to drizzle, hurrying to pack up my equipment before it got too wet. The WWTV meteorologist, Bernard, had been pretty hyped up that morning, which was never a good sign—especially when I had an outdoor event to cover. When I left that morning, he was frantically waving his arms in front of the chromakey, telling our viewers, "Everyone in our viewing area needs to be on high alert today, folks."

He was simultaneously recording live on Facebook that day, which Meghan pulled up on her phone when we got in the car. "We're under a tornado warning now," she mumbled, barely opening her mouth.

"Then it's probably safe to assume the picnic at the senior center is canceled, right?"

I hoped that would cheer her up, considering she'd grumbled about having to cover two outdoor events in a row. But she was still gloomy as ever, frowning as she watched Bernard pace from one side of the screen to the other with his weather map zoomed in on our county.

When Meghan remained quiet, I glanced out the window at the darkening clouds and said, "Doesn't look too bad here. Do you want to grab a coffee on the way back? My treat, if you'll let me." I hadn't seen her smile once that day, which was okay—but maybe an iced coffee could help turn things around. At the very least, it would give her a moment to breathe.

I was sort of counting on her to turn down the offer, but she let out a heavy sigh and flipped her phone over, saying, "Coffee sounds fine."

Without hesitation, I took a right, driving us in the direction of downtown. Meghan slumped further in the passenger seat, pulling that pendant up to her face to rub it along her bottom lip, just like I'd seen her do a hundred times.

The short trees lining the Riverside drive-thru were blowing at a sixty-degree angle, making me second-guess the decision to roll down my window in the rain that was now falling more steadily. Not quite a downpour, but it was getting there. Keeping an eye on the clouds above, I opened my mouth to ask her what drink she wanted when our phones simultaneously sounded an alert, startling both of us. With mine tucked in a bag in the backseat, I waited for Meghan to fumble with hers, the color draining from her face when she read the words on the screen. "Confirmed, large tornado. On the ground."

"Shit. Where?"

"Here!"

For a few seconds, I was paralyzed with fear and indecision, my hands firmly gripping the steering wheel.

Meghan reached over to squeeze my arm with her left hand, staring at her screen. "It's crossing the river now. Chase, help me think—where can we go to get a good shot of it?"

Was she out of her mind?! Ignoring her question, I drove right over the lipped curb between two of the trees in the grass which now looked like they might be ripped from the ground at any second. I sped down the alley behind the row of buildings, making a split-second decision about which way to turn when I got to the side street.

The library.

The library had a basement, and it was only two blocks from us.

"Where are you going?" Meghan asked, reaching for the handle above her head when I ran a stop sign. It didn't matter. Not right now. Not when it was raining so hard we wouldn't be able to spot the tornado if it were twenty yards in front of us. Meghan sat up straighter, twisting her body to look out the rear window. "Chase! Don't you want to get it on video?"

"No, I honestly don't," I said, the front end of the car scraping the ground as we turned into the library parking lot. I had one goal, and it was to get Meghan somewhere safe. I parked diagonally between two yellow lines, but there was no time to correct it. "Are you ready to run?"

Meghan's eyes grew wide. "No! Chase, we have to report on this—it's our job!"

"Come on, Meg, no story is worth our lives. We can't report anything if we get sucked up in a tornado, can we?" Tiny pellets of hail pelted the windshield. "Now, are you ready?" My fingers rested on my door handle, but Meghan wasn't budging. Between the hail and the wind, I could barely hear my own words. "Meghan!"

"Don't scream at me!"

"I have to scream because of the—" I rolled my eyes, knowing I couldn't persuade her with words alone. I pushed open the door and ran around the front of the car as quickly as I could, nearly slipping on the hail accumulating on the concrete just as I reached Meghan's door. "Fuck," I muttered, yanking her door open.

"What are—"

Before she could get her words out, I leaned across her lap and unbuckled her seatbelt. Offering up: I was fully prepared to throw her over my shoulder and carry her inside, but the deafening crack of an oak tree limb falling in the courtyard ahead of us snapped her into action. I held out my hand, and she took it in hers without protest. I yanked her out of the car and shoved the door shut before running up the sidewalk with her, our fingers interlocked the entire way. When we made it to the small alcove by the main doors, I pulled on the handle, but the door wouldn't budge. Neither would the other one when I tried it.

"Are they locked?" Meghan yelled with panicked eyes, her hair plastered to her face in wild, wet strands.

I didn't answer. Instead, I let go of her hand and grabbed the door handle with both of mine. The pressure fought against me, but I mentally counted to three to give it one more try. In the final second, Meghan's hands joined mine on the handle. "Pull *now!*" I hollered over the sound of the wind and rain. And though we both grunted and pulled with all our might, the door still wouldn't move. "It's the pressure!"

Meghan smacked the glass, either trying to show it who's boss or to get the attention of someone inside. Surely everyone was already downstairs, though. Just as I was beginning to contemplate how safe we'd be from a tornado in that little inlet, the door burst open.

"Get in, get in!" One of the librarians, a kindhearted old man whose name I could never remember, ushered us into the building. The door slammed shut behind us, and the three of us jogged toward the stairs to the archive department in the basement. The lights in the antique chandeliers flickered above our heads like something out of a horror film.

My wet shoes squeaked with every step down into the room below, where a few library workers and patrons had already gathered. A woman was seated on an ottoman with a little girl on her lap, pointing out the pictures in a book in an attempt to distract her from the chaos happening outside. Eyeing the little window at the top of the wall facing the library parking lot, I instinctively reached for Meghan's wrist and pulled her the opposite direction. "Over here," I said, leading her around the corner in the L-shaped room, where two loveseats faced one another in a sort of cozy reading spot.

The second we sank into one of the seats, the lights went completely out—and stayed out this time. The only light in our section of the room was from Meghan's phone screen. "I have no service," she said, giving me a desperate look. "I hate not knowing what's going on out there."

I just nodded, listening to the sound of heavy rain hitting the building. It seemed to come in waves. Beside me, Meghan slouched lower into the seat, burying her head in her hands with loud, panicked breaths. Without knowing what else to say, I whispered, "We're okay down here."

"I'm not worried about us. I'm worried about Lenny."

Oh. With a soft, low, voice, I said, "Hey. That building is sturdy as fuck. Look how long it's been standing, and how many storms it must have been through. Even a fire couldn't take it out. I'm sure Lenny's safe." As I spoke, Meghan lowered her hands from her face, and she began to slowly nod like she might actually believe me. God, I hoped I wasn't wrong.

She hugged herself, checking her phone again, as though it might suddenly start working. Still nothing. She heaved a loud sigh, momentarily distracted by one of the librarians laughing about the little girl's light-up shoes. The group around the corner didn't sound nearly as concerned about the tornado as we were, but then again, they might have just been playing down their fear for the sake of the kid.

"I bet Wanda is terrified right now," Meghan said, turning to me.

"Do you want to check on her when this is over?"

After giving me a little nod, Meghan leaned her body against mine, pressing her forehead against my shoulder. I inhaled, unsure of how I should react to her sudden display of intimacy. It was the closest she'd been to me in years, and I could smell her perfume, the spicy scent that once lingered on my pillow. Without thinking, I turned my head slightly, just enough for my lips to graze the wet strands of her hair. God, I could almost kiss the top of her head right now—the compulsion to do it was so strong, I had to force myself to stay still.

And then, in a moment of bravery—or maybe stupidity—I rested my hand on her knee and gave it a small, reassuring squeeze. Before I could move my hand away, she placed hers on top, threading her fingers between mine. The breath she let out was one of relief, like this had a calming effect on her.

On the other side of that loveseat, my heart was beating so fast, I wouldn't have been surprised if I dropped dead right then and there from cardiac arrest.

The moment would have been perfect if it weren't for the knowledge that some neighborhood in Woodvale was probably getting shredded by a massive tornado.

The wind and rain had seemingly died down, and the commotion around the corner picked up—it sounded like a couple of librarians were venturing upstairs to check things out. Meghan lifted her head. "Should we go? We have work to do. I can't let Xander get this story."

I couldn't help but smile, staring back into her eyes, mere inches from mine. "You don't even know what the story is yet."

She didn't respond right away. Instead, she looked deep into my eyes, her gaze lingering in a way that made my pulse race all over again. Her hand still rested on mine over her knee, and I knew it was only there because she wanted it there as much as I did. The realization floored me—because the Meghan from a few weeks ago would have been disgusted by my touch. Repulsed. But this version of her, the one whose pinky finger was lightly tracing the inside of my thumb, looked at me like I was someone she trusted.

Something between us had shifted, and I knew, without a sliver of doubt, she was feeling it, too.

She finally broke the silence. "Let's go," she said, pulling up to her feet. I followed her up the stairs, where the library staff was gathering around the main doors, repeating "wow" as they looked out at the fallen branches. "Thank you for letting us take cover in here, Diana," Meghan said, waving at the library director before we walked outside.

It was only sprinkling now, and a bit of sunshine peeked through the clouds in the western sky. Other than the massive limb in the courtyard and branches scattered around the parking lot, the damage seemed minimal. "Maybe it missed us," I offered.

"Or it was just really weak." Meghan walked down the sidewalk, taking a big step to avoid getting her strappy heels wet in a puddle. She took a couple pictures of the courtyard with her phone. "Maybe this is the worst of it."

"Hopefully," I answered with my hands on my hips. It didn't seem like there was much of a story here, at least not beyond what Bernard was already covering at the studio, so I didn't bother to get my camera equipment out of the car.

Meghan's phone rang. "Oh good, I have service!" She held the phone to her ear. "Hey, Graham."

I bent over to pull a branch off the sidewalk into the grass nearby as Meghan spoke with Graham. One of the ladies inside the library held the door open and hollered a "thank you!" my direction. I winced, realizing they couldn't see their courtyard from where they stood. Just as I lifted my hand to wave for them to come outside and take a look, I caught a glimpse of Meghan's horror-stricken face.

"We have to get to Grissom," she said, lowering her phone slowly.

"The elementary school?" I took a step closer. "Why?"

Meghan licked her lips, her eyebrows drawing together at the corners. "Because they just took a direct hit."

chapter seventeen

meghan

My stomach churned with every swerve of the car as Chase drove around fallen limbs and chunks of debris. I attempted to swallow the acid in my throat, almost choking when I saw the damage to some of the houses on our way to the school; roofs missing, entire walls collapsed. I could barely make out what looked like pieces of a metal car frame wrapped around a tree.

"I can't go this way," Chase said, throwing the car in reverse. The road ahead was blocked by downed trees. A family stood on their porch, looking up from the shingles scattered across their yard to watch us make a three-point turn in their driveway.

It took Chase three attempts to find a side street that wasn't blocked by trees or traffic. It looked like half the town was trying to get to the school, and there were sirens coming from every direction. Chase pulled to the side of the road, wincing as the tires rolled over a thick branch, to allow a firetruck to pass. "Follow him," I urged.

"What?" Chase looked over with wide eyes.

"He's making a path—go!"

"I can't just-"

"We're the news. They'll see the logo and understand. Do it, Chase!"

He didn't waste another second. Chase put the pedal to the metal to catch up to the speeding firetruck, following it past the line of cars trying to get to Grissom. "This feels wrong," he whispered, pulling his hand from the steering wheel to wipe it on his jeans.

When Grissom Elementary came into view, I couldn't decide whether I should feel relieved or concerned. Three-fourths of the brick building looked okay, aside from some dangling gutters. But one end of the school, where the gymnasium stood, had been completely obliterated.

I held onto the tiniest bit of hope that no students or staff were in that end of the building when the tornado hit. The roof had been wiped clean off, leaving beams of twisted metal behind. Chunks of debris were scattered all over the playground and baseball field behind the building.

The school garden, which I had reported on numerous times, was unrecognizable. The trellises were gone, and all the plants were flattened or uprooted. Everything they'd worked toward had been destroyed—but then again, that was probably the least of their worries.

"Should I go all the way up there, or—?" Chase's knuckles were white.

We'd reached the main driveway leading up to the school, where the digital sign, which typically displayed reminders about picture days and book fairs, was shattered. There was still a line of cars in front of us trying to get to the school, but there were two police cars up ahead stopping everyone. However, all the cars made room for the firetruck in front of us. "No harm in trying, right?"

Chase nodded, gunning it to catch up to the firetruck. He stared straight ahead when we drove past the police, pretending he had the authority to be there. Disaster situations like this were often tricky to navigate. There was a fine line between informing the public and being intrusive, a boundary

Xander and Jillian probably had more experience with than either of us. But there we were, arriving on the scene at the same time as the first responders.

Chase gave the emergency vehicles room, parking along the curb at the edge of the parking lot. Before I could move to gather my things, he reached toward me, his big hand closing around my wrist, gentle yet firm.

"Hey," he said, the softness of his tone making me pause. "We could see something we don't want to see here. Are you… going to be okay with this?"

I understood what he meant. "I just want to do my job," I answered, though my voice trembled. "I'll be okay."

He gave my wrist a little squeeze before letting go. "'Kay. Let's do this." We gathered our things—my notebook and Nikon, his camera and tripod—and walked up to the front of the school, where the fire chief was talking to a rattled and wide-eyed Principal Sarah Gardner. The chief's hands were on her shoulders as he gave her instructions, and she repeatedly nodded at his words.

I'd interviewed Chief Wade Ruger more times than I could count. I was never quite sure how to take the man. He was a kind person, but he was always so serious, and often too busy to talk to me. Jillian told me she once witnessed him get a little tipsy at a gala and tell an inappropriate joke, but the man I was looking at now was all business.

"Room by room, wing by wing," we heard him tell Sarah, "starting with the classrooms on the west side of the building, where the structure isn't secure." He motioned toward the lot at the other end of the school—the non-destroyed half, that is— toward the bus-loading zone. "And we'll tape the area off to designate it as the pick-up zone. I recommend staggering the release."

Sarah nodded again.

Beside me, Chase already had his camera out. Propping it up on his shoulder, he recorded the damage, panning over after a few seconds to show the line of parents' cars trying to reach their children.

Chief Ruger gave Sarah some final words before sending her back inside: "You did everything right, and you kept them safe. Now let's get them home."

Sarah chewed on her bottom lip, nodding one last time before she pulled a walkie-talkie from her dress pocket and went back into the building to begin the evacuation process.

"Chief," I said, planting myself in front of him before he could walk away.

He looked slightly annoyed, but he at least stopped on the pavement. His eyes shifted from me to Chase, who was pointing the camera at him now. I didn't even have to ask—the chief knew exactly which info we wanted. "All of the children here at Grissom are unharmed, thanks to the fast thinking of their principal and staff."

"So, there are no injuries?" Chase questioned.

Wade stared at Chase, his lips parting, and my stomach sank when more seconds passed than necessary. "I don't have any further information at this time. Together with Principal Gardner, we'll work on a safe evacuation for the-"

Chase pulled his face away from the camera. "You didn't say all the staff members were unharmed."

I inhaled when I noticed an ambulance emerging from the backside of the building, coming from the direction of the gym. When they hit the parking lot, they threw on their lights and sirens, making a beeline for the street. The ambulance turned in the direction of the hospital.

"Sir, can you confirm that at least one adult is injured?" Chase was relentless. Still recording, still giving the fire chief the staredown of his life.

But Wade, beginning to step away, just said, "I'll have more information soon. Let us get the evacuation straightened out, alright?"

He turned around and walked away, joining some other firefighters who were preparing to enter the building. When I looked around, all I saw was chaos. Parents parking their cars on the street and running up to the school. Police radioing each other. A sheet of metal dangling from the side of the gym, looking like it would crash to the ground below at any second. And a white SUV cutting across the grassy median that divided the school parking lot and the street, disregarding the police officer's waving arms. Whoever was driving that Volvo started a trend—two, then three cars followed before the police could put a stop to it.

The white Volvo pulled up right behind the firetruck on the curb. I wasn't sure who I expected to step out of the vehicle after all that, but Owen Gardner probably would have been my last guess. Then again, I knew exactly why he was here. His business partner was with him, and the two of them jogged up to join us on the sidewalk.

"I just saw Sarah," I quickly said, and I could see the relief etched into Owen's face as he bent over with his hands on his knees. "She's okay. The kids are all safe."

Mason, fidgeting with the buttons on his flannel shirt, looked too shaken up to even speak.

Owen straightened up, putting his hands on his head. "How did she look?"

"Sarah?" I tucked my loose hair behind my ear. "She looked a little rattled, but she's handling it."

Again, Owen bent over to put his hands on his knees and took a couple of slow, deep breaths. Was this guy going to throw up? "She doesn't need this right now," I heard him whisper. I glanced at Chase, who had been filming Owen and Mason since their arrival, and he quickly panned to the damaged end of the school instead.

Before long, kids began emerging in straight lines from the side door of the school, guided by their teachers and firefighters. They were seated in rows on the pavement, with Sarah pointing and directing everyone where to go.

"I see Finley," Mason said, clutching his stomach. "And Kendall."

Those must be his daughters, I thought. A second later, a teacher I recognized waved our direction, and I suddenly remembered her name—Kendall Devin. I'd interviewed her last October at the school's fall festival. When I looked over at Mason, he was making a heart with his hands against his chest, a gesture Kendall returned.

Was he-? Were they-?

I didn't have time to contemplate their relationship, because Chase got Mason's attention and asked him for an interview. "As a parent of a child who goes here, would you mind sharing your thoughts right now?"

Mason seemed hesitant at first, but he ultimately agreed, nodding his head as he glanced in the direction of his daughter. I hit the record button on my phone and stood back as Mason spoke into the camera about him and Owen getting the alert on their phones, just like us. The second they heard the tornado touched down in this part of town, they hopped in Owen's car and headed to the school.

"I broke several traffic laws to get here," Owen interjected, standing beside Mason with his arms crossed. His eyes flashed with panic. "Um, that's off the record."

Chase laughed, assuring Owen he'd cut that part. Their conversation wrapped up when the kindergarteners were released to parents, and Chase filmed Mason scooping up his daughter in his arms. He hugged the teacher, too, before taking the little girl to Owen's car.

While I got a couple of quotes from parents waiting their turn to pick up their kids, Chase set up his camera on the tripod and connected with the studio to do a live report—which was somewhat rare for him. He seamlessly switched into newscaster mode, highlighting the efforts of Principal Gardner, the Grissom staff, and the first responders for keeping the kids safe. I noticed the careful way he mentioned he was still waiting on an update from Chief Ruger regarding the staff and other adults in the building. "But stay tuned to WWTV, as Jillian will have the full report tonight."

I'd been watching him so closely, I almost forgot I'd been talking to a mom who'd just spelled her name for me. I was going to have to ask her to do it a second time.

Later, I sat on the curb, crafting up a quick post for social media, promising a more detailed report on the website later. We probably had hours of work ahead of us. I sent Graham a quick text to check in and took time to gloat to Xander that I'd beat him to breaking news.

Xander: I've been getting minute-by-minute updates from my source at the school this entire time. With permission to use her photos of the damage from the inside. Nice try, though.

153

Of course. I should've known he would have checked on Abigail by now, and she was giving him firsthand details. "Motherf-"

chapter eighteen

chase

"The fire chief has an update for us," I told Meghan, waving for her to follow me over to the firetruck near the school's entrance. We weren't the only journalists on the scene anymore. I recognized some reporters from the next town over, and some independent photojournalists were beginning to wander around. Chief Ruger rounded us all up. I was ready with my mic, and Meghan with her phone and notebook.

"To provide an update now that the family has been notified," the chief began, "I can confirm that there has been one injury here at Grissom Elementary. The school custodian, Russell Stout, sustained critical injuries when a section of the wall collapsed. He has been transported to the hospital, and at this time, that's all the information we have available."

With a nod, he started to walk away, but Meghan stepped forward, touching the chief on the arm. "Chief." He turned back around, his expression stoic. "Will the students be able to return to school in the coming days?"

The man let out a heavy sigh. "Doubtful. The gym has considerable damage, obviously—and on top of that, the rest of the structure will need to be assessed before students can safely return. My guess is the superintendent will be looking at alternative options like e-learning or what-have-you."

His statement made me thankful there was no such thing as e-learning when a pipe burst in my elementary school back in the day. I got a couple of days off, just me and my Nintendo 64, with all the ramen noodles I could convince my older sister to cook for me. Zoom didn't exist back then, either.

These poor kids.

"I wonder what else we can find out about Russell's condition?" I wondered aloud to Meghan, who was still writing down some notes.

"Sarah should be our go-to for that info in the coming days. She'll know," she said, tucking her pen in the spiral of her notebook to rub her eyes. I'd never seen her look so tired. At least the negative feedback on her Lenny article was far from her mind at the moment.

After scanning the scene, I couldn't come up with any reason for us to stay. We had all the information and coverage we needed for our reports, and we'd both interviewed a handful of people. Now that parents were coming through to pick up their kids, we were only getting in the way. "Hey, what do you say we go check on Wanda?"

Meghan looked up at my face, and I tried not to grin at the smeared mascara beneath her right eye. It did absolutely nothing to take away from her beauty. "That sounds like a fabulous idea," she said, opening her mouth wide to yawn.

Wanda was asleep on Meghan's bed when we got to her apartment, curled up between a pillow and the headboard. I wasn't sure if I should follow Meghan all the way into her bedroom, so I lingered at the doorway with my hands in my pockets. "She seems unfazed," I noted, watching the cat nuzzle against Meghan's legs at the foot of the bed.

"Can you hear her purring?"

I took two cautious steps forward, listening. "Yeah, I can," I said, watching Meghan kick off her shoes and lie on her side, scratching Wanda just above her tail. She yawned, rapidly blinking her watery, sleepy eyes. Her messy hair spilled onto the dark, moon-print bedspread, and with one hand tucked beneath her cheek, she looked like she'd probably fall asleep within minutes if I left her alone.

"Hey, why don't I leave you here for a bit so you can rest?" I quietly suggested, stepping forward to pet Wanda between her ears. "I can come back in a couple—"

"But I need to write."

"You need to nap."

To my surprise, she didn't argue. Instead, she opened her mouth to yawn again, trying to cover it with her hand, like she was embarrassed. "Okay. Just give me twenty minutes."

I smiled. "Okay," I said, curling my fingers around the keys in my pocket. I could probably get some work done in the car while she rested.

When I turned to go, Meghan lifted her head and said, "Just stay."

I looked from her face to the cat to the empty side of her queen-sized bed. "Here?"

"As long as it's okay with Wanda," Meghan said, following my gaze to the silver, satin pillow next to her head. It did look soft and inviting, and I couldn't ignore my own exhaustion much longer.

I moved closer to the bed, my knees pressing against the side of the mattress as I stroked Wanda's little head. The cat closed her eyes, leaning into my touch, and purred even louder. It appeared I had her permission—and Meghan's—to lie here. Yet still I hesitated, feeling like there was an invisible line I was about to cross. I envisioned that line down the center of the bed as I knelt on the bedspread, removing my glasses. I set them on her bedside table and lay on my back with my head on my interlocked hands, completely still.

It wasn't that I worried I'd be tempted to touch her. I wouldn't make a move, not now—not when she was in such a fatigued state. But this gesture, as innocuous as it was, further confirmed something: She no longer hated me. In fact, I was feeling pretty confident that she might even *like* me a little.

At the very least, she felt safe with me.

Wanda settled between us, pressing her paws into the bedspread a few times before curling up into a little ball against me—just the way she used to when the three of us shared a bed years ago. I let out a quiet chuckle, turning my head to see Meghan's reaction. But her eyes were closed, and her breathing had slowed.

I assumed she was asleep until she whispered, "Do you think Lenny's okay?"

"I think it missed that side of town," I said, swallowing. She kept her eyes closed, but she nodded. I rolled all the way onto my side, so we were facing each other. "He's probably already collecting metal debris to take to the scrapyard."

Meghan smiled, slowly opening her eyes. We stared at each other for a few seconds in the quiet of that dark bedroom, her blinds blocking the afternoon sun. With a soft exhale, she closed her eyes again, relaxing into the pillow. As she shifted her position, her socked foot grazed my leg and settled there, her bent toes pressing against my ankle. I held my breath as I watched her fall asleep, thinking to myself that this wasn't exactly what I fantasized about when I imagined *sleeping with Meghan*, but it was actually better.

My God, I love this woman.

chapter nineteen

meghan

"Meghan."

I jolted awake, finding Chase kneeling on the bed beside me, his hand resting on my shoulder. The room was darker than it should have been. I shot up straight, wiping the dot of drool from the corner of my mouth. Good God, how embarrassing. "What time is it?"

"It's almost five. We slept for an hour, and your phone keeps ringing." I scrambled for it beneath my pillow, my phone's usual spot, but Chase handed it to me. "It was in the living room."

I had two missed calls from Graham and a text from Xander, who wondered where I was. My phone rang again before I could answer either of them, and it was Xander this time.

"Xan, I'm sorry—I came back to my apartment to rest. What's going on?"

"Our lovely editor is insisting you and I consolidate our info and collaborate on this tornado story for the front page. When the hell will you be back?"

Still half-asleep, I could barely process his words. "But who gets credit?"

"We'll share the byline. Not like we haven't done that before."

"No, I mean, in the competition," I said, picking my shoes up from the floor. Chase was sitting at the foot of the bed with Wanda in his lap, staring at his own phone. "Who gets the points?"

Xander let out an exasperated sigh. "He said breaking news doesn't count. Will you just get here so we can write this thing? And send me what you've got while you're on your way." And with that, he hung up.

"Ugh," I groaned.

Chase looked up from his own phone, swiping Wanda's tail away from his face. "What's wrong?"

"Graham says breaking news doesn't count in the competition with Xander. So what's the point?"

Chase stared at me with a couple of slow blinks. "Informing the public…?"

"Yeah, yeah," I muttered, pulling my knee up to my chest to fasten the strap of one of my sandals. My left hand felt tingly and weak from sleeping on it, making me struggle with the second shoe. "Shit," I whispered.

Chase nudged Wanda off his lap and slid off the bed onto the floor to kneel in front of my feet. He rolled his eyes, grinning at the way I tried to pull my foot away. Did he think I was a toddler? "Just let me help you, dammit," he insisted, with one hand on the back of my ankle, the other on the bottom of my shoe, to bring my foot to his thigh. As he took the strap in his hand, he stared up into my eyes, his fingers tickling the back of my ankle when he moved them away. The sensation sent a tingly feeling all the way up my leg as he lowered his eyes to concentrate on the buckle.

Fuck, I really didn't mind the sight of him kneeling at my feet.

He let out a quiet grunt, adjusting the placement of my foot on his lap. It shouldn't have been so difficult to simply buckle a shoe, but maybe he was taking his time on purpose. My mind went to a dirty place, imagining him pushing me back on the bed and climbing atop me like he had so many times before. The memory of the weight of his body pressing down on mine made my heart race. Could he hear how fast I was breathing?

"You okay?"

Shit, he *could* hear it. I yanked my foot away the second he tucked the strap behind the little black loop. "Yes. Let's go." I couldn't look him in the eye as I gathered my things, almost forgetting my phone on the bed. When I reached for it, Chase stood up and grabbed me by the wrist. I held my breath, half afraid he was about to kiss me, and half afraid of how badly I wanted to let him.

But he said, "Please don't take offense when I say this, but you should probably look in a mirror before we go." His eyes lingered on my hair, which had been secured in a perfect bun that morning. That felt like an eternity ago, and I imagined I probably looked exactly how someone who'd been through a tornado would look.

I sighed, letting out a nervous laugh to cover my sudden, inexplicable nervousness. "Right. Good call." I pulled my wrist from his grip, brushing past him toward the mirror above my dresser. My hair had come unraveled, dark strands falling around my face in a wild, tangled mess. I tried to adjust it with my fingers, tucking pieces back in here and there, ultimately deciding to let my hair down completely. From the corner of my eye, I saw Chase standing behind me, watching with that familiar, infuriatingly patient expression on his face. He wasn't rushing me, but the intensity of his gaze made me feel even more flustered.

I wasn't one to show up at work with a sloppy hairdo, but then again, a tornado wasn't a bad excuse, was it? I reached for a claw clip, taking two seconds to gather all my hair at the back of my head. Then I grabbed a make-up wipe, quickly removing the smudges from beneath my eyes as I made my way to the bedroom door. I paused, turning to face Chase. "Do I look decent?"

He wasn't smiling, but the expression on his face was warm, nonetheless. "Decent?" He shook his head. "Meghan, the way you look after surviving a tornado is what most people strive for on their best day."

I fought the compulsion to giggle like—well, like a schoolgirl—and pretended to be annoyed instead. "Whatever. Don't try to flatter me," I muttered, squeezing past him on my way through the bedroom door. He could see right through the facade, though, grinning as he followed me out.

What a long, confusing day this had been.

**

In the days that followed, our work shifted to round-the-clock tornado relief coverage, forcing us to push most of our other assignments aside so we could give it our full attention. Most of the events on our schedule were canceled, anyway, as the entire town focused on the storm's aftermath. Clean-up efforts were underway, and local businesses had stepped up, offering supplies and meals to those affected.

The National Weather Service classified the tornado as an EF-3. Thankfully, there were no deaths, and only a few injuries, including the school custodian. In my phone interview with Sarah two days after the tornado, she let me know Russell had suffered a collapsed lung and a lot of broken bones, but he was already taken off the ventilator and breathing on his own. "He's going to make a full recovery," she said.

My mind wandered to the day I had to make the decision to take my mom off her ventilator, knowing she would never breathe on her own again. The memory of the sound of the machine in her hospital room made me lose my train of thought for a moment.

Memories like that hit me like a freight train sometimes. It didn't matter where I was or what I was doing. Grief didn't wait. It just barreled on through, dragging me back to that hospital room, where I watched helplessly as my mom succumbed to pneumonia after the cancer had already ravaged her body. I had to shake my head, like I could physically push the memory away. *Not now*, I told myself.

"I'm sorry," I said, adjusting the phone against my ear. I clenched my eyes shut, trying to picture Sarah's face instead of my mother's. "There's so much going on here, it's hard to stay focused. But I wanted to ask about your plan for moving forward. Um, let's see…" I flipped through my notes, trying to get myself back on track. "Have you been given a timeline for when students can return, and what they will do in the meantime? E-learning, I assume?"

There was a heavy sigh on Sarah's end. "Unfortunately, I received some bad news this morning. Much of the school's roof suffered damage, not just the gymnasium. The structure isn't safe. It might be weeks before we're back at Grissom. We are moving to e-learning for the time-being, but I'm working with Superintendent Delgado to look at other options."

I tapped my pen on my notebook. "Like alternative buildings?"

"Yes, exactly," Sarah said. "Because here's the thing—for some of these children, their only complete meal of the day is our school lunch. I've also been in conversation with many parents who don't know what they're going to do for childcare. And the kids who view the school as their only safe place *have* no safe place now. That's why I'm going to push for in-person schooling, one way or another."

I jotted down Sarah's words, my hand moving as fast as my thoughts. I'd sort of developed my own language when it came to taking notes during phone interviews; a combination of abbreviations and shorthand that would make the pages of this notebook indecipherable to anyone else.

It reminded me a little of the strange, rune-like symbols I'd discovered doodled inside Fannie's journal. There were six of them across the top of one of the pages, with a few similar markings spread throughout the book. I'd meant to research the meaning behind those symbols the day the tornado hit, but—well, things had gotten a little hectic since then.

My pen hovered over the last word as I considered Sarah's concerns, finally processing what she'd just said. Those kids needed a place for in-person instruction. What better than an old school?

Between our newspaper staff, the TV news crew, and the radio guys up on the third floor, we took up less than half the building, even counting the offices and storage. As far as I knew, the cafeteria was still functional, and so were the bathrooms. We couldn't fit the entire Grissom student body in this building, but we could probably accommodate a good number of them.

"Sarah, has anyone spoken to Silas Brown?"

"He's… the head of your news network, isn't he? I don't think so."

"Well," I said, sitting up a little straighter. "I'm not sure if you're aware, but we moved our offices into the old Clark Elementary building not long ago, and there's still a lot of unused space. That might be exactly what you're looking for."

Sarah had a lot of questions for me. Was the building accessible? Did all the rooms have working air conditioners. Were the words "FUCK ENZO" ever removed from the side of the gymnasium? All the important things. I was able to give her some answers before passing along Silas's contact info.

The second I hung up, I was startled by Xander's brooding presence over the side of the cubicle. His hands gripped the top of the wall, and he was looking at me like I was a bug he wanted to squash. "Are you out of your damn mind?"

"I'm sorry?" I spun in my chair to face him.

"You want to bring a bunch of noisy-ass kids into this building? Do you have any idea what that'll mean for us? Extra security, no more coming and going as we please, and sharing a bathroom with a bunch of toddlers who'll piss on the floor?"

"Toddlers don't go to elementary school," I said, holding back a laugh.

He ignored me, nodding toward my phone on the desk. "Call Sarah back right now and tell her you spoke to Silas yourself. Tell her it's not going to work."

I set my pen down and folded my arms. "You should've heard how stressed Sarah sounded. This is going to help her out, and isn't she your friend's wife? What would Owen think of this reaction?"

That got him to close his mouth, at least momentarily. "There are other buildings," he mumbled.

Another realization struck me. I leaned back in my chair, a slow smile stretching across my face. "I wonder," I said, touching my chin with my pointer finger, "if your beloved librarian would move into this building. You'd probably get to see her every weekday, wouldn't you?"

Xander's face softened, and his eyes dropped to the floor. He could deny his affection for Abigail all day, but his love for her was written all over his face. After a moment, his jaw clenched again, and he disappeared from my view. I heard the squeak of his desk chair as he sank into it, having changed his mind.

"That's what I thought," I hollered over the cubicle wall. Xander was probably just bitter about our competition being put on hold while we covered tornado-related news. Graham told us we could return to our regularly scheduled assignments in a week.

I'd also seen less of Chase than normal over the past couple of days. Our reporting required us to be in different places at odd times, often with little notice.

Sitting alone in my quiet cubicle, staring at the blank document before me, I found myself missing Chase. Actually, truly missing him. A hollow ache settled in my stomach, and it wasn't from hunger or anxiety, the usual culprits. It wasn't grief, either—no tears came when I stared at the picture of my parents on my desk.

That ache deep within my body? It was *longing*.

chapter twenty

chase

Meghan beat me to our meeting place on Monday morning, and she'd stolen my usual spot, too. Perched on the desk with her legs crossed, her black skirt pooling around her, she perked up when I came through the doorway. "Guess what?"

I could already tell her mood had improved from last week. Sometimes, when Meghan shifted into one of her heavy, sad moods, she tended to linger there for a while. To see her smiling again was a welcome relief.

But I'd take her either way.

I stopped and scanned her from her bare feet right up to the sheer collar of her blouse, held together with a pearl button against her neck. She looked beautiful in it, like an actress plucked from an old black-and-white film, but I couldn't let the opportunity to tease her pass. "You stole your outfit from a Victorian ghost?" I guessed.

Meghan tilted her chin downward to shoot me an annoyed look, but her smile never went away. "No. The parks department is having a big bash in June to celebrate the new skate park, and we've got dibs on the story."

I nodded in approval, dropping my heavy backpack on the desk beside her.

"Whatcha got in there, rocks?" she joked.

"Actually, yes." I quickly unzipped the bag and reached inside, pulling out a flat stone. I finally got a hold of the kid who had found weird rocks in the area the Woodvale Witch frequented, and he'd let me borrow them to research the symbols etched into them. For days, I'd been meaning to contact a friend of mine who was an expert on runes and symbols, but the tornado had kind of forced me to put most of my hobbies on hold.

Meghan let out a cute chuckle when I pulled out the second stone, but when I flipped them both over to reveal the symbols, her laughter came to an abrupt stop. She yanked one of the rocks from my hand, staring at the symbol in confusion. "Where did these come from?"

"The Woodvale Witch, apparently."

"Shut the fuck up," she whispered, turning the stone counterclockwise between her fingers. She took the other one, examining it just as closely. "Be serious, Chase."

"I am serious," I said, pulling out more stones. I laid all six of them all out on the desk between her and my backpack. "These were dug up where historians think Evelyn's witch hut used to stand."

Meghan's eyes drifted up to mine, as if waiting for me to laugh and say "gotcha!" When I didn't, she turned her attention to the stones on the desk, lightly touching a couple of them with her fingertips.

"Do you recognize these symbols?"

She didn't answer. Instead, she turned around and reached for her notebooks, pulling the old musty one out from the middle. I watched her open it on her lap, flipping toward the back of the journal and turning the last pages slowly to find just the right one. She picked up one of the rocks, holding it beside the page, glancing back and forth between the two. She didn't utter a word, but her mouth dropped open. I could guess why.

"Let me see," I said, sliding my butt onto the edge of the desk as I carefully took the journal from her. Just as I expected, there in Fannie's notebook was the same symbol as the stone in Meghan's hand. The crisscrossed lines, as random as they seemed, were identical. I'd sort of thought the etchings on the rocks were more like unplanned scribbles, but there were three more symbols on this page matching some of the stones.

It made the hair on the back of my neck stand up.

"I am beyond perplexed right now," Meghan said, her eyes darting from the stone to the journal again.

"Are you sure you haven't been carrying around the old witch's journal this whole time?"

"I'm sure. Fannie signed her name at the bottom of some of her journal entries."

I scooted closer, reaching across her to pick up another stone. Again, this one's symbol was identical to one of the jagged, pointy drawings in Fannie's journal. "Evelyn and Fannie were alive at the same time. Maybe these markings were popular symbols back then."

"All of them? I doubt it. They're too unique. Too... random." Meghan shook her head, moving closer to me to peer over my shoulder at the stone in my hand. "Where were these rocks found, exactly?"

Luckily for her, the guy who found them had provided the exact coordinates. Sean and I had plans to investigate the area someday, but maybe Meghan and I could get to it sooner. "I could show you, if you want to go-"

"Yes," she said, immediately sliding off the desk. "Let's go."

I had to laugh, holding the journal flat against my chest. "Easy, Wednesday. We have other priorities today."

"Let's give the candy shop story to Xander and Jill. And nothing else is time sensitive. If anyone asks what we're doing, we can say it's for a story." She was talking a mile a minute, slipping her feet into her shoes. I swallowed, somewhat disappointed she wasn't wearing the ones with the buckles that day. "How far into the woods is it? Do I need to wear boots?"

I just licked my lips and grinned, letting her take the journal from my hands. "You didn't look at our shared calendar, did you?" I asked.

Her eyes found mine. "Why? Am I forgetting something?"

"Someone promised they'd accompany me to my tattoo appointment..."

Meghan blinked. "Is that today?"

I looked down at the knees of my worn jeans, almost wishing I hadn't reminded her. Truthfully, I was having second thoughts, despite Mae's enthusiasm in our DM exchange. While I loved her concept—a creepy old house with ghosts flying out from the windows—the thought of having my skin pricked repeatedly by a needle was freaking me out. "I could cancel it."

"What? Why?" she questioned, her whining, disappointed tone making me grin even more. "Don't tell me you're chickening out."

"But I am."

"It won't hurt as bad as you think. Where were you planning on getting it?"

"I hadn't really decided. Was going to ask you what you thought." I put my hand on my right arm, just below my shoulder. "Maybe here?"

I held my breath as Meghan reached for my arm, her fingers grazing my skin as she pulled my shirt sleeve higher. "No one will ever see it if it's up here."

I swallowed. Still perched on that desk, I was at her eye level, and she was standing so close I could smell whatever product she had in her hair. I heard her inhale as her hand dropped lower on my bicep, her fingers pressing just a bit harder into my skin. If I didn't know any better, I'd think she was feeling up my muscles. We were both holding our breath, the only sound in the room coming from the still-ticking but inaccurate clock on the wall.

I wanted to touch her, to put my hand on her waist and pull her down to kiss me. But even after all our pleasant interactions as of late, I still feared she'd push me away. Maybe even slap me in the name of self-defense. I kept my hand glued to the desk, choosing instead to make a dumb joke. "I'll cut off all my sleeves so everyone can see my ink. Especially when I report live."

Meghan smiled, that dimple on her cheek popping as she stared into my eyes. Lowering her hand on my bicep, she inhaled to speak, but the sound of approaching footsteps distracted us both. Principal Sarah Gardner strolled into the room, followed by Silas Brown, the school superintendent, and another man I didn't recognize. The four of them looked just as confused to find us there as we were to see them.

Meghan quickly pulled away, stepping back from me like we'd been caught doing something far more scandalous than discussing a tattoo. Principal Gardner's eyes flickered between us, her eyebrow raising ever so slightly, but Silas was the first to speak.

"Chase, Meghan," he said, his tone polite but his expression unreadable, "I hope we're not interrupting anything." He eyed my still rolled-up sleeve before switching his gaze to the pile of weird rocks on the desk beside me.

I opened my mouth, completely unsure of how to explain this without sounding like a lunatic. But Meghan, always quick on her feet, beat me to it.

"Oh, not at all," she said, her voice confident. "I'm sure this looks odd, but we're doing some research for our next story—about the Woodvale Witch." I blinked, knowing full well that was not part of our plan. But Meghan didn't even flinch, catching my eye as she lied again. "We thought the town could use something fun and light to read about after all the tornado chaos."

Damn, she was good.

"I'm sorry, the 'Woodvale Witch'?" Silas questioned, his brows furrowed in confusion. Having lived in Woodvale for less than a year, it was no surprise he'd never heard of her.

Principal Gardner smiled, turning from Meghan to Silas. "Oh, it's a Woodvale legend," she said. I got the impression she could sense the awkward tension between us and Silas. "A woman accused of poisoning her husband was publicly hanged here centuries ago, and rumor has it, her ghost haunts the woods."

Silas nodded, shifting on his feet like he was bored already. "Interesting," he said, exchanging a glance with the superintendent, who shrugged.

Tucking her hair behind her ear, Sarah turned back to us. "I love your Sunday column, Meghan. I can't wait to read this one."

Meghan let out a nervous chuckle, probably coming to the realization she was going to have to actually write this. She uttered a quiet thank you before helping me put all the rocks back in my bag.

"We'll get out of your hair," I said, zipping up the backpack. Why these four people would be in this room together confounded me. When Meghan and I got to the hallway, she tucked her hand beneath her bangs, shaking her head at herself, clearly just as embarrassed as I was. "So, what do you think that's all about?" I asked her on the stairwell.

"I think Grissom's temporarily relocating here."

"Really?" That made a lot of sense, actually, and I wasn't surprised she'd already figured that out. My head immediately filled with questions, like—where would Meghan and I have our meetings now? Would I have to deal with school traffic when I arrived in the mornings? And could I still play basketball (badly) in the old gym to let off steam in the middle of the day? "I wonder whose idea that was. I can't see Silas offering that up."

"Mine, actually," Meghan said, "but I doubt he'll give me any credit for it. Anyway, are we headed straight to the woods, or are we going to the tattoo parlor first?"

"I don't know," I said, pausing on the second landing of the stairwell. "I'm not sure I can do this."

Meghan stopped walking and put a hand on her hip, the sweet smirk on her face indicating she was either going to insult me or flirt with me. The lines tended to blur between the two lately, so I was prepared either way. "What if I let you hold my hand?"

"Okay," I blurted, like an obedient golden retriever with a treat dangled in front of him. It made Meghan laugh the rest of the way down the stairs, that familiarly sexy cackle slipping through, like she loved how easy I was to manipulate.

I was putty in her hands.

chapter twenty-one

meghan

Mae had the patience of a saint.

Chase didn't chicken out completely, but he started second-guessing the size of the tattoo when he sat down, worrying it was too ambitious for his first one. Mae tried to gently coax him into it, but he kept looking at me like a little kid in a dentist's chair, waiting for his mom to speak up for him. I asked Mae if she could come up with a more simplified version, and she pulled out her stencil paper and drew a tiny outline of a ghost. It reminded me of the Snapchat logo.

"Does that work?" she asked him.

He looked at me.

"Chase," I laughed. "It's your skin, not mine. Do you want it or not?"

After waffling it over for a minute, Chase finally decided that yes, he did want it. As Mae got her tools ready, she warned Chase she couldn't refund the money he prepaid just because he'd downgraded his tattoo. Shop policy, she said. And that was when Chase asked, "Could you apply it to her next one, then?" He nodded toward me.

I started to protest, but Mae looked over her shoulder as she put on her gloves, saying, "Well, is there something small you'd want to get today?"

"Oh, I—that's okay."

"What if you got a little ghost like his, but with a bow on it?"

"That sounds adorable, but I—no, he's the one getting tatted up today. Not me."

"Are you really going to turn down a free tattoo, Meg?" Chase asked, watching Mae prep his skin with an alcohol swab. Butterflies fluttered in my stomach every time he called me by my nickname, and this time was no different.

"I'll think about it." I watched Mae apply the stencil to Chase's bicep in the exact spot I'd told him to get the tattoo. I had a feeling that if I asked Chase to jump off a bridge, he'd shrug and say, "okay," before leaping to his death.

He handled the tattoo better than I expected, taking slow, deep breaths as he watched the needle poke his skin. I hadn't forgotten the words I'd said that convinced him to come here, so I slipped my hand inside his on the black leather seat. "Here," I said, "you can squeeze my hand if you need to." Like he was afraid to move too much, Chase nodded his head slightly, his hand tightening around mine.

How did we get here? How did we reach this point where we had now held hands not once, but twice? A few weeks ago, I had contemplated running him over with my car after he said he wished I'd die in a fiery crash. Now, I couldn't decide if holding his hand felt too familiar or too foreign. Familiar in the sense that I knew Chase better than I knew almost anyone, but foreign because we hadn't been this close in more than three years. Watching his thumb subtly caressing mine, I could almost forget all the heartache this man had put me through.

The memory of his nonchalance when I left him made my smile fade for a few minutes. How could he act like this with me now—like he was falling back in love with me—when three years ago, he didn't care whether I was in his life or not?

I swallowed, trying not to think about it.

Chase's tattoo was so simple, Mae was done in twenty minutes. She wiped Chase's skin clean and inspected the tattoo, asking him what he thought. He looked down at his new ink, then up at Mae's face. "It's pretty badass."

"Right?" Mae asked with a giggle, "Now we need to convince your girlfriend to get one."

"Ex," Chase and I blurted in unison.

Mae looked as embarrassed as she did confused, her cheeks turning as pink as the left side of her hair. "Oh my gosh, I am so sorry. I guess I just misread the vibe. You probably don't want a matching ghost, then, or-?"

Did I need a reminder of Chase forever etched on my skin? Then again, a little ghost with a bow fit my aesthetic perfectly, and I didn't *have* to associate it with him. And once I saw Mae's drawing of the girl ghost, the words "alright, let's do it" left my lips before I had the chance to second-guess myself.

I opted to get it on my collarbone, the one that wasn't already covered in ink. I pulled off my sheer top and lowered the straps of my black tank and bra, noticing the way Chase looked down at the ground, like he was seeing something he shouldn't. But when Mae began her work, and I closed my eyes from the stinging sensation, Chase's hand quietly found mine.

Poor Mae—she was probably going to spend the rest of the day wondering about the dynamics of our relationship. Then again, so would we.

We both tipped her on our way out, and when we stepped into the cool air outside, Chase turned to me, his eyes wide. He looked down at his upper arm, wrapped in clear plastic, before turning back to me. "So. We just got matching tattoos."

I pressed my lips together tight, meeting his eyes, and nodded. I was too stunned by my own actions to even speak. It wasn't my first impulsive tattoo—I had an owl on one of my calves I wished I could erase. My owl phase was short-lived, but the reminder of it was permanent.

One look at Chase's sexy smirk told me this phase, when it inevitably ended, would leave an even bigger mark on me.

******

Chase parked on Persimmon Road, just behind the football field of the high school, at the edge of Ackerman Woods. The park, with its winding hiking trails, led to a set of double waterfalls. One of them was forty feet tall, although when the weather was dry, it was no more than a disappointing trickle. It used to be private land until five years ago, and if you asked me, the parks department missed a big opportunity by not playing up the Woodvale Witch lore. They seemed to want to bury Woodvale's dark past, but they underestimated just how many people would have flocked to the park for a chance to spot the ghost of a supposed witch.

My goal for the afternoon was to figure out how long it would have taken Fannie to walk from her home—or at least where we assumed her home had been—to the spot where Chase's YouTube fan claimed to have found the rocks. I wanted to rule out the possibility Fannie could have buried them there herself. Because, after all, that would be more believable than the idea that she and Evelyn were somehow both connected to weird symbols.

"Here we are, trespassing like the old days," Chase said, as we trudged through a yet-to-be-plowed cornfield. The dead, broken cornstalks jutted out of the ground like jagged spears, and the dirt beneath was still soggy from last week's rain. It made me glad we stopped at my apartment on the way so I could change into boots. I was still in my long skirt, hiking it up in front so it wouldn't snag on the sharp, brittle stalks. "Between this and the tattoo," Chase continued, "I feel like an outlaw."

"An outlaw? Please," I said, rolling my eyes at him. "You've never even gotten a speeding ticket."

"Hey—I got a warning that one time. You were with me."

I couldn't help but throw my head back and laugh as we traipsed through the muddy field. "Yeah, for driving erratically while playing Pokémon Go. Not exactly something to brag about, is it?"

He just shrugged, unashamed. We reached the edge of the woods at the end of the field, forging our own path through the budding trees. Pale green grass scattered with violets poked through the dead leaves on the ground, and a brief memory of picking a handful of them for my mom as a little girl flashed through my mind. She pressed one in my dad's old dictionary, the massive red book that always sat on a shelf in our living room. I found it after she died. One of these days, I would have a piece of jewelry made out of it. But for now, I clutched my obsidian pendant with one hand, taking Chase's outreached hand with the other as I stepped over a fallen log.

He used his phone's GPS to guide us to the exact location where that kid found the rocks. I imagined we were walking the same path Fannie would have traveled if she were visiting the waterfall. Did this area look the same back then?

There probably wouldn't have been a discarded Mountain Dew bottle wedged between a couple of rocks, that's for sure.

"You doing okay?" Chase asked me, watching me hike up my skirt to step over some thick tree roots. "You know, jeans might have been a better choice…"

"I feel like I'm in a romantasy novel with this skirt on, so shut your mouth." I kept walking, but Chase came to an abrupt halt. I didn't like the look of his smirk when I turned around. "Why do you look so amused?"

"You said 'romantasy.'" He paused, running his hand through his hair. "You could've just said 'fantasy', but you said—"

A rush of warmth flooded my cheeks. "I know what I said," I snapped, continuing on my way. My skirt snagged on a pointy piece of bark, and I struggled to yank it free. With each tug, it only seemed to catch the jagged wood even worse. Chase, still grinning, bent over to work the black fabric free. I let out a whine when I saw the tiny hole the bark left behind.

"Like I said. Jeans," Chase muttered as he straightened back up, his face only a few inches from mine. Caged between him and the tree, I swallowed hard, feeling the heat between our bodies. My chest heaved with my spine pressed against the bark, and I dared him with my eyes to make a move. *Take it there. Do it.*

But he didn't. He glanced away, his jaw tightening, and the moment slipped away. I pushed off the tree, my stomach sinking with disappointment.

We continued walking in silence, and it was hard not to notice how he wouldn't look at me anymore. Maybe he was too afraid. I'd been too mean to him, hadn't I? Pushing him away at every turn. Why would he make a move now, when I was the one who decided to leave in the first place? Really, the ball was in my court. But I wasn't going to make the move either.

It was probably for the best.

We reached the creek, the sound of rushing water growing louder as we came upon the double falls. We were at the top of the forty-foot drop, with a smaller waterfall just a few steps away. The storms from the week before made the water flow fast and fierce.

I eyed the creek, where a series of large rocks seemed to form a rugged, natural bridge across the shallow water, only a few yards from the drop-off. We'd strayed from the marked trail, and now it seemed like our only option was to cross here. Chase glanced at the map on his phone and then out at the water before turning back to me.

"Let's walk upstream to get across. This looks a little dangerous."

I ignored him, carefully stepping onto the first slippery rock. "Thought you were an outlaw."

"Seriously, Meghan," Chase called after me. "If you fall…" He didn't finish that thought.

"Then there would be two ghosts haunting these woods," I quipped, taking another step. The water splashed against the soles of my boots.

Chase let out a heavy sigh, giving in, like usual. He joined me in the creek, stepping across the rocks with his hands in his pockets like he did this kind of thing all the time. "You're exhausting," he said.

"Thanks," I tossed back with a smirk.

"When are you going to stop taking my insults as compliments?"

I turned around to shoot him a smart reply, but my foot slipped on a loose rock, making me teeter back and forth dangerously. Before I could react, Chase lunged forward, grabbing me by the waist to steady me. My hands instinctively reached for his arms, gripping him as I tried to regain my balance.

"I wasn't going to fall," I assured him, even though my heart was pounding in my chest.

"Right. Maybe next time, I'll just let you plummet to your death, if you're going to be stubborn like that."

"Yeah? You'd like that, wouldn't you?"

He stepped closer, his grip still firm on my waist. "Is that what you think?" His voice softened, and he glanced down at his feet as he moved onto the rock closest to mine. "I'm surprised you haven't pushed me over the edge of the waterfall already."

"I'm thinking about it," I said, trying not to smile.

"Well, if I go down now, you're going down with me." His hands felt heavy on my hips, holding me into place. Inching closer on that mossy rock, his palms slipped around to my backside until he was pulling my body secure against his. Hips against bony hips, chest against heaving chest.

We drew our foreheads close together, and I could feel one of his hands cupping the back of my neck. "Meg," he whispered, his voice hoarse and desperate. I took in all of the features I hadn't seen this close in a long time—his impossibly long eyelashes behind his glasses, the single freckle on his left cheekbone, and the soft lips I'd missed more than I realized. He leaned into me some more, those lips finally crashing into mine like we had no time to waste. With my arms wrapping around his body, I let out the softest whimper, parting my lips for him. He used his hand to tilt my head back like he needed to get a better taste. The man who couldn't make a decision to save his life was confident in the way he kissed, his tongue thrashing against mine with purpose. The sensation sent an electric spark through my core that settled between my legs. *God, that tongue…*

This wasn't the same man who knelt at my feet. The one kissing me now didn't have to beg. He knew what he wanted, and he knew he had me. I could feel his lips tug upward in a smile before he deepened the kiss, his fist tightening around the hair at the base of my neck.

I breathlessly pulled away, opening my eyes to find him looking right back at me. "What are we doing?" I breathed out.

"I believe it's called kissing."

I took a step back from him, feeling his hands drop from my body. "You and I don't *kiss*."

"Then color me confused, because you just had your tongue in my mouth." He glanced at my lips like he wanted to kiss me all over again. I resisted the urge to let him, taking another careful step backward.

The vulnerability of the moment hit me, knowing I'd just admitted my feelings without saying a single word. Feelings I hadn't even come to terms with myself. Now that my guard was down, I felt exposed to Chase, completely. I could no longer pretend I didn't like him, could I?

Dammit.

I clenched the fabric of my skirt, hiking it up again as I turned around. "Anyway, let's go."

If Chase's feelings were hurt, he didn't let it show. To my surprise, he chuckled as he came up behind me. It was like he saw my deflection as an amusing challenge he had to overcome.

The two of us were quiet as we made our way up a steep embankment to the flattened trail on the other side of the creek. And we were still silent as we followed it the rest of the way to the probable location of Evelyn's old cottage. I knew why I wasn't speaking, but Chase's silence had more of a nervous, excited energy which probably had very little to do with the witch and everything to do with kissing me.

My pulse refused to slow down to a normal rate as we walked. *What does this mean?* That was the question that repeated itself over and over in my brain. He had to be asking himself the same thing—and my stomach sank when I realized our answers to that question were, most likely, vastly different.

Staring at the map app on his phone, Chase strayed from the path. "That kid said he found the rocks over this way," Chase said, nodding for me to follow him. He led me ten or so yards from the trail, stopping when he reached a fat, fallen log covered in turkey-tail mushrooms. I watched him stare down at the ground, moving some loose dirt with his foot. "I think I can see where he dug up the rocks."

"What was he doing out here, anyway?"

"I'm not totally sure, but I think he's really been getting into all the Evelyn lore and was hoping he'd find something. When he did, he contacted his favorite local paranormal expert," Chase said, "and now we're here."

I walked around the area, expecting to find something that would give me an answer—but I wasn't even sure what the question was. Just beyond a freshly fallen tree, there was a short section of a crumbling stone fence covered in moss and lichen protruding from a bank of dirt. It struck me as odd to come across a man-made structure here in the middle of the woods. But now, finding it so close to where the rocks were buried, it was like it meant something.

I ran my hand along the soft moss on the old stone fence, knowing Evelyn's old cottage must have been around here. That was no secret, though—while the exact location would never be known, everyone presumed her house was in this general section of Ackerman Woods. I felt a prickle at the back of my neck as I made my way past the fence, like I was standing where Evelyn once stood herself. If I mentioned that eerie feeling to Chase, he'd try to convince me Evelyn's ghost was with us, so I kept my mouth shut as I took a few more steps. The white blossoms on the trees up ahead caught my eye. They weren't Bradford pears, thank goodness—but definitely some kind of fruit tree. Apple trees, maybe? There were at least a dozen of them in the area, haphazardly spaced out like they could've sprouted from seedlings of older apple trees.

My breath caught in my throat. *"Perhaps a sip of apple brandy would do wonders to calm their nerves."* Where did Fannie get that apple brandy she told the Woodvale Times about, anyway?

I turned with a gasp, startled by how close Chase was standing. His eyes were wide as he gazed all around us. "I have such an eerie feeling in the back of my neck right now," he said, rubbing his arms like he suddenly felt a chill.

"Me too. Because I've just figured it out—Evelyn and Fannie *were* friends. I knew it."

His eyebrows lifted in confusion. "Yeah?"

"Close friends," I added, slipping my hand beneath my bangs and pacing. With the rocks being found so close to where Evelyn's cottage stood, it couldn't be a coincidence. I knew it. I felt it deep in my bones. Both women were connected to those symbols, and the apple trees in the middle of the woods only solidified my theory.

My mumbling turned into whispers as I tried to fit the pieces together. Evelyn was executed in 1846. Fannie died in 1849. Neither of them had children, and it was clear they were both outcasts in Woodvale. It made sense that they would be drawn to each other.

It was probably just my imagination running wild, but I just knew in my heart those women got drunk on apple brandy one evening and developed a secret code for communicating with each other. The thought made me smile, because it sounded like something Jillian and I might have done before our lives got too hectic.

"Hey, so…" Chase cleared his throat, absentmindedly scratching the edge of the plastic wrap around his arm. "Did you suddenly obtain some psychic abilities out here, or am I missing something?"

I shook my head. My fixation on Fannie had been a convenient distraction from the emotions I wasn't ready to face, but I knew I could only avoid them for so long. Chase just stood there, waiting patiently.

"Sorry for being incredibly weird right now," I said, fidgeting with my necklace against my chest.

Chase put his thumbs in his pockets, his eyes softening as he took in my wild appearance—the muddy boots, the holey skirt, the flyaways sticking out here and there, and the shiny plastic wrap on my collarbone that was visible beneath my sheer top. "It's okay," he said, "I like you weird."

Hearing those words grounded me. All of this reminded me of our old blog days—one of us would always be rambling about our current nerdy hyperfixation while the other one patiently waited it out.

But what would happen the next time I went on a grief spiral? Those days were few and far between now, but they still occurred. We were coming up on my mom's birthday, a day I'd already scheduled off, just like I had for the past three years. I was going to eat her favorite cake, stare at pictures of her, and cry. That was, quite literally, my entire plan for the day. But in my shared calendar with Chase, I'd entered "appointment in Indy" as a cover-up for being gone that day. A lie. The last thing I needed was for Chase to tell me I was grieving wrong, as gently as he might try to approach it.

The closest thing Chase had ever come to loss was his childhood dog, who died from old age when he was in the eighth grade. He still had his parents and all four grandparents. He didn't know.

And I still didn't know if I could trust him to handle the darkest parts of me. He liked me "weird," but did he like me when I was curled up in the fetal position listening to the same Fleetwood Mac song for the ninetieth time, crying into my mom's old cardigan because it no longer smelled like her? Could he handle that?

I just wasn't sure if I was ready to find out the hard way that he couldn't.

chapter twenty-two

chase

Never in my life had I wished I could read minds more than I did in the quiet car ride back to the studio with Meghan. Then again, I didn't need to be Professor X to sense she was regretting that kiss. She fidgeted with the hole in her skirt, stretching it and making it bigger, while gazing out the passenger window like she couldn't bear to look at me.

I couldn't decide whether I should turn the music on to fill the silence or leave it off in case she wanted to speak. When the silence stretched on for too long, and it became apparent she wasn't going to talk, I figured the ball was probably in my court and I needed to do something about it.

I cleared my throat, glancing her direction a couple of times as I drove, taking a deep breath. But before any words escaped my mouth, Meghan spoke first, slowly turning toward me with a gentle, "Chase…"

"You don't have to say it," I interrupted, cutting her off before she could even begin.

A crinkle formed between her brows. "I don't?"

I shook my head, trying to keep my voice steady. "No, I get it. The kiss was a mistake, right? And I know you're sitting over there stewing, trying to figure out how to walk it back. But you don't have to—it's okay."

I thought I'd save us both some time by making the rejection a little smoother. I wasn't sure what kind of response I expected from her, maybe a heavy sigh or even a "thank you" for understanding. Instead, she turned back to the window again, staring at the snapped and uprooted trees in quiet contemplation. And then, without warning, she shifted in her seat, crossed her arms, and said, "You've got me all figured out, don't you?"

"Tell me I'm wrong."

But her lips parted before slowly coming back together, because we both knew I was right. "I'm just confused. You and I—" She stopped abruptly, letting out another loud sigh.

"What? Me and you… what?"

"There's so much history. So much… hurt. I can't just forget all of that, and I know you can't, either." Meghan stared at the now gaping hole in her skirt. "Tell *me* I'm wrong."

She wasn't.

I bit the inside of my cheek, feeling the weight of her words settling in. "I bet you're wishing you'd pushed me off that waterfall, huh?" I said, trying to keep my tone light, but the sting of her almost-rejection was a little hard to mask.

Meghan kept her eyes on my face as I drove. "You go down, I go down with you." In the corner of my eye, I caught the flicker of a smile on her face, and that was enough to give me the tiniest sliver of hope.

**

Back in the newsroom, I stared at my computer screen daydreaming about Meghan for God knew how long. Five minutes? Ten minutes? A fucking hour? And when I finally managed to think about work, I noticed she'd renamed our shared folder *Feel-Good Stories & Other Bullshit*, and all hope was lost. While Bernard was over there talking about a 20% chance of rain, there was a zero percent chance of productivity for me that afternoon.

I didn't snap out of it until Jillian flounced into the newsroom in a pink pantsuit, returning from her assignment with Xander. When she spotted me working at my desk, she pivoted, making her way over toward me. "Candy?"

She held up a white box from Coleman's Candies, their gold logo glinting beneath the overhead lights, popping off the lid as she made her way toward me. Inside was an array of assorted chocolates that looked too tempting to pass up. "Wow, Meghan's going to wish she hadn't passed the story onto you guys," I said, taking what I hoped was a plain milk chocolate piece.

"Yeah, what the hell's that all about?" she asked with a laugh, setting the chocolates down on my desk. She helped herself to one, using her free hand to take off her heels. "She said something about going to the woods?"

"That we did. And," I said, reaching for my sleeve, "we got matching tattoos." I removed the clear wrap, unable to remember a word Mae said about the aftercare because I was too busy internally screaming about holding hands with Meghan.

Jill wiped caramel from her lip, leaning around my monitor to get a closer look. "Aww, I love it," she said, flipping her hair off her shoulder. "And I'm sorry, hon, but it sounded like you said 'matching tattoos'? I know I'm hearing things wrong."

"You're not." I was desperate to tell her—or anyone—about the kiss, but that wasn't my news to share.

She finished the chocolate in her hands and swallowed. "There's no way Meghan got a matching tattoo with you today."

"Ask her," I said, leaning back in my desk chair with my hands folded behind my head. Jillian squinted at me, calling my bluff, but I could only laugh. "Why would I lie about this? She got a tattoo on her… chestal region."

Jill pulled her phone from her pocket to send Meghan a quick text. "I told her to get down here right now. She would never get a tattoo without consulting with me first."

"'Kay. Let's wait."

As we waited for Meghan to come downstairs, Jillian shared more chocolates with me. I always liked Jill. When Meghan and I ended things, Jill was obviously on Meg's side, but she didn't display any animosity toward me at work. She kept things professional, and I treated her with the same level of respect I always had.

Jillian had just handed me another chocolate when Silas strolled in with his usual cloud of self-importance. He paused just inside the studio, eyeing the two of us. Jill immediately stiffened, her discomfort almost palpable when she said, "Hi Silas, do you want to try a chocolate from one of our local businesses?" She picked up the box from my desk. "Chase and I may have just devoured the best pieces, but they're all good."

Silas fidgeted with the button on his sport coat, hesitating like he would rather be anywhere else in the world than associating with us. But he took Jill up on her offer, walking over to accept a chocolate. And then, after the subtlest of glances at Jill's hips in those pink pants, he said, "I would've thought you'd have to be on a strict diet—I mean, what is the expression? 'The camera adds ten pounds'?" He chuckled, staring at the candy in his hand, but never taking a bite. "Better be careful, yeah?"

I almost choked on the raspberry creme in my mouth. Jill let out a tight, forced chuckle, but she was too stunned by Silas's comment to speak. But I wasn't. "What a weird thing to say to the face of our network," I blurted, maintaining eye contact with the guy, as uncomfortable as his long stare was making me feel. I knew I'd chosen just the right words to get under his skin without getting myself in trouble. Did I call him a misogynist? No. Did I say he was rude? Nope. But *"weird"* felt like the perfect word to rattle him without crossing any lines.

I wished I would've had the nerve to speak up when he chastised Meghan in front of me, but at least I was saying something now. And if nobody ever shut him down, he was probably just going to get worse.

"Uh—" Silas opened his mouth to start what might have been a half-assed apology, when two men confidently stepped into the room behind him. It was the superintendent again, this time with a member of the school board. Their arrival saved Silas from having to own up to his body-shaming remark. Without another word, he quickly ushered them to the conference room at the far end of the studio.

Jill was a statue, staring down at the box of chocolates in her hands. "I hate that bastard," she whispered. I nodded in agreement just as Meghan took a cautious step into the room. My heart forgot how to beat for a second when she came into view.

"Jill? What's with the 911 text?"

Jillian dropped the box of chocolates on my desk, closing her eyes with a deep inhale, like she was resetting her thoughts after that encounter with Silas. When she turned around, she put one hand on her hip and demanded, "Show me your chest."

Meghan looked from me to her overly brazen friend, a smile stretching across her face. "Wow, Jill, that's a whole new level of forwardness, even for you." With a playful roll of her eyes, she glanced over at Bernard and his cameraman to make sure they were distracted before pulling up her sheer top to reveal her ghost tattoo. "It's still a little red, but here it is."

Jill stared at Meghan with wide eyes. "Okay—that's different for you, but I like it," she said, nodding her head a lot. "So, you two actually got matching tattoos. There's a lot to unpack there."

I really hoped she wouldn't. Not now. Thankfully, Xander chose that moment to pass by the newsroom door and came to a halt when he saw the women standing in front of my desk. He lifted one eyebrow in curiosity as he stepped all the way into the room. "What's going on in here?"

"Meghan and Chase got matching tattoos," Jillian answered.

Xander's eye lingering on Jill for a couple of seconds before he was distracted by the men behind the soundproof glass wall in the conference room. "Thought I smelled something," he muttered, narrowing his eyes at them. "Guess they're moving forward with Grissom relocating here, huh?"

"Looks like it," I said. "I think they're fine-tuning all the details."

"Then why isn't Sarah Gardner in there with them?" Jillian wondered aloud, looking at each of us before staring at the group of men behind the glass.

"Because she's a woman," Meghan said. "And Silas Brown doesn't respect women."

Jillian, casting a subtle glance my direction, sighed and said, "You're telling me. He just came in here and body-shamed me."

"Are you fucking kidding me?" Meghan blurted, her face turning red with anger. "What'd he say? Tell me what he said, Jill."

Jillian shook her head, glancing at the floor. "Just something about how I need to be careful because the camera adds ten pounds."

"That's pretty rich coming from a guy with a receding hairline and three failed marriages," Xander noted. He crossed his arms as he stared at the three men in suits who appeared to be exchanging documents across the table. "Look at them. Birds of a feather flock together. Noah Sherman's a fucking misogynistic prick, too. Oh, and fun fact—my report about his sexist Facebook posts getting brought up at the school board meeting has been wiped from the website."

"What do you mean?" I asked. "Who deleted it?"

"Good question. Graham didn't know anything about it when I asked, but I found out Silas golfed with the guy the next day." Xander nodded toward the men in the conference room. "Interesting, isn't it?"

"So, he's protecting his little buddy," Meghan scoffed.

"When he's not protecting his buddies, he's forcing us to paint them in a positive light," Jillian said, detailing how Silas approached her about covering a locally hated real estate developer who'd just wiped out a wooded area and a few houses to build another strip mall. When Jill expressed concern the town might not respond well to a feature on the man responsible for literal destruction, Silas persuaded her to twist the narrative. "He told me to focus on how it boosted the economy instead of all the trees and homes that were destroyed."

I let out a sharp exhale. "Our CEO is manipulating the news to suit him. Somebody needs to do something about this."

Instinctively, we all looked at Xander, who had a history of meddling with controversial politicians when he worked for the Chicago Tribune. But he shook his head, saying, "Don't look at me. You want me to go after the CEO? Sure, let me just dust off my resume first, because that'd be the last you'd see of me around here."

A silence fell over us as we watched the men chuckle and grin at each other behind the glass, that kind of casual laugh that only came from men who knew they were untouchable. Silas's cozy relationship with the very administrators we were supposed to hold accountable was just another red flag. He had the reins of the local news, steering it exactly where he wanted, and there was nothing any of us could do about it.

When our conversation wrapped up, Meghan asked Jill to take a walk with her. She cast the tiniest, subtlest grin in my direction before the two of them linked arms and rounded the corner into the hallway like a couple of middle schoolers getting ready to gab about a crush. I was sure Meghan had a lot to say, and I was already bracing myself for Jill's over-the-top reaction when she returned.

With the two of them gone, that left me alone with Xander, whose presence wasn't quite as foreboding as Silas's, but it came pretty close. I hoped he would walk away, but he made himself comfortable instead, sitting on the corner of my desk.

"Bust any ghosts lately?"

I rested my arms on my desk, blinking up at him in annoyance. "Do you need something?"

"Yes, actually." He stole a quick glance at Silas and the other men before turning back to me. "Heard you were throwing some kind of nerd convention?"

"Comic con. Why, need some help with your Kylo Ren cosplay?"

Xander smirked. "I'll get back to you on that. Anyway, I want the story. Let's set up an exclusive interview."

"Oh. I sort of assumed I'd handle the coverage myself, like I always do. And Meghan would be the one to do the write-up."

Xander absentmindedly turned my Ant-man bobblehead around to face him. "Probably a conflict of interest to have you do your own reporting on it, right?"

"You just want to beat Meghan in this little competition."

"If she really wanted to win, she wouldn't be handing me her stories so she could run around the woods with you, would she? And let's face it, I'm not expecting a mass influx of subscriptions by writing about lightsaber-wielding basement dwellers." He paused to look in my eyes, smiling from one side of his mouth like he didn't fully mean the insult. "Seriously, though, I'll give you a decent write-up, and Jill can probably get you guys a primetime spot. Sound good?"

It almost sounded like he was doing me a favor, but I accepted it with a wary nod. "Then there's really nothing in it for you?"

"Not at all," he said, standing up to stretch. And then he dropped his arms at his sides, rolling his eyes. "Okay, there's actually one thing."

"Yeah?"

Xander scratched his temple with his thumb as he stared down at his feet, his usual cocky demeanor melting before me. What could he possibly need from me? And why was he having such a hard time saying it? "Think I could have a one-on-one with Ethan Killian the day of the event?"

I couldn't decide what was more amusing, the fact that Xander knew who Ethan Killian was, or that he was embarrassed to admit he was a fan. As tempting as it was to laugh in his face, especially after the "basement dwellers" comment, I managed to keep my reaction to an amused grin. "Don't tell me you've watched *Starlight*."

"I never said that."

I licked my lips, deciding to have a little fun with this. "Did you hear they're rebooting it?"

Xander's mouth slowly fell open. "Are you serious? When? Is that confirmed?"

"I'm lying. But your reaction tells me… a lot."

Xander's eyes narrowed as a smirk tugged at the corners of his lips. "Fuck you," he muttered, turning to walk away with his hands in his pockets.

Finally, I let out the laugh I'd been holding. "You can have your exclusive interview with Ethan. But hey, there's something else you could do for me." I waited for him to turn back around and took a deep breath, deciding to be vulnerable for a second. "Could you talk me up to Meghan a little? I know she respects you, so, you know—put in a good word for me, I guess."

His eyes locked on mine for a moment. "She got a matching tattoo with you today, my guy. You don't need my help." And with a little shrug, Xander turned and walked out of the studio.

chapter twenty-three

meghan

I hadn't anticipated all the screaming.

The energy inside our building shifted once Grissom officially moved in. It only took them one week to figure out all the logistics. And I had to admit, I was impressed with how efficiently it all came together—moving furniture, coordinating bus schedules, installing new security measures at all the entrances. Our building would temporarily house kindergarten through second grade, while the other half of the student body was relocated to a nearby church. From my vantage point, it looked like their first day was going pretty smoothly.

But the noise level as the kids filed into the building that morning was deafening. I arrived at work during peak drop-off time, and I made a mental note to never do that again, considering I almost got swept up in the sea of screaming kids packing the hallway.

Jillian ate it up, planting herself outside the studio door to high-five the kids as they passed. *"You're the lady from TV!" "I saw you on a billboard this morning!"* She loved the attention, even tearing up when she told me about a kindergartener calling her pretty. "I hope they never leave!"

Xander, on the other hand, was handling the situation… differently.

"That's it. I'm calling in an anonymous bomb threat," he yelled from his cubicle when the hallway filled up with noisy kids again at lunchtime. He'd already been stopped by Sarah for not wearing his district-provided lanyard—Graham said we were all required to have them as part of the building's new security measures. Xander didn't hate the lanyards as much as he loathed having to wait for the school secretary to let him into the building. The only thing preventing him from quitting on the spot was the presence of a certain redheaded librarian who parked her book cart outside our newsroom door to playfully pester Xander in his cubicle.

I smiled as I typed, overhearing the way Abigail giggled at his bomb proclamation, and how his voice pitched up when he spoke to her. Was she even aware of the hold she had on him?

Between their hushed conversation and the growing noise just outside our newsroom door, it became difficult to concentrate on my write-up of the board of works. And then, the ultimate distraction came in the form of a text from Chase:

Chase: Since our meeting spot has been overrun by tiny humans, let's grab coffee at Riverside

I was a little taken aback by his boldness. As tempting as it was to call him out on the audacity of assuming I'd want to do such a thing, my thumbs typed an "ok" instead.

I would just have to make it very clear from the get-go that this was in no way, shape, or form a "coffee date." For the past few days, Chase had been giving me this quiet, puppy-dog-eyed look every time I talked, as though I were on the verge of asking him if he'd rather make out instead of conducting an interview with me.

I couldn't deny my feelings. Not to him, and not to myself. My mind wandered with curious thoughts, an endless stream of "what if?" questions that kept me awake at night. As good as it felt to get cozy with him again, it also left me feeling vulnerable. After everything we'd been through, this—whatever it was—was just as scary as it was exciting. I wasn't ready to jump in headfirst.

At least he seemed to understand my need to take a step back without my having to say the words out loud. At the coffee shop, when I asked him to let me pay for my own drink, he didn't fight me on it. He graciously stepped aside, only casting the tiniest, subtlest eyeroll at my stubbornness.

There weren't any empty tables on that Monday morning, so we had no choice but to sit on the worn leather loveseat in the corner. The seat had a lot of give, maybe too much, sinking us closer together than either of us intended. I pretended not to notice, crossing my feet at the ankles as I tugged on the hem of my skirt.

"I've got something for you," Chase said, unzipping the backpack between his feet. He set his coffee down on the table in front of us and pulled a packet of papers from his bag.

"What's this?"

"You left Fannie's journal in my car last week, and I scanned the pages and did some heavy-handed editing to increase the contrast, so her writing is actually legible. And then, I had an AI program convert the text."

A small gasp escaped my lips as I flipped through the pages on my lap, the once-illegible scrawls now clean, clear words in front of me. "Chase," I said, his name coming out in a whisper. When I turned my head to look at his face, dropping my eyes to stare at the crease on his chin where I used to kiss him, I was so overcome with gratitude I couldn't speak.

"I only skimmed through it, so there might be some inaccuracies. I didn't want to take the enjoyment of reading the entries for the first time away from you."

I could kiss you right now.

With a grin, I moved my eyes in a triangle from each eye to his lips. "Why did you do this?"

"Because I know it's important to you." He swallowed, maintaining eye contact with me. "And now you've got me obsessing over it, too. I need answers."

On second thought, take off your pants.

It was probably best I kept those thoughts to myself. I pulled my eyes away, bringing my iced latte to my lips for my first sip. "Thank you," I said, flipping the pages back. "I can't wait to dive in. I wish we didn't have a billion things on our agenda today."

"You mean you don't want to pass them off on Xander and Jill?"

"Not this time." I tilted my head back with a groan. Xander was in the lead again, thanks to that feature on the town's beloved candy store. "I'm starting to lose hope of ever getting to that conference in NYC. Xander pretty much has this in the bag."

"Don't say that. We've still got a couple weeks. And who knows, your witch story just might blow everything he's written out of the water."

I gave him a doubtful glance as I carefully inserted the Fannie printouts in the front of my notebook in my bag. And then, pulling out my phone, I opened up our shared calendar. Our day was filled with a ribbon-cutting, a quilt-a-thon, and an interview with the mayor about the ongoing tornado recovery efforts. To close out the day, we were covering a tornado relief art show fundraiser at the high school, which meant we'd be writing and editing late into the evening. I was already exhausted just thinking about it all.

However, being with Chase made it all a little easier. Easier than it would have been if I were on my own, that is. I had someone I could whisper my judgmental comments to—someone who could make me grin with only a knowing, wide-eyed stare. After years of working solo, having someone to debrief with at the end of an event made even the dull moments more bearable. And something like a quilt-a-thon would have been a challenge for me to get through without zoning out, but watching Chase charm those ladies with his compliments on their craftsmanship had me holding back a smile.

"I genuinely think you could've gone home with Gladys," I told Chase as we made our way between the rows of tulips on the walkway up to City Hall.

"Gladys? I had my eye on Shirley. She could take me for a ride on her rollator anytime."

I clutched my stomach, unable to hold back my laughter as he held the door open for me. "Well, either way, they'll keep you warm at night with their quilts, won't they?"

Chase gave me a playful grin as we walked through the vestibule leading to the mayor's office. "Someone's got to. The right side of my bed has been awfully cold lately." His teasing tone didn't quite match the flicker of sincerity in his eyes as he opened the second set of doors for me.

I used to occupy that space on the right side of his bed.

That thought lingered for a moment as we entered Mayor Michaels' office, shook her hand, and took our seats. Chase opted not to record the interview, choosing instead to set up his camera outside afterward with City Hall as the backdrop, where he'd summarize the mayor's statements in his own words.

The mayor spoke about how the community had come together in the aftermath of the storm, how neighbors helped neighbors, and how donations had poured in from across the state. "And thanks to the generosity of First United Methodist Church, and of course, the Woodvale News Network," she said, nodding toward us, "our students have the vital opportunity to continue their in-person education, even in these unprecedented circumstances. Silas Brown has been especially instrumental in getting the ball rolling with that."

I couldn't help but roll my eyes, a gesture the mayor most certainly noticed, based on the way she contorted her face to hold back a smile. There was no doubt in my mind she'd observed how pretentious and self-serving Silas was. She'd never say it out loud, but the look of validation she gave me was enough.

Chase picked up on it, too. "Do you get the impression the mayor's not a Silas Brown fan?" he asked me outside, extending the legs of his tripod.

"I think she would've had a hell of a lot to say if I hadn't been recording," I muttered, eyeing the pair of white butterflies flitting around above the tulips. I felt a quick pang of sadness deep in the pit of my chest. Spring was always my mom's favorite season, when everything was blooming and full of life again. The daffodils in her yard bloomed the day I handed the key to her house over to the realtor and said my final goodbye to the place. I was screaming on the inside because my mom never knew that last spring when she looked at her daffodils it would be her very last time.

"At least we know she can't be swayed by him and his checkbook," Chase said, snapping me out of my daydream. It took a full five seconds before I remembered we were talking about Silas and the mayor. I nodded, watching him twist a knob on the tripod to secure his camera. I opened my mouth to agree when I noticed a honeybee on the back of his collar.

"Hey, Chase?" I licked my lips. "Do you have your EpiPen?"

"Yeah, why?" He cupped his hand over the screen on the back of his camera to shield it from the sun, sighing in frustration as he panned to the left to reframe his shot. And as the honeybee crawled to the edge of his collar, its front legs touching the back of his neck, Chase froze. Slowly, he turned his head toward me, and it only took one look at the sheer panic in his eyes for me to take action. Without giving it a second thought, I sprang forward to slowly and carefully slide the corner of my notebook between the bee and Chase's neck, shaking the entire time.

He'd never been stung when he was with me, but he and his mom both told me the story of how he almost lost his life from a single bee sting when he was fourteen. It was all I could think about as I inched the notebook closer to the stubborn bee, which crawled even further up the back of Chase's neck. I bit my lip, willing it to crawl on to the paper instead of stinging him. "You motherfucker," I whispered, trying not to tremble so much I startled the damn thing.

And finally—*finally*—the little guy turned around and crawled onto the notebook. I almost cried out in relief as I pulled the notebook away. The relief came too soon, though— because the bee decided to retaliate against this rude relocation by buzzing toward my thumb to sting me. My notebook fell to the ground just as sharp, burning pain shot through my thumb. I sucked air in through my teeth as Chase whipped around to face me with his hand on the back of his neck like he was double-checking it was gone.

"Did it get you?"

I gave my hand a shake. "Yes. But it's fine," I lied, as though there wasn't a fiery sensation pulsating through my entire hand. I lifted my eyes to meet his. "I wasn't about to let this become a *My Girl* moment."

"God, I feel terrible." He touched his forehead, his brows furrowed with worry. "What do I—should I get something? What do normal, non-allergic people do for bee stings?"

"I don't know, suffer?" I answered with a laugh.

"Fuck, Meghan, I'm sorry."

"Why are you apologizing? You didn't sting me," I teased, grinning at him so he understood it wasn't a big deal. He stepped closer, lifting my hand in both of his to get a closer look, frowning at my reddening thumb. He reached for his wallet in his back pocket, unfolding it to pull out a credit card. I knew exactly what he was doing, but I still tried to lighten the mood with another joke. "Are you compensating me for my troubles?"

Chase paused, his lips twitching like he was trying to suppress a smile. His eyes narrowed playfully as he shook his head, but the hint of amusement didn't leave his face. "Funny," he muttered, glancing at me with a smirk before turning his attention back to my hand. I held my breath as he carefully angled the edge of the credit card against my skin, his fingers brushing mine as he worked to scrape the stinger free. I felt the warmth of his body against mine the entire time, which might have been the reason I stopped breathing. "There. Think it's out."

As he straightened his body, he didn't let go of my hand or step away. With an exhale, I got lost in Chase's green eyes, more mesmerized by them than the way he delicately stroked my thumb with his. "Thanks," I said, and it made him shake his head with a smile. "What?"

Rather than answer, he yanked me toward him, lowering my hand to his hip like that's where it belonged. And without a second of hesitation, he placed one palm against my cheek and kissed my lips. His other hand roamed up my side, resting just below the curve of my breast. Right here in front of City Hall, between the rows of tulips, Chase was two short inches from feeling me up through the silky fabric of my top.

And I did nothing to stop him. No, I had wandering hands of my own, one of them slipping into the back pocket of his jeans. This kiss felt right and wrong at the same time—right because he made me feel good and warm and loved, but wrong because he was the person responsible for the third-worst heartbreak of my life.

When the doors of City Hall swung open and the mayor's assistant stepped out, we jerked apart like a couple of teenagers caught in the act. Chase returned to his camera and I bent over to pick up my notebook, nodding a hello to the man as he passed us. It was hard to determine the cause for the heat rushing to my cheeks— my embarrassment or the warmth that still lingered from that kiss.

Chase bent over to pull his microphone from his bag, wiping his mouth with one hand as he finished setting up. Before he started rolling, he licked his lips and said, "You know you don't have to keep coming up with all these dangerous, elaborate ways to get me to kiss you, right? Deadly waterfalls, bees…"

"I'll keep it simple next time."

"As long as there's a next time," he murmured under his breath as he swiveled the pop-out screen on his camera to face the front. I watched him bite his bottom lip as he got into position for his report, my heart threatening to beat right out of my chest over the two words we'd both just said.

Next time.

Logically, I knew kissing him again without confronting all the pain from our past was probably not the best idea. But logic had nothing to do with the parts of my body that throbbed and *ached* with need for this man. *Oh, there is most definitely going to be a next time.*

chapter twenty-four

chase

Next time, I'd be sure to do a lot more than kiss her.

If she'd let me, of course. With every moment we spent together, I grew more confident this might actually turn into something meaningful. It felt like I had Meghan back, or at least I was on the cusp of getting her back. She had no idea what she was doing to me every time we touched, how the front of my pants tightened around my dick when we kissed outside of City Hall. When she was close to me, it took every last bit of strength to fight the animalistic urges I had to do more. Touch her more.

Next time, I wouldn't hold back, no matter where we were. Ribbon-cutting? Art show? *Shield your eyes, everyone. I've waited long enough. We're the art show now.*

That ridiculous thought made me smile while I culled and trimmed footage that evening. Meghan always wanted to explore her exhibitionist side, although I was quite certain that wasn't what she had in mind. We did it in front of an open window at our old house once, and I swore our neighbors never looked us in the eye after that. But the memory of her smile and flushed cheeks right before she came, the sheer curtains blowing apart to expose us even more, made every bit of awkwardness worth it.

Get it together, idiot, I told myself, adjusting the front of my pants as I waited for my edited files to upload. It was well after dark, and it was rare I was the only person left in the studio. The room was eerily silent. Jillian, Marco, and the others had left nearly an hour ago, but I had too much work to do to call it a night. I had to get this footage ready for the next morning's briefs.

My phone buzzed on the edge of my desk. It was Sean with an updated schedule for the Comic Con. Now that we had Ethan Killian on board, he'd done a little adjusting to make sure the people waiting in line for him wouldn't miss Owen's live podcast recording. I sent him a quick reply to acknowledge I agreed with the changes. I watched the three dots appear on the screen and disappear five or six times before a longer text appeared.

> **Sean:** I need to be totally up front about something. I think it's time for me to pull back from paranormal investigating. Between this and running the store and trying to be a good dad and husband, I've gotta give something up. I haven't been sure how to bring this up to you, but I hope you understand. Life's just too much right now, man. I'm sorry.

My heart sank as I reread the message. It wasn't a surprise, really—I'd been noticing for a while now that Sean was getting pulled in many different directions. Too many. He hadn't been himself for several weeks, so I sort of saw this coming. I wondered just how long he'd been waffling over this decision— and I hated that he'd been stressed about telling me. I quickly typed a response so he wouldn't worry any longer.

> **Chase:** I completely understand. Those other things take precedence. You do what you need to do to be a better dad. And hey,

maybe when he's old enough he can join us
on a ghost stakeout. Lol

Sean: He'll be talking to ghosts before he
can ride a bike

Despite the positive message, I laid my phone on my desk and stared at it for a few moments, contemplating what this change meant for my life. This probably signified the death of the YouTube channel. It was just like Owen said—the banter with Sean was the reason most people watched. I wasn't sure I could carry our show on my own.

I sighed, glancing up at my laptop to find the very last file had finally uploaded. Closing my laptop, I grabbed my phone and keys from my desk and headed toward the door. Outside, only one streetlight illuminated the parking lot. I kept my head down as I trudged along, absentmindedly hitting the unlock button on my key fob as I trudged down the sidewalk. Something made me look up, and I spotted Meghan's car just a few spaces over from mine. I peered up at the second floor, where only one window was lit up. She had four or five articles to write, after all, so it was no surprise she was still up there working.

I re-locked my car and turned around, hating the thought of Meghan walking through the parking lot alone on such a dark night. They really needed to install better lights out there. Jillian was there before sunrise every morning, too, but I guess Silas Brown hadn't thought of that. He prioritized sleek office furniture in the conference room over safety measures like lighting.

Maybe Principal Gardner could get it done. As I re-entered the building, I made a mental note to ask her about it next time I saw her.

I lightly knocked on the newsroom door so I wouldn't startle Meghan. "Hello?" I called out.

She peeked over the top of her cubicle, her face softening when she saw me. "Oh good, it's just you." The room was dark, other than a small, warm light coming from her space.

"What's with the mood lighting over here?" I asked, coming around the back of her cubicle. I wasn't surprised to find a black welcome mat just outside her cubicle that said, "GO AWAY."

"The fluorescents drove me crazy, so I got this," she said, nodding at the little lamp on her desk. "Xander hated it at first, but now he's on the lamp train, too. We all are."

I smiled, crossing my arms as I leaned against the side of her cubicle. Her hair had mostly fallen out of the messy bun, with strands framing her face in a way that caught the warm light from the lamp just right. "Did you get all your articles done?" I asked, eyeing her laptop, which was open to a Wikipedia page.

"Uhh," she started, smoothing her hair down with one hand as she swiveled her chair to face her desk. "No, I did not. I've been somewhat distracted by Fannie's journal, now that I can actually read it." She nodded toward the packet of papers I'd printed for her.

I held up my pointer finger for her to wait and ventured into Xander's cubicle to steal his desk chair. "Anything juicy?" I asked, rolling the chair up beside hers.

Meghan dipped her chin and blinked at me. "This lady was obsessed with her chickens. Listen to this." She flipped back a page to read one of the entries aloud. "'Miss Red refused to lay eggs today, and I fear something is upsetting her. I will need to sit with her tonight, stroke her feathers, and assure her that all is well.'" She stopped reading to look at me with wide eyes. "She was having therapy sessions with her hens."

"No different than how you are with Wanda," I teased, making her roll her eyes with a grin. I nodded toward the printed journal. "Read me some more of it."

Meghan flipped forward a couple of pages, squinting at the text. "Haven't read this one yet. 'May 17th: I believe the radishes will be ripe in a matter of days. I think Evvy and I shall have a nice radish salad on the…'" Her voice trailed off and she sat up straighter, rereading the last sentence in a whisper. "Evvy and I shall have a nice radish salad on the tree trunk by the waterfall."

"Evvy?" I scooted closer to see the journal entry myself, distracted by Meghan's wide eyes. "Is that Evelyn?"

"It must be," she said, staring over at me with wide, twinkling eyes. The two women were friends, just like she suspected, and I could almost feel the excitement radiating from her as she frantically flipped through the pages, hoping to find another occurrence of Evelyn's nickname. "Oh my God, I feel like Nicolas Cage when he found that secret map on the back of the Declaration of Independence."

Laughter erupted from my chest. "Wow, just when I thought you couldn't get any nerdier…"

"Says the guy who has an *Infinity* gauntlet replica on his nightstand," she said, shooting me a teasing smile.

"Hey, you don't know what's on my nightstand." I swallowed, deciding against letting her know the gauntlet now had a permanent home on my dresser—that information wouldn't do much to prove I wasn't a nerd. Instead, feeling a surge of courage, I reached down to squeeze her behind her knee. "I know what's in the top drawer of yours, though."

Meghan's mouth dropped open as she pulled her leg away. "Chase!" I took her smile as an invitation to tickle the smooth, silky skin on the back of her knee some more, delighting in the way it made her squirm. She jerked away with a laugh, closing her laptop and the packet of Fannie's printed journal pages. "Well, since you're not going to let me concentrate anymore, I guess I should call it a night."

I sat back and watched her gather her things with my hands folded across my stomach. She stood directly in front of me and bent over to slip her laptop into her tote bag, my eyes catching the way the hem of her skirt hiked up just enough to tease me. When she bent down further, giving me just the smallest glimpse of the edges of her light blue panties hugging her where her ass met her thighs, I knew the teasing was intentional. She'd wanted me to see.

As she turned around, draping her bag over her shoulder, I grabbed her by the wrist and yanked her toward my chair. "Put down the bag."

The tote bag hit the floor with a soft thud. Standing between my knees, her pretty eyes concentrated on mine, awaiting my next command.

"You think you're going to just walk out of here after teasing me like that?" I asked, my voice low as I leaned forward to slide my hands up the backs of her thighs. With a firm grip, I tugged her closer, guiding her hips toward me.

She gasped, and without breaking eye contact, she followed my lead, slowly lowering herself onto my lap. The absence of arms on the chair made it easy for her to straddle me, and I couldn't help but smile as she settled perfectly against me, her hands draping around my neck. "Pretty smooth for a nerd," she said, biting her bottom lip.

Her body pressed against mine, and as she adjusted herself on my lap, I felt the slow, subtle movement of her hips. I closed my eyes, focusing on the gentle grind that sent a rush of heat through my entire body. When I opened my eyes again, hers stayed locked on mine, and I could see a flicker of mischief there. She knew exactly what she was doing to me.

I was already hard beneath her, the pressure and warmth making it impossible to hide my reaction. "Feel what you do to me, Meg?" I murmured, working with her movements to press my erection against her center.

Her lips curved into a teasing smile as she tilted her hips in a way that made me let out a low, rough groan. I moved one hand to the back of her neck and pulled her in, crushing my mouth against hers as her hips rolled slowly over my lap. Our tongues moved together in a rhythm that matched the way she moved her body. A sudden hiss of air expelled from the chair as it lowered beneath our weight. We might have just broken it, but it didn't slow either of us down. Gripping her waist tight, I guided her movement as she pressed against my arousal.

She tilted her head back, breaking away from the kiss, her breathing ragged as she concentrated on my face. "Chase," she whispered, her chest rising and falling with each breath. "I'm still not sure what I want. I can't give you any answers about the future and I just—I don't want you to feel used. It wouldn't be fair."

The words stung, but I ignored my feelings. "Use me," I said, my voice hoarse as she continued to grind against me. My forehead pressed against hers, and I squeezed her ass, fighting to hold back. "On second thought," I rasped, my control slipping with each roll of her hips, "you'd better stop doing… that."

She slid off my lap, but I didn't let her get very far before I grabbed her by the hips. Sliding both hands to the soft skin on the back of her thighs, I pulled her in just a little closer, tucking my fingers beneath the sides of her panties to pull them down— I needed them out of my way as quickly as possible. She appeared to have the same goal, helping me guide them down her thighs, and then her knees, until she used one hand to tug them away from her black wedge shoes.

I pressed my forehead against her lower abdomen, inhaling her scent as my hands found their way to her ass. Meghan lifted my chin with one hand, and without a word, she removed my glasses, setting them on the desk beside us. I closed my eyes and she cradled my head against her body, running her fingers through my hair with a tender, caring touch. With one hand still cupping her ass, I slid the other between her thighs, feeling the dampness of her arousal on her smooth skin.

The familiar, breathy moan she emitted when my middle finger grazed over her clit was music to my ears. *Fuck,* I'd missed that sound. With every pass of my finger against her sensitive bundle of nerves, I became more eager to taste her. I *needed* it.

I tilted my head back, gazing up at her eyes. "Use my face."

Her hands rested on either side of my jaw. "What?"

In one sweeping movement, I slid out of the chair and pushed it away to give myself room on the floor. I lowered my body all the way down, my shoulder pressed against the side of her leg. "Use my face," I repeated, running my fingers along the inside of her ankle with a delicate stroke. "Let me make you come with my tongue. I want your juices all over my chin, Meg. Please."

She gazed down at me, sucking on her bottom lip like she was doing her best to hold back a smile. Meghan wanted this just as much as I did, but her stubborn streak wouldn't let her admit it so easily. She had to at least make it look like she was weighing her options. "Chase, I can't just—I—you'll suffocate down there."

"We both know I won't, and what do I always say?" I grinned up at her, struggling to swallow. I was speaking in the present tense as though we hadn't spent three years apart.

Not what I always *said*. What I always *say*.

Because this is happening right now.

"Not a bad way to go," she and I said in unison. I licked my lips in anticipation as her fingers slid beneath the hem of her skirt, inching it up her thighs. I took a couple of deep breaths as she stepped over my body, hiking her skirt all the way up to her hips.

I barely had time to react to the beautiful, glistening pussy hovering above me before she lowered herself, resting a knee on either side of my head. Bracing her hands on the desk in front of her, she still hesitated, like she was scared to put the full weight of her body on me. "Let me taste you," I demanded, gripping the backs of her thighs. I kissed her silky skin—the part of her I could reach—and breathed her in.

Finally, she inched forward, settling her warm, wet core against my mouth. My dick strained against my jeans as I pressed my tongue flat against her clit, taking my time with slow, firm movements—just how I knew she liked me to get started. She tasted sweeter than the ripest peach, combined with a flavor that was uniquely her own—and even better than I remembered.

Meghan still wasn't putting all her weight down on me. I gently nudged her backward, catching my breath to say, "Come on, use me. Ride my face."

That was all the coaxing she needed to take control, guiding where my tongue went next by grinding forwards and backwards against my mouth. I wrapped my arms around her hips, feeling her body tense and then relax again and again. Her breaths became more shallow, and I knew when she slapped the desk she was getting close. "Oh my God, Chase, Chase, *Chase*," she exclaimed in a whine. I loved the sound of my name on her lips so much it almost distracted me from the job at hand. I held the pace, licking her clit with deliberate strokes. Meghan's body twitched, one hand clutching my hair as she cried out. She trembled on top of me, her arousal coating my chin.

And then, with a deep, lingering sigh, she lifted herself off me and collapsed beside me on the floor. I struggled to catch my breath, turning my head to look at her. Her eyes were clenched shut, her hand resting on her chest as she, too, fought for air. At some point during that face ride, she'd let her hair down. and now it was splayed out all around her on the floor of her cubicle. "I knew you liked me," I said, pulling myself up onto my elbows.

She turned to me with an unconvincing scowl that did *nothing* to hide the look of pleasure in her eyes. "Shut up."

chapter twenty-five

meghan

"Someone fucked with my chair."

Shit. I swiveled around to see Xander standing outside my cubicle with his hands on his hips. With his brows furrowed, he looked even grumpier than usual. "What do you mean?" I asked, trying to sound innocent.

"The damn thing sinks every time I sit down. The lever's broken, and I know for a fact it wasn't like that when I left yesterday."

"Weird, but that happens sometimes," I said, glancing at the time on my phone. We had a staff meeting in the conference room downstairs in about fifteen minutes, and I was eager to see Chase. My brain was still a little broken after last night. Every time I closed my eyes, it was like I could see the desperate, hungry look in his eyes when he begged me to ride his face. And I actually fucking did it, despite every instinct telling me not to let this go that far because it would only end in pain.

But I had gone from *"I'm not sure what I want"* to asking him if I could return the favor pretty quickly. Suddenly, I was clawing at his zipper like I couldn't wait to get my hands on his dick. And if it weren't for the cleaning crew arriving to mop the hallway floors, who knew what might have happened?

I had thought Xander went back to his own cubicle, but he appeared by my side, still frowning, clearly more upset about his broken chair than I realized. He bent over my desk, leaning on his elbows. "Someone attempted to get into my Google account five times yesterday, too," he said, speaking low enough that Devonte and Byron wouldn't hear. "I was locked out for half the day after so many failed attempts. Couldn't access any of my files, emails. Someone's actively trying to see what I'm working on, and now they've resorted to coming into my cubicle and going through my stuff."

I looked over at him with a sheepish grin. "The person who broke your chair isn't the same one trying to hack your account."

"I think they are. And-"

"It was me and Chase," I blurted. "On your chair. At the… same time."

Xander's lips came back together slowly, and he squinted at me like he didn't quite believe me. But when I didn't laugh it off or confess it was a joke, he shook his head. "Okay, so, I'll be burning that chair…"

"We didn't actually do much *on* the chair, we—"

"I don't need the details. And you owe me a chair."

"Okay. But aren't you at least relieved someone's not trying to spy on you and sabotage your files?"

Xander pursed his lips, staring down at his crossed arms on my desk. "Yeah, maybe," he said slowly, "but I still don't think it's a coincidence that someone tried to get into my account. I'm working on something that Silas isn't going to like—and he might already know."

I raised an eyebrow. "What are you working on?"

He leaned in closer, his voice dropping even lower. "I've been investigating the contractors hired by Weston Properties for that new apartment complex. They've been using building materials that got soaked from all the snow over the winter, and now there's black mold spreading. People who move into these apartments are going to get sick, but John Weston doesn't give two shits."

John Weston was the same shady real estate developer Silas made Jill do that fluff piece on. His last name was all over Woodvale, considering he owned about half the town. Like Silas, it seemed like he had a lot of people over a barrel, making his influence questionable. "Is this what you were referring to when you said your story was going to send the town into a frenzy?"

Xander exhaled. "Yeah. I've talked to some contractors, a couple of tenants that have moved into the completed buildings—I'm close to publishing this. And I know for a fact Weston's hot on my tail, which means Silas probably is, too."

"Does Graham know what you're working on?"

"No. That fucking brown-noser… I'm not exactly sure this is the kind of controversy he wanted us to find."

"Probably not."

I eyed my Fannie papers, feeling pretty safe with this story. It wasn't like a tale of two women from 170 years ago was going to ruffle any feathers. While Xander was out there doing some investigative journalism about actual, living people, I was traipsing through creeks and carrying around a stinky old journal. And what did I have to show for it? Proof that two women who lived in the same town at the same time knew each other?

Fascinating.

My shoulders slumped as Xander walked back to his own cubicle muttering about a chair replacement. He was four subscriptions ahead of me in the contest, and I could feel my motivation slipping away. If anyone belonged at that journalism conference this summer, it was Xander. Not me.

**

The conference room smelled like fresh coffee and sugar-glazed donuts—an obvious attempt by Silas to sweeten us up before whatever nonsense he was about to throw at us. I grabbed a paper cup and poured myself some coffee, glancing at the assortment of donuts on the table at the side of the room. They were from Dunkin', I noticed—meaning Silas had sent someone an hour away to pick them up instead of supporting our local donut shop.

No surprise there.

"Think he brought any fruit for me?" Jillian muttered under her breath as she joined me at the donut table. Before I could even process her comment or what she might be hinting at, Chase strolled through the door running his hand through his hair, his other hand clutching a notebook at his side. He greeted one of the radio guys from the third floor, making some joke about them coming out of their cave for free food.

His eyes caught mine as he walked across the room toward the donut table, and all I could think about was the satisfied grin on his face when I lowered myself onto him the night before. "Morning," he said, flashing me that exact grin.

"Morning." I quickly took a sip of my piping hot coffee to cover the heat rising in my cheeks, but Jillian was already watching me with an amused smirk. She knew me too well.

Chase and I settled into two chairs near the middle of the long conference table. Xander strode in last and bypassed the donuts completely, dropping into the chair next to Jillian with a sigh. He was already crossing his arms, radiating defiance like Judd Nelson in *The Breakfast Club*.

His eyes darted from me to Chase, a subtle half-grin spreading across his face as he leaned over to whisper something in Jillian's ear. She bit her lip, clearly amused, while Xander cast a glance back in our direction.

Was he seriously gossiping about me right now? Wait, of course he was. Gossip was literally his job. I'd have to remember to keep my secrets to myself.

Chase gently nudged my elbow. "Did you sleep okay?"

I managed a quick nod. "Yeah."

"Good."

There was a beat of silence. "Did you?" I asked, keeping my eyes locked on him, because it felt like everyone in the room could tell this man had me screaming his name just one floor up from where we currently sat.

"Yeah, I did."

"Good," I said, tucking my hair behind my ears. What the hell was this? Why did we sound like two robots trying to remember how to speak? Across the table, Xander and Jillian were grinning at us like they'd just heard the punchline of some private joke.

"What?" I mumbled, trying to sound casual as I avoided looking directly at her.

Before she could answer, Silas's voice boomed from the head of the table. "Alright, everyone, let's get started. Take your seats."

The last couple of stragglers found their seats at the long conference table, donuts in hand, and the murmuring in the room faded. Silas, standing up at the head of the table, adjusted his tie as he stared down at a printout of his notes. The way he towered over everyone, like he needed to remind all of us who was in charge, made me uneasy. Graham sat to Silas's immediate left, refusing to meet the man's eye. I couldn't blame him for that.

"Let's start with the good," Silas began. "We've had some successes as of late, especially when it comes to our growing list of investors. But one of the biggest wins, which I think deserves some recognition, is the hybrid content strategy."

Silas paused like he was waiting for some kind of applause, but he was met only with a silent group of people exchanging uncomfortable glances. Did he think we couldn't tell he was just patting himself on the back?

"When we launched that initiative several weeks ago," he continued, "a lot of people were skeptical. But our web traffic has doubled since then. That's right—doubled. We've made our content more dynamic, more engaging, and the numbers don't lie. It's a testament to the kind of innovative thinking that's going to keep us on top. Which brings me to the next step we need to take to ensure that growth continues."

The discomfort in the room was palpable. Not wanting to draw attention to myself, I didn't dare turn my head to look at Chase, but Jill and I exchanged a curious glance from across the table.

"It's about more than just the numbers, right?" Nobody nodded in agreement. "It's about credibility and transparency. People are scrutinizing us more closely than ever, which means we need to focus our efforts on content that matters to our consumers."

Consumers. Like we were selling a product.

Silas cleared his throat, running his hand over his tie. "This is why, effective immediately, leadership will be more involved in selecting the content we cover to ensure our stories reflect the concerns of the community."

Xander let out a small chuckle across the table, and if he was trying to be subtle, it didn't work. Silas, narrowing his eyes, turned to him immediately. He crossed his arms against his chest, saying, "Let's start with you, Mr. Pierce."

"Start with me… how?"

"I'd like to go around the table and have everyone pitch some story ideas. Whatcha workin' on, huh? Got anything up your sleeve?" It was obvious in his aggressive tone and cocky stance he knew exactly what Xander had been investigating.

Though Xander's jaw clenched, he casually folded his hands on the table in front of him as he said, "Well, the new four-way stop on Poplar Road is causing quite a stir. Looks like it might be causing more accidents than it's preventing. Our *consumers* are going to eat that story right up."

The staredown that followed sent a shiver down my spine. Beside me, Chase whispered, "I hope they have a duel," and I quietly shushed him.

Silas's back stiffened. "That the only story you're working on?"

"I've also got some pothole repairs to follow up on— pretty exciting stuff."

"Maybe I should be talking to your hybrid partner instead," Silas said, turning to Jillian. "Surely there's more to report on than traffic lights and potholes? Tell me you have more."

Jillian, pushing her half-eaten donut away, sat up straighter. "Yes, um," she started, glancing at Xander, who stared at the table, "we're actually working on a feature about a local dentist's office that's making special accommodations for kids with sensory needs. I think it could resonate with a lot of families."

Silas gave her a curt nod before glancing down at his printed agenda. "I like it. Devonte, what have you got?"

Devonte leaned back in his chair. "Well, baseball season is in full swing. I'm also, uh," he took a beat to scratch one of his sideburns, breaking eye contact with Silas. I couldn't blame him—our CEO was like a vulture at the end of the table, waiting to swoop down on the first sign of weakness. "I'm going to be highlighting a local swimmer who's been breaking lots of records. Should be an inspiring piece."

"Good, good," Silas said, his tone still clipped as he continued around the table. He zeroed in on Byron, who was using a napkin to dab jelly from his donut off his sweater vest. "Byron, what about you?

Byron blinked a few times, startled to be called on so abruptly. "Oh, uh, just the usual," he stammered. "A lot of babies were born. Obviously. Oh and… my church is having a bake sale?"

Silas nodded. "That's all fine, but let's mix it up a little, shall we? I'd like for you to talk to John Weston about the new income-based apartment complex going up. Let's highlight his tremendous generosity and commitment to making Woodvale an affordable place for more families. Can you handle that?

Byron glanced at Graham with a nervous nod before answering. "Y-yes, I can handle it. Of course."

"Good," Silas said with a smug grin. "Glad to hear it." He turned his gaze briefly toward Xander, giving him a knowing smirk that made it all too clear what this was really about. He wanted the coverage about the apartment complex to be safe and sanitized.

Silas continued around the table, the meeting dragging on as people outlined their upcoming stories. Finally, it was Chase's turn.

He took a deep breath, leaning forward slightly to see Silas better. "Meghan and I are following up on tornado relief efforts, mostly. We're also going to be talking to the Humane Society about the feral cats plaguing the old mill." He didn't mention a word about Fannie or Evelyn, and for a moment, I was relieved. The last thing I wanted was to stumble through an explanation of why two old friends from the 1800s were worth anyone's time. But that feeling quickly dissipated when Silas's gaze shifted toward me.

"Meghan," he said, a hint of condescension creeping into his tone. "That 'witch' story you mentioned a couple weeks ago—is that for your historical column?" I didn't like the way he emphasized the word "witch" or the subtle way he smirked when he said it.

I cast a quick glance in Chase's direction before answering. "No, actually. It's going to be a feature. We're planning a deep dive into her life, her friendships, and the role she played in the town's early history."

Silas didn't even bother to hide his dismissiveness, waving a hand as if to shoo the idea away. "But that's not news, right? I say we leave that to your editorial column to free up space for current events. Anyway," he said, looking up at the guys from the third floor who were huddled together at the end of the table, both of them dunking their donuts in their coffee, "let's move on. Radio guys, give it to me."

His tone changed completely as he addressed the DJs, and the men all chuckled together at their idiotic inside jokes. I felt the heat rising to my cheeks. My fingers curled around the edge of the table as I fought to keep my expression neutral. Chase's hand found my knee under the table, and all at once, the tension in my chest began to loosen.

A little.

I glanced across the table at Graham, who was staring down at the table with his brows furrowed, his knee bouncing restlessly. He looked like he was about to say something, his jaw set in anger, but he kept quiet as Silas wrapped things up.

"Alright, that's all for today, everyone," he said, shuffling the papers in front of him. "Oh, and one more thing—these meetings will be weekly from now on to ensure everyone is held accountable. Expect more frequent check-ins to keep things on track." His gaze swept across the table, landing on each of us like he was daring anyone to protest.

But besides the radio guys, who were evidently part of Silas's boys' club, we were all speechless.

**

The second we made it back to the newspaper offices, Xander, Byron, and I descended on Graham like a pack of wolves. That spineless little wiener.

Byron clenched two fistfuls of hair—what hair he had left, that is. "Hey boss, I don't know if I'm cut out for this kind of story—"

"It's *my* story," Xander snapped. "He's making Byron turn it into a fluff piece to keep me away. I've got some dirt on Weston, and he knows it."

"Why's he controlling what we cover if *you're* the hybrid content coordinator?" I took a step closer to Graham, who had literally backed into a corner. "Doesn't that bother you?"

"He's driving our paper into the ground," Xander added, crossing his arms, "and you're just going to roll over and let him do it?"

Graham backed up even more, his shoulder nudging the doorframe as he held up his hands in a calming gesture. "Whoa, whoa, okay—everybody just take a breath. I get it, alright? I know it's frustrating. But there's only so much I can do right now."

"Why?" I shot back, narrowing my eyes at him. "Why can't you do anything?"

He let out a long sigh, his shoulders slumping as if the weight of it all had finally settled in. "Look, I have to pick my battles, okay? Silas has got these new investors eating out of his hand. If I push back too hard right now, I risk getting our whole department shut down." He glanced at the three of us, his eyes pleading for understanding. "I have too much to lose—we all do."

Xander let out a frustrated huff and shook his head. "This is bullshit," he muttered again before sauntering off to his cubicle. Graham watched him go, then turned to Byron, who was chewing on his bottom lip.

"First of all—Byron, I have faith in you for this Weston piece," Graham said, his tone softening. "And I'm here for support if you need it. We'll make sure it's solid."

Byron's shoulders visibly relaxed, and he nodded quickly. "Thanks, boss. I appreciate it." He gave Graham a small, relieved smile before heading off, clearly grateful to have some of the pressure lifted.

I stayed rooted in place, my hands on my hips as I leveled a hard stare at Graham. "Don't look at me like that," he said, his voice low and weary. "I'll fix this."

"When?" I shot back.

He ran his hand through his hair and sighed again. "Soon. Just… give me time, alright?"

I wasn't so sure. "In the meantime, you're just going to let the guy kill every story that doesn't fit his agenda?"

Graham's jaw tightened, but he shook his head. "Look, I'm not even sure he's wrong about the witch story, Meghan. The truth is… this paper rewrites the story on the Woodvale Witch once every decade or so. Hell, I even did a feature on her myself when I first started here. I love your enthusiasm, but it's kind of a tired topic. I'm sorry. There's nothing new to say."

Oh, how I loved proving men wrong. "Actually," I began, "I acquired an old journal that mentions her, and someone found some buried rocks in the woods with symbols on them that match the symbols in the journal."

"Symbols?"

"Yeah, all these weird, jagged lines. Like nothing I've ever seen before."

"Could they be… sigils?"

I shrugged one shoulder. "I mean, yeah, I suppose."

Graham crossed his arms, blinking at me in curiosity. "Huh. Then you need to contact Cadence at the Historical Society."

"Why?" I didn't want to give up Fannie's journal. At least, not yet.

"Because Evelyn's personal effects were collected at the time of her execution," Graham said, locking eyes with me to make sure I was paying attention, "and among them was a sigil decoder."

My heart sped up the second the words left Graham's mouth. I wasn't aware such a thing existed. Could this actually give me the answers I'd been desperate for?

"You may be the first person in over a century to uncover something new about that witch, Meghan."

chapter twenty-six
chase

Meghan and I didn't have to travel far for our assignment that afternoon—Grissom Elementary's garden club was planting a small garden on the grounds of the old school, and Sarah asked us to come outside to document the occasion.

She teared up during her interview, taking almost a full minute's pause to collect herself. I shut the camera off, shooting Meghan an uncertain glance. Sarah wiped her nose with the back of her hand. "I'm so sorry for getting emotional. It's just been a tough semester, and this little garden… well, it just means a lot. It's the first time I've felt a sliver of hope in a little while."

"Don't apologize for having emotions," Meghan said, lowering her phone. She wasn't recording anymore, either.

I nodded in agreement. "A tornado ripped apart your school. I think you're allowed to have the occasional breakdown."

Sarah forced out a small chuckle, dabbing at her eyes with the collar of her Grissom t-shirt. "Thank you," she said, taking a couple of deep breaths. She shook her hands out like she was resetting herself before letting us know she was ready to continue.

As we wrapped up, I felt Meghan's eyes on me. We hadn't had any sort of conversation about what happened between us the night before. Besides a few typo-riddled, rambling text messages about a sigil decoder, I hadn't heard from her since the meeting that morning.

But I knew she had to be thinking about it as much as I was.

As we made our way down the winding path toward the front of the building, I spotted a four-leaf clover near the edge of the sidewalk and bent over to pluck it from the grass. I'd always had a knack for spotting them without really trying—a useless skill I inherited from my dad. It always amused Meghan, though, who kept every clover I ever gave her, pressed between the pages of an old, heavy dictionary, something she inherited from *her* dad.

She'd probably thrown them out by now. Maybe even used them in a spell to hex me.

But when I silently extended my hand to give it to her, a small grin tugged at the corners of her mouth as she said, "I'll add it to the collection."

I tried not to react, but I was fighting a smile even harder than she was. Moments like this with Meghan made me feel like I did when we first began dating in college. The rush of excitement when she revealed her inner nerd, the disbelief that I'd somehow won over the cute emo girl in my ethics class— this all felt very familiar.

"Speaking of collections," I said, pausing in front of the steps leading up to the school, "when did you say you're going to get to the Historical Society?"

Meghan stepped up onto the first stair and turned around. "Cadence said I could stop by on Thursday afternoon," she answered with a sigh. "I'd planned to take that day off, but I'm too eager to get my hands on that sigil decoder."

"Why were you going to take Thursday off?"

Meghan hesitated for a second, her hand trailing along the railing. "It's my mom's birthday," she said, her voice softer than before.

I swallowed, feeling like I should have remembered that. "Oh." I adjusted the camera bag on my shoulder. "Do you want me to pick it up so you can still take the day off? I can drop it off at your apartment."

With her feet on the bottom step, her eyes were level with mine. "No, I can do it. I think… I think I'm just going to try to work like normal that day."

"That's good," I said with a nod. "It's probably better to stay busy than to, you know, sit around and think about it too much."

I caught a flicker of something on Meghan's face, an emotion I couldn't quite pinpoint, as she looked down at her feet on that step. I winced, realizing my comment might have come out a little insensitive.

"I'm sorry," I rushed out. "I just meant it might be healthier to keep yourself distracted."

I had thought that explanation made it better, but Meghan lifted her chin to give me a subtle scowl. "Staying home and thinking about it can be healthy, too. Crying is healthy. I mean, what'd you just tell Sarah?" She forced out a little laugh, but she wasn't amused.

"I know, I know. You're right. Wrong choice of words," I said, wanting to explain myself even more, but I knew I'd only dig the hole I was standing in even deeper. I reached for her arm, sliding my hand down her wrist until I was holding her hand. She squeezed my fingers, sending a wave of relief through my body. "However you choose to spend that day is okay. Obviously. It's not up to me."

Christ, stop talking.

Her grip tightened even more. "I want to spend it decoding sigils."

"Okay." I lifted my free hand, placing it on her hip. Before I could talk myself out of it, I stepped closer and whispered, "Nerd." Then I brushed my lips against hers—a brief, feather-light kiss, followed by a second, deeper one. That kiss lingered a little longer, making the tension and awkwardness from a moment ago melt away.

We pulled apart when a couple kids came into view, chasing an empty topsoil bag that blew across the school lawn. Meghan let out a giggle as we watched one of them tackle it. "They're so cute."

"Have you changed your mind about never wanting kids?"

She turned to me in horror. "Oh God, no. I said they're cute, not that I wanted one."

I laughed. Having kids was something Meghan and I discussed years ago. Or rather, the choice to never, ever become parents. We liked our lazy weekends too much, and neither of us had the patience to deal with dirty diapers and Cheerio-covered car seats.

Meghan started to turn to go up the steps, and I followed her through the doors of the building. "Hey," she said, turning to me outside the double doors leading into the studio. "I thought of something that will give me an edge on Xander in this contest, especially now that it looks like he's not going to get to do this Weston story."

"Yeah?"

"Let's give people a sneak peek of what they can expect at the Woodvale Comic Con, maybe even talk to a couple of the comic book artists and authors who will be—" She came to an abrupt halt when she saw the way I was wincing at her. "What is it?"

I was about to disappoint her. Again. "I kind of… gave Xander the exclusive on the Con. I'm talking to him and Jill at Sean's store in just a little bit, actually."

"Tell me you're joking."

"Unfortunately, I'm not. Xander's a closet *Starlight* fan and he approached me. Wouldn't it be a conflict of interest if I report on myself, anyway?"

Meghan let out an annoyed sigh. "I guess. I just don't know how I'm supposed to win this contest. He's the better journalist, anyway, so I'm not sure why I bother trying to keep up."

I blinked, caught off guard by this crack in her confidence that seemed to come out of nowhere. "Hey, whoa— Xander's good, but so are you. Look at the impact your Lenny story had."

Meghan rolled her eyes. "Yeah, if by 'impact' you mean people hated it."

"Come on, don't worry about the opinions of a few idiots on Facebook with their collective five brain cells. You can't focus on the loudest complainers while ignoring everyone who gave you accolades for that story."

"You say that like it's easy."

"Seems like it takes more effort to zero in on the bad stuff and miss everything else. You're not doing yourself any favors."

Shit. Talking like this with Meghan felt like tiptoeing through a minefield, and judging from the look in her eyes, I'd just jumped on one with both feet. I'd meant to be encouraging, not condescending, but I'd missed the mark. Again.

"Thanks, Dr. Phil. All better now."

I opened my mouth to apologize once more, but to my relief, Meghan's lips curled upward in a small, reluctant smile, easing the knot in my chest.

Just down the hall, a young, blonde teacher emerged from a classroom holding a set of keys and an iced coffee. Meghan returned her wave before turning to me to say, "I'd better go write. Good luck with Xander and Jill."

"Thanks," I said, wanting to kiss her again. I probably would have, too, if it weren't for that teacher walking past us down the hallway. I settled for a quick goodbye, watching her hips swing from side to side as she walked up the stairs.

She's a challenge, I thought, enjoying the way she smirked at me as she slipped around the corner of the stairwell, *but she's worth it.*

**

"This is Ethan Killian?" Jill turned her phone screen around to face me, her eyes wide with delight. "You guys didn't mention he was ruggedly handsome."

Xander and I exchanged looks over the row of comic books between us. "Oh, did I not mention that?" Xander raised an eyebrow at Jill, making her grin. "Must've slipped my mind."

"You guys will have a half hour with him the day of the con," I said, "before he starts signing autographs. Is that enough?"

Jill's grin widened. "Oh, a half hour will be plenty."

"Keep your pants on," Xander said, crossing his arms, his eyes trailing down her body. She caught him, too, but it didn't seem to bother her. The two of them locked eyes, making me feel like I was intruding on something I wasn't meant to be a part of.

I turned and watched Sean, who was ringing up the sole customer in the store. Jill's cameraman was setting up his gear near the back of the store, preparing to use the Justice League mural on the exposed brick wall as a backdrop for our interview.

"You know what?" Jill pulled out a compact mirror to check her hair. "I just realized none of us mentioned this feature to Silas."

"Fuck Silas," Xander said.

Sean told his customer to have a good day and joined us in the middle of the store. "Are you guys talking about your CEO?"

"Silas Brown? Yeah," I answered. I'd vented about him to Sean a couple of times, but I hadn't really mentioned him by name. I usually stuck to *our dumbass CEO.*

"That dude was nosing around here the other day," Sean said, pressing a comic book back into place in the bin in front of him. He had our full attention now. "With John Weston, who owns like half the buildings on this block. Weston's been trying to buy me out for years, but he's been relentless about it lately. Wants to knock down that wall and extend the unit next door."

"Cool, now what about Silas?" Xander nodded him along, clearly anxious for him to get to the point.

"Weston's had your CEO over there in the empty unit with him a couple of times, and yesterday they stood out on the sidewalk and stared at me like a couple of fucking weirdo vultures."

"Did you hear anything they said?" I asked.

"Not a lot, just something about offices."

Xander squinted at him. "Offices for what?"

"Maybe they're turning it into one of those trendy co-working spaces?" Jillian suggested with a hint of optimism no one else in our group shared. "You know, hipster-style. Rent by the hour, free kombucha on tap. They're huge in big cities."

"This is Woodvale, Indiana we're talkin' about here." I raised an eyebrow at her. "The majority of the people in this town can't pronounce kombucha."

"True," she conceded with a laugh.

"Or maybe he's planning to downgrade the news network again," Xander said, his tone the complete opposite of Jillian's. "Which could mean layoffs."

The three of us exchanged looks of concern, and Sean piped in with, "Sounds like Silas is running that place into the ground."

None of us disagreed.

chapter twenty-seven

meghan

All the firsts were the hardest.

The first Christmas without my mom almost killed me. There was no stocking with my name hanging by the fireplace, which she always pretended wasn't from her. "Look what Santa brought you!" she'd say with that mischievous grin, even when I was in my twenties.

Then came the first birthday without her Facebook post, timestamped one minute after midnight because she insisted on being the first every year. And on the first anniversary of her death, I couldn't stop reliving the horror of her final days.

It wasn't like that after my dad's heart attack when I was in the fifth grade, because we had each other. People rallied around us, too, making sure all of those "firsts" were filled with joy and distractions. My birthday party that year was the biggest I'd ever had, and my mom's best friend sent us on a cruise for Christmas. It didn't even feel like a holiday because we were somewhere completely new.

The grief after losing my mom was lonelier. In the quiet moments, I found myself wondering what my mom and I would be doing on this day if she were alive.

On her birthday, I knew we'd be eating carrot cake and watching *Practical Magic* together—our shared favorites. I wouldn't be sitting at a picnic table alone with Stevie Nicks drifting through my AirPods, struggling to swallow the lump in my throat. I kept glancing up at the classrooms above, half-expecting to see the faces of little kids laughing at the sad, lonely lady in the schoolyard.

I was halfway through my Uncrustable when I heard voices behind me. I looked over my shoulder to see Sarah Gardner and Kendall Devin walking in my direction carrying their own lunch boxes and gigantic pastel cups. I started to gather my things when Sarah said, "Don't get up—can we sit with you?"

"Yeah, of course." I took my AirPods out and put them back in their case and Sarah and Kendall sat down across from me. I smiled as I brushed the crumbs off my lap, sitting up a little straighter. "How's the day going? Surviving the chaos?"

"Barely," Kendall said, unscrewing the top of a thermos. "I had to ban farm animal noises today. It started with one—and it's always the same one, of course—and before long they were all mooing and neighing and cock-a-doodle-doing. I can still hear the echoes."

I laughed. "That seems… exhausting. I could never be a teacher."

"We question choosing a career in education every day," Sarah said with a chuckle. She looked past me like someone was behind me, and sure enough, Abigail walked up and took the spot next to me on the bench. She had two yellow pencils securing her long, red hair in a bun, which seemed like a very "librarian" hairstyle to me.

"Okay, I am dying to know," she said, turning to me the second she sat down, "what's it like to work with Xander day after day?" Abigail's bubbly, high-pitched voice reminded me of a mouse—it was impossibly endearing.

"Well," I started, staring down at my water bottle. "Sometimes I want to kill him…? He can be a real ass, but I honestly think it's just for show."

"That checks out," Sarah said, swallowing a bite of her sandwich. Kendall nodded beside her, widening her eyes.

"He's always been like that," Abigail said. "He's all talk. Really, he's just a big ol' sweetie-pie."

That statement nearly made me choke on my water. My reaction had the same effect on Sarah, and before long, the others were laughing, too. "I think you're the only person in the entire world who thinks Xander Pierce is a 'sweetie-pie', Abigail," Sarah said.

"He is," she insisted. "You just have to get to know him. Anyway…" She trailed off, shifting gears as her attention turned to Sarah. "How are you holding up with everything?"

Sarah's smile faltered for a split second. "I'm okay," she said, tucking a loose strand of hair behind her ear. "I've just been keeping myself distracted with books."

Kendall turned to Sarah with her eyebrows lifted in curiosity. "*What* books?" Her tone was suspicious- almost accusatory—but in a teasing way.

Sarah hesitated, glancing between us, then reached into her bag and pulled out a paperback. She held it up sheepishly, revealing the cover of a true crime book about a man who annihilated his entire family.

"Sweetie," Abigail said, reaching diagonally across the table to touch Sarah's hand. "If you're trying to de-stress, you're doing it all wrong. You need to be reading smut. Like me."

"I second that," Kendall said, lifting her soup spoon in solidarity.

As someone with a Kindle library that would make most people clutch their pearls, I couldn't help but jump in. "Smut is always a good distraction. The smuttier, the better."

"Okay, do you see what's happening here?" Abigail moved her hand in a circle between the four of us. "We're forming a smutty book club. Right here, right now. Everyone in?"

"I don't think we have a choice," Sarah answered with a laugh.

"I'm in," Kendall said, taking a sip from her giant cup. "We can call ourselves the Woodvale Smut Sluts."

Abigail clapped. "I love it. Let's get shirts made!"

"Can we add a fifth?" I glanced around at the three of them. "Jillian Taylor would be all over this." They all excitedly agreed, so I sent Jill a quick text.

Meghan: Do you want to join the
Woodvale Smut Sluts?

Jill: Only if I can be president.

She didn't even ask any questions, but that didn't really surprise me. "She's in," I told them. Sarah wondered if we'd want to get together to choose our first book that evening. "Owen's having the guys over for poker, and—"

"The guys?" Abigail asked, and I was glad she did, because I was wondering, too.

"Xander and Mason," Sarah said, continuing, "and I can send them to the dining room while we all hang out on the patio. Sound good?"

I bit my bottom lip. I'd already canceled dinner with Jill that night, planning to wallow in my room and watch *Practical*

Magic alone, but this sounded like a better use of my time. "Perfect."

As I finished my Uncrustable, I noticed the lump in my throat was long gone. Maybe this night at Sarah's would be exactly what I needed. When I looked up again, Kendall and Sarah were staring past my head. Abigail looked over her shoulder before turning back around to say, "God, there are *far* too many hot people working in this building."

My curiosity got the best of me, so I turned around, too. My stomach did a little flip when I saw Chase approaching, fiddling with his lanyard, like he couldn't quite get used to wearing it. His steps slowed as he got closer. He seemed nervous, but then again, I couldn't imagine there were too many times that Chase approached a table of women like this. He stopped at the edge of the picnic table and shoved his hands in his pockets. "Ladies."

"Have I seen you on the news?" Abigail asked.

"If it was the America's Most Wanted segment, then no," he quipped, darting his eyes back and forth. The other women laughed, but I just looked up at him, returning his tight-lipped grin. He was so proud of his little joke—it was adorable. "Meghan, did you want me to go with you to the Historical Society?"

"I'd love that."

"Okay." He glanced at the trash in front of me on the table, fidgeting with his lanyard again. "Are you ready now, or-?"

I gathered up my stuff at lightning speed, throwing a quick goodbye to the others. "I'll DM you the details about the Smut Sluts," Sarah called out as I joined Chase on the sidewalk to the parking lot.

"Smut Sluts?" Chase asked as I waited for him to unlock the car. "That the name of your new coven?"

"Something like that."

**

The Woodvale Historical Society was headquartered in an old Victorian house a few blocks from Grissom Elementary. With slate blue siding and gray scalloped eaves, I'd admired it since I was a little girl. I'd even insisted on having my senior pictures taken in front of it.

It made my heart sink to see how it looked after the tornado came through, with chunks of the gutter and pieces of siding completely ripped away. Inside, Cadence told us they were looking to brighten up the paint job on the outside anyway. "We're going to bring it back to its original cerulean color," she said, leading us to the reception counter, flipping her dark hair over her shoulder.

"Cerulean? The Concerned Citizens of Woodvale will be—well, concerned," Chase said.

Cadence grinned as she pulled a yellow clasp envelope from below the counter. "I welcome their fury."

I watched Cadence's meticulously manicured nails closely as she opened the clasp and pulled out what looked like a wooden coaster. The sigil decoder was round, about the size of my palm, and made from smooth, aged wood. The letters of the alphabet had been carved around the edge, softened with time but still legible.

"This was in Evelyn Stewart's dress pocket when she was taken to jail."

"Is it a replica?"

"No, this is the real deal," Cadence said, meeting my eye. She had a twinkle in hers like she understood how special this was. I held my breath as I took it from her hands, like I didn't deserve to touch it. It felt like I was holding a magical tool, but in a way, I suppose that's what it was.

"I'll get the form for you to sign it out."

"Wait, I can borrow it?" I assumed Chase and I would only be allowed to take pictures of it.

"I trust you," she said. "And I trust that you'll share your findings with me. I can't wait to see what you discover."

Neither could I.

I was shaking as we walked back to the car, holding the yellow envelope close to my chest like it was something sacred. Chase opened the driver's side door and leaned over the roof of the car, taking in my dazed appearance with an amused smile. "Do you want to head to the library to work on it? We've got the whole day, no assignments."

I hesitated, feeling the words forming before I even realized what I was saying. "Would you be comfortable if we just went to my place?"

Chase tapped his fingers on the roof of the car, staring at me like he was waiting for me to change my mind. "Uh, yeah. Your place. Your place is good." He covered up his awkwardness by rushing out the words, "Because I know Wanda misses me."

"Uh huh." I rolled my eyes as we both got into the car. I hoped he didn't expect anything more than a nerdy sigil-decoding session, because it was all I could think about.

chapter twenty-eight

meghan

Back at my apartment, I hoisted the coffee table onto the couch to clear space on my living room rug. It was one of my favorite possessions—it was black with ornate flowers framing two intertwined snakes mirrored perfectly in the center. The rug was equal parts elegant and eerie, which was kind of my entire vibe.

Chase stared down at the rug, scratching his temple with his thumb. "This is unsettling."

"Thanks," I said, spreading out everything we needed to get started—Fannie's journal, the sigil decoder, and a spare notebook for Chase. He lowered himself to the rug, taking his bag off his shoulders to unzip it. "Are you still sure you want to help me with this?"

Now that we weren't allowed to make this one of our hybrid features, I wasn't sure what direction I was taking with it. It was beginning to feel more like a personal project than a professional one. "I'm just as curious as you are," Chase said, spreading out some of the sigil-etched stones on the rug.

I sat cross-legged in my black cigarette pants, carefully pulling the sigil decoder out of the envelope. "What if this is a big nothing-burger and we can't make sense of it?"

"We'll at least know we tried," he said. "And hey, we might stumble across something cool."

I watched Chase tear out a blank page from the notebook and place it over the sigil decoder, smoothing it flat with his palm. I was confused until I saw him pull a pencil from his bag and begin to make a rubbing of the decoder. The circular pattern of the decoder was faint, but just clear enough to make out the letters. "So we can translate at the same time," Chase explained.

We decided to start with the six sigils that appeared both in Fannie's journal and on Evelyn's stones, since those seemed to be the symbols that connected them. I could get to the others that were sporadically spread out in Fannie's journal later.

It took a while to figure out how the sigil decoder lined up. The letters weren't in order, so it was difficult to determine where to even start. It wasn't until I noticed the tiny notch carved above the letter "A" that I realized it should be turned to the 12:00 position on the top. Finally, the pattern made sense. I followed the jagged lines of the first sigil, tracing across the decoder with my finger until, finally, it spelled a word.

I gasped, drawing my hand to my chest to clutch my pendant. "Chase, I think this one spells 'only'." I waited for him to look up and traced the letters again. "Look. The 'A' goes at the top. You start with one end of the symbol and follow the lines across the circle."

He shifted closer, putting his hand on my knee as he watched me do it once more. "Got it." He turned his rubbing of the decoder counterclockwise, lining up the letters the way I'd shown him.

Chase grabbed the stone with the simplest sigil—the one with a simple V-shape etched into it—and held it up to the journal, flipping through Fannie's scrawled notes. He glanced from the stone to his paper, working through the lines slowly. I figured it out a second before he did, but instead of saying it, I watched his expression, waiting to see if he'd get it, too.

His lips parted as the realization hit him. "'My'?"

"I think you're right."

Chase leaned back on his hands. "So, we have 'only' and 'my.' That's cryptic."

"But we're getting there," I said. My heart was racing. Now that we knew how the sigil decoder worked—and we'd actually used it to form some words—my excitement level reached an all-time high. The rest of the words came even faster. When we combined our efforts, the six words were:

my

only

beats

heart

you

for

"Only my heart beats for you?" Chase asked at the same time I slapped his knee and declared, "My heart beats only for you!"

He blinked at me a couple of times. "Yeah, let's go with yours."

My heart practically exploded. "Chase! Do you realize what this means?!" I gripped his arm so tight I was probably digging my nails into his skin, but he didn't seem to care. The pieces were clicking into place in my mind, faster than I could say them. "This… this wasn't just some random spell or something. This was personal. Fannie *loved* her." I pointed at the journal, at the sigils on the stones. "This message—it's a love note. A secret one."

Chase raised his eyebrows at me, still trying to keep up. "You think Fannie and Evelyn—"

"They were in love!" I interrupted, unable to contain myself. "This was their way of keeping it hidden. They communicated through sigils—codes no one else could figure out!" I rose to my feet and began to pace. "Oh my God, it's not just folklore, it's a love story. A real-life lesbian love story. They couldn't be together because of the times, but they met in secret and drank apple brandy and ate the vegetables from Fannie's garden-"

"And made out by the waterfall," Chase interrupted.

"And declared their love with a secret code."

"And poisoned Evelyn's husband," Chase reminded me, lowering his chin to give me this come-back-to-earth look. Oops, I'd sort of forgotten about the whole murder thing. I hadn't meant to romanticize a murderer, but maybe there was more to that crime than met the eye. "Do you think Fannie went to the public hanging?"

"Records show there were ten thousand people from around the state in attendance," I said. "Who knows if Fannie was one of them."

"Did she write about it?"

I shook my head. "She stopped writing in the journal almost a year before the execution." I sat down again, pulling the printout of Fannie's journal onto my lap. There were still some entries I hadn't read yet, and some I gave up on because they didn't fully make sense. Chase's AI tool seemed to have about a 75% accuracy rate. I turned to her last journal entry, dated December 1845. It was pretty mundane, just talking about the frost patterns on her windowpane.

Chase pulled out his phone beside me. I couldn't see his screen, but I watched him adjust his glasses as he scrolled and read something. In the meantime, I flipped backward a few journal entries and read and reread one of the jumbled sentences.

The fore in the heart matches the heat in my lains—for both, I have Envy to thank. How I wish she didn't hove to go nome so soon.

Envy was obviously meant to be Evvy. I reread the first sentence again and again, trying to make sense of the words Chase's translator didn't get right. "Fore in the heart" could mean "fire in the hearth," couldn't it? But... *lains?*

And then it hit me: *loins.*

"'The fire in the hearth matches the heat in my loins,'" I read aloud, grinning like I'd stumbled upon some 1800s erotica.

That caught Chase's attention. He raised one eyebrow at me, asking, "What about your loins?"

"Fannie's loins. Evvy had her all hot and bothered in her bloomers."

Chase snickered. "Could you imagine all the layers of clothing they had to peel off just to get to the goods? I think I'd give up."

"No, you wouldn't."

He just smiled, knowing I was right. "Okay, now let me show you what I found." He flipped his phone screen around to show me a death record on one of the ancestry sites I frequented myself. "Evelyn's husband was murdered the same month Fannie's journal stops, and the trial was the following spring."

"Interesting. They would've been separated. Maybe she just couldn't bear to pick up her pen."

"I was going to theorize that the poor man could've been poisoned with something from Fannie's garden, and she was crushed with guilt," Chase suggested. "She ever mention poppies? I mean, they produce opium."

I flipped back to an entry about the flowers Fannie planted the spring before. "No. She just mentioned cosmos, daisies, foxglove, and lavender."

"Ding, ding, ding," Chase said. "Foxglove causes instantaneous cardiac arrest when ingested."

"How the hell do you know that?"

"Agatha Christie," he said with confidence, like it was common knowledge. "Anyway, that could be where Evelyn got the poison. Those two might've been in on it together."

I bit my bottom lip, trying to hold back a smile. "Is it bad that I'm still kind of rooting for them?"

"You know how this ends, right?" He rested his hand on my knee like he was trying to gently rein me back in. After all, this was a tragedy, not a love story. "How do you think the historically open-minded people of Woodvale are going to react to this? I mean, is this all going in your column?"

With a deep inhale, I looked at everything scattered on the rug in front of us and considered the best way to get Fannie and Evelyn's story into the world. There was too much to cover for my Sunday column. I turned toward Chase, an idea forming. "What if we bring the blog back and post it there?"

Chase's lip parted, and his eyes bounced from one of mine to the other, as though he wasn't sure I meant it.

"We'll make Silas regret telling us this can't be a hybrid feature when he sees how much attention it gets."

"That *would* be extremely satisfying," Chase said, staring down at his folded hands on his lap. "I could take my gear out to the woods and see if I can make contact with their spirits."

In the past, I'd often met Chase's interest in the paranormal with skepticism, knowing he played it up a little for views—that and because he *wanted* to believe it was true. But in that moment, so did I. If there was any chance at all Fannie or Evelyn's spirits lingered in the woods, I wanted to find them. "Can I come?"

Chase didn't answer me with words. Instead, he stared into my eyes as he took my face in his hand, his fingers grazing the side of my neck. I instinctively leaned my body toward his, and when his lips pressed into mine, I slid one arm around his midsection to pull him in even closer. I wanted to feel his warmth, his weight. He gave my inner thigh a firm squeeze like he needed more, too. I melted into him, threading my fingers through the back of his hair, tugging just enough to draw a low hum from him. His lips moved hungrily against mine, and when he gently bit my bottom lip, I gasped, pressing closer until there was no space left between us.

Still, I needed more.

I breathlessly tugged away and rose to my feet, reaching down to pull him up off the rug. He didn't question it, he simply sprang up and let me drag him into the bedroom, where the afternoon sun spilled through my open blinds. "Get out of here," I yelled at Wanda, who glanced up at us from beneath her back leg as she licked her crotch. She didn't budge until Chase backed me against the bed and practically fell on top of me. As the cat scampered away, Chase looked down at me with a wicked grin, his fingers slipping beneath the hem of my shirt. "Did reading about the Fannie's fiery loins get you all hot and bothered?"

"No," I said, sticking both hands up the back of his shirt as I pulled him against my body. "It was all you."

Chase showered me with a few hard, aggressive kisses, his hands roaming as if he couldn't decide which part of me to touch first. Then, with a low hum of satisfaction, he pushed himself up to tug my shirt over my head. His gaze landed on my black lace bra, and he froze for a beat, staring at my chest like he'd just unwrapped the perfect Christmas gift. "Christ Almighty," he muttered, as though he hadn't seen my breasts before.

Before I could even tease him, he lowered himself again, his lips brushing slow, deliberate kisses along my collarbone. The warmth of his breath sent shivers across my skin. He painted my neck and shoulder with his tongue, while one of his hands cupped my breast through the lace, his thumb pressing firm against my nipple. His lips trailed back up to my neck, where he nibbled the spot just below my ear that always drove me wild. An involuntary, dorky giggle escaped from my lips.

I felt his smile on my neck. "There she is," he whispered, his voice low and teasing. "God, I love those little noises you make." His hand slid beneath the lace, his fingers grazing bare skin now, and I arched my back. "Think I could make you do that again?" he murmured, his thumb and forefinger rolling my nipple with just the right amount of pressure. "Yeah, I know exactly how to get you there."

Chase nipped at my ear, his breath hot against my skin. I let out a loud, satisfied sigh, a noise he seemed to appreciate even more than the laugh. His hips pressed closer against my body, and I could feel the hard length of him against my thigh. "Chase," I rasped, tucking my fingertips beneath the waistband of his jeans. "I need you."

Just like Chase knew how to get me going, I understood how to work him, too. I knew what he liked to hear, which words unlocked the animal in him. Chase tore the rest of my clothes off like they were in his way, delighting in the way my breasts sprang from the black lace for one, lingering second before sliding off my pants and underwear together. With the same sense of urgency, I helped him remove his own clothes, my fingers scrambling to peel off his jeans. He pulled back from the bed to kick them all the way off, yanking his briefs down after. And then he was on top of me again, skin against skin, his solid dick pushing against my core. He kissed my breasts, pausing between them to whisper, "Do you still have that thing in your arm?"

He meant my birth control implant. "Yes," I gasped out, tracing my fingernails down the center of his back.

Chase groaned, the sound low and dangerous, as he rolled his hips just enough to tease me, his dick sliding against my slick skin. "Good," he murmured, brushing his lips against mine without quite kissing me, "because I don't plan on holding back."

Finally, he let me kiss him, rolling his tongue around mine, with one of his big hands holding both of my wrists down above my head on the pillow.

"And don't you hold back on those pretty sounds you make, either," he said, rubbing the tip of his nose against mine, "because I'm going to keep going until I hear them."

He kissed his way down to my breasts, giving one nipple a slow flick with his tongue. And then he lifted himself up, sliding into me slowly with his eyes locked on mine. My breath hitched as he filled me inch by inch, not stopping until his hips were flush against mine. His eyes drifted shut like he was savoring the moment. When he opened them again, he lowered his upper body to kiss my lips.

"I missed you," he whispered, before pulling part of the way out. He kept his thrusts slow and deliberate for a while, taking his time to kiss me and caress my skin, giving me reminders of what had been missing from my life for the past three years with every touch. I had no idea where this was going or what it meant, but the uncertainty only added to the thrill.

Squeezing my legs around him tight, I tugged on his hair, enjoying the way it made him grin. He picked up the pace, reaching behind him to give my thigh a hard squeeze. His hand slid up to my knee, fingers curling around it before he pushed my leg farther away, opening me up beneath him. The new angle sent a bolt of pleasure through me, and I couldn't hold back the soft, needy moan that escaped my lips. "That's it, sweetheart," he murmured, thrusting faster now. God, I couldn't take it when he called me *sweetheart*. The only thing better was when he called me— "God, Meg," he whispered, like he could read my mind, pushing his sweaty forehead against mine. He slowed the pace, closing his eyes. "I don't want to come yet."

"Please don't stop. You're making me feel so good."

Chase's eyes shot open and he licked his lips. I followed his gaze to my bedside table. "I want you to get one of the toys I know you keep in that drawer," he said with a slow thrust, "and I want you to use it on your clit while I'm inside you."

With a shaky breath, I reached over to the nightstand, fumbling to get the drawer open. My fingers found the small vibrator immediately—muscle memory, I guess. Chase watched me turn it to a medium speed setting and lower it between us, pressing it just above where he entered me. My head fell back against the pillow as Chase's hips rolled into me again, the sensation of him inside me combined with the toy threatening to send me over the edge within minutes. Chase's groans were in sync with my whimpers, and my mind drifted to my retired neighbors who were always home around this time. Oh well, they were probably just glad to hear a second voice in the room this time.

The thought almost made me laugh, but it was quickly drowned out by the way Chase thrust into me again, harder this time, making the vibrator buzz even closer against me.

"Chase." My eyes widened as the heat began to coil low in my belly—and it was building fast.

He looked down at me with that cocky grin that always made me weak. "That's it, sweetheart. Come for me."

And just like that, I felt myself unraveling beneath him. I gasped, digging my fingernails into his back. I dropped the vibrator from my other hand—I didn't need it anymore—and tugged on his hair, as the pleasure low in my belly began to pulsate through my entire core. My thighs trembled on either side of Chase as he slammed into me. "Fuck, Meg—" His voice was a strained growl, and that was all it took. I shattered beneath him, a scream ripping from my throat as the orgasm crashed through me.

Chase wasn't far behind, his hips shaking as he buried himself deep with a guttural groan, coming right along with me.

As our breathing slowed, he stayed inside of me, squeezing a fistful of my hair in his hand. My skin was still buzzing from the pleasure.

After a moment, he collapsed onto the mattress beside me, dragging a hand through his messy hair. I rolled onto my side, catching my breath just as a low buzzing noise made both of us freeze. Chase shifted, and with a lopsided grin, he pulled the vibrator out from beneath his back and turned it off. We looked into each other's eyes and laughed.

He lazily draped one arm over my waist, and we stared at each other just like that for a little while. I pressed a kiss against his shoulder, taking in the sandalwood scent of his deodorant.

Wanda leapt onto the bed with a chirpy meow, digging her claws into the comforter as she stretched. "C'mere," Chase said, clicking his tongue. She listened, purring as she cuddled up against his bare chest.

And suddenly, it was like no time had passed between us at all—like we were just picking up where we left off. Back before everything went wrong.

chapter twenty-nine

chase

"I need to start getting ready," Meghan called out from the bathroom. She'd left me with Wanda on the bed in my underwear while she peed and cleaned herself up.

"What for? Your coven meeting?" I teased.

"No," she said, letting out a laugh. I heard the toilet flush. "It's a book club meeting at Sarah Gardner's house."

"You should try to get the tea on what really happened between Owen and the high school football coach, Sarah's ex," I said, scratching Wanda just above her tail, making her purr louder by the second. "I heard they got into a fist fight once."

"Really, Chase? Owen Gardner would never get in a fist fight," she said, opening the bathroom door to look at me. She was wearing a black bathrobe, and her hair was pinned back with a clip. "You shouldn't believe everything you read on Concerned Citizens of Woodvale."

She was probably right. Maybe she should heed that advice herself the next time she published an article that divided people.

"Owen, Xander, and Mason are playing poker at the Gardners' tonight," she added, stepping out of the bathroom. "You should come."

I leaned back against the headboard, trying not to laugh. "I'm not just going to show up at the Gardners' house uninvited."

Meghan shook her head, already pulling her phone from the pocket of her robe. "I'm sure it'd be fine," she insisted.

Her thumbs tapped rapidly over the screen, and I heard the familiar whoosh of a text being sent. A few seconds later, her phone buzzed, and she glanced down with a smug grin.

"Sarah said Owen told her, 'absolutely.' See?"

I had to admit, the thought of playing poker with those guys was pretty enticing. It'd been years since I played with my dad and his brothers, though, and I might have been a little rusty. "I don't know. I don't want to ruin the vibe."

Meghan crawled onto the bed, kneeling beside me. "Xander's going to be present. The vibe is already a little iffy."

I chuckled, eyeing the way her robe gaped open to reveal part of her thigh. As she stroked Wanda between the ears, her eyes lifted to meet mine, making me aware I'd been staring. There was a thoughtful look on her face—the face she wore when something was on her mind, but she couldn't say the words.

I cleared my throat. "Do we… do we want to arrive together?"

"Like a couple?"

"Yeah. Is that what you want?"

Meghan's hand came to a stop, making the cat let out a disgruntled chirp and twitch her tail in an attempt to get her attention. But Meghan didn't notice, holding my gaze as a heavy silence stretched between us. And the longer it went on, the louder it became. Why was she hesitating?

"Forget I said that."

"No, it's—"

"I'm not trying to move things along too fast. Really."

Meghan shifted beside me, her lips pressing together like she was trying to decide if she wanted to say something else or let the silence win. Her hand returned to Wanda's fur, stroking absentmindedly now, but her gaze never left mine. "It's just… complicated," she said.

Complicated. I hated that word. I nodded, pretending to understand. "I know."

After a moment's pause, I pushed myself up from the bed and grabbed my jeans, pulling them on. "We can just play it by ear. It's totally—" I paused, suddenly needing to swallow, "—fine." I swallowed. Why did I have so much trouble getting that last word out?

Maybe because it wasn't true.

I buttoned my jeans slowly like I was stalling for time. I knew I should just leave the conversation at that. We were in a good place. Fragile, but good. Before I could stop myself, I blurted, "Can I just ask—what's holding you back?"

I regretted the question the second the words tumbled out of my mouth. Did I even want the answer?

The way Meghan frowned down at her lap, rubbing the sash from her bathrobe between two fingers, told me I didn't. "I just… I know I'm a lot to handle," she started. "I *still* am. Even though today ended up being pretty easy, I barely thought about my mom at all—which is something I'll probably feel guilty about later—I still have dark days. Like I did before. I'm still the same, sad girl."

She paused to look at my face, watching me as I slid onto the edge of the bed beside her.

"You probably think I'm this changed, healed person, but I'm not. I don't want to be a burden on someone else."

"Meg," I said, giving her bare knee a squeeze. "You'd never be a burden to me."

"But I *was*," she said quickly, making my heart feel like it leapt up to my throat. She shook her head, staring down at her silk sash again. "I *was* a burden to you."

"Come on, no you weren't. It was a challenging time, yes, but I—"

"Chase," Meghan interrupted, rolling her eyes. "I could feel the resentment rolling off of you every time you walked in the door and saw me crying again. Maybe you never said it out loud, but I could feel it."

I wasn't quite sure how to defend myself without making it worse. I squeezed her knee harder, like somehow my true emotions would translate. "I'm sorry, but you misread me. Your grief never burdened me. I just felt ill-equipped to handle it. I felt… inadequate. I kept trying to do my best, but it was like everything I tried was just… wrong. You would only push me farther and farther away. In fact, I felt like I was burdening *you*."

"Of course you weren't."

I picked my shirt up off the floor and held it between my knees, still perched on the edge of her bed. Right there was another opportunity to let the conversation drop, but once again, my big stupid mouth had to push things too far. "You know, you hurt me, too," I mumbled, barely opening my mouth.

Maybe it didn't need to be said. Maybe she already knew. But just in case she wasn't aware, it was out in the open now.

"I just—" Meghan sucked in a shaky breath like she was holding back a sob. "I just had to let you go because I knew you deserved better. Someone happy."

"I didn't want happy. I wanted you."

Her lips trembled as she hugged her knees to her chest. It dawned on me then that we'd had this same argument before, both of us attempting to make these very same points during the break-up, when everything was still raw. Now that we'd had time to reflect and mature, we could finally *hear* each other. Despite what she might believe, she wasn't the same person she was three years ago, and neither was I. But that was a good thing.

Because maybe the new versions of us could finally get this right.

I stood up to go, turning toward her to cup her face in my hand. She leaned into the touch as I slid my thumb along her cheekbone. "Look. We'll figure this out."

Meghan nodded. That was a relief.

I bent down to kiss the top of her head. "I'll see you at the Gardners tonight," I whispered, pulling my hand away from her soft cheek. The corners of Meghan's lips turned upward in a tiny smile, and I hurried out of there before I had the chance to say something stupid. I couldn't lose her again.

My heart beats only for you, I thought as I picked my bag up off of Meghan's living room rug. Those 1800s lesbians were a little dramatic with their love proclamations, but then again, I could relate.

chapter thirty

meghan

The Gardners lived in a newer subdivision—the kind with clean sidewalks, matching mailboxes, and meticulously trimmed lawns. Their house was the biggest one on the street, with a two-car garage and landscaping that looked straight out of a *Better Homes and Gardens* spread. As Sarah led me through the house toward her patio, I felt a little out of place. I'd never been one for big, beautiful homes like this. I preferred old houses with history, ones with a little charm and a lot of creaky floorboards. But there was no denying it: The Gardners' house was impressive. I followed Sarah through her immaculate, neutral-toned kitchen, where the guys stood around the island with beers in their hands. Owen tapped a deck of cards against the granite countertop, glancing at me with a quick and friendly, "Hey."

And then there was Chase. He lifted his fingers in a lazy wave from the neck of his bottle, like he hadn't had me gasping beneath him just a couple of hours ago. I gave him an innocent little smile as I walked past. His lips twitched, as if fighting back a grin, before he turned his attention back to the conversation.

Sarah opened the sliding glass door to her backyard, and it was like stepping into a Pinterest board labeled "Backyard Goals." Warm patio lights crisscrossed above us beneath the white-painted pergola. A sprawling outdoor sectional wrapped around a sleek fire pit, with an arched stone pattern forming the perfect centerpiece beneath it all.

"There's my girl!" Jill hollered, clutching the stem of a giant margarita glass that was already half-empty. She patted the cushion beside her, waving for me to join her on the sectional. Between her enthusiasm and the frozen strawberry margarita Sarah handed me, the tension began to melt away.

The conversation flowed easily, with spicy book recommendations, talk of our favorite and most hated tropes, and comparing the kinkiest scenes we'd read lately. Jill, of course, took center stage, gesturing obscenely as she described a particularly memorable scene from a dark romance she'd just finished. She even acted it out for us, making Abigail cover her face with a pillow to stifle her laughter.

But as much as I tried to keep my attention on the conversation, I kept glancing back toward the house. Through the glass, I could see the guys at the dining room table, deep into their poker game.

My chest tightened as I watched Chase, wondering if he was doing okay in there. Did he feel out of place, like I had when I first stepped inside?

And was Xander being nice?

Sarah leaned back on the sectional, laughing at Jill's antics as she tucked her feet beneath her. "Okay, okay," she said, holding her La Croix can on her lap, "we still haven't picked a damn book for our next meeting. How about we go with a romantic suspense? That way, it's spicy *and* has an edge. Win-win, right?"

We all murmured in agreement, and Abigail scrolled through her TBR list, throwing out a few recommendations. It took a while, but we finally agreed on a book about a homicide detective falling in love with one of his suspects.

Sarah got up, announcing she was going to bring some snacks outside before the guys ate them all. As she went inside, Kendall and Abigail quickly fell into a conversation about one of the students at their school. I stared into margarita glass just as Jill's hand wrapped around my arm. "Hey, I need to talk to you," she said, nodding toward the other end of the backyard.

She took me by the hand and led me off the patio across the grass to the corner of the privacy fence. "You're scaring me," I said.

But she was smiling. "It's not scary. Well, maybe it is. Depends on your reaction." Her mischievous giggle was unsettling.

"Say it, Jill," I said, holding my stomach, bracing myself for whatever news she had to spill. "Just tell me."

"You and I might get to be hybrid partners after all," she said, trying not to smile.

I blinked at her, confused. "Really? Why?"

"Because," she said, pausing for emphasis, "it might be somewhat unethical to sleep with your hybrid partner, and..." Jill bit her bottom lip.

I glanced toward the sliding glass door, where I could barely make out the guys playing cards. "Dammit," I groaned, narrowing my eyes at Xander. "I knew he told you."

Jill raised one eyebrow at me. "What do you mean he *told* me?" She glanced from side to side. "I mean, I was kind of there."

Now it was my turn to look confused. "Wait, what?"

Jill took a step back, holding her margarita glass out to the side. "Wait, what?"

Oh. *Oh, no.* "Jill!" My mouth fell open. "Are you saying you slept with Xander?"

"Let's do you first. I knew you kissed, but—you *slept* with Chase?"

I shushed her, catching Kendall and Abigail peeking over the back of the sectional in our direction. Leaning in closer, I lowered my voice to a near whisper. "Okay, yes. Chase and I have… hooked up a couple of times. We're taking it slow, and it's just been… weird."

Jill stared back at me with a grin that said *I knew it.* "Oh my God," she said, "I am so, so happy this is finally happening."

"Sorry, aren't you the one who helped me burn his Ramones t-shirt after the break-up?"

She shrugged. "Yes, but I've always hoped you two would find your way back to each other. That boy loves you so much, and he always has. Seriously, I wish I had someone who looked at me the way he stares at you—all starry-eyed like he wants to gobble you up."

"Uh-huh. And does Xander look at *you* like that?"

Her naughty smile returned. "Sometimes, especially when I'm riding h-"

"Stop it right there," I begged with a laugh. "He's like my brother. You'd better not tell me anything that's going to make it hard for me to work beside him."

"I'm sorry," she giggled. "I know it's crazy and reckless, but it's been so fun, and we just can't *stop.*" She shivered, like the memory of one of their encounters was running through her mind. "Which is why I think we're going to have to quit working together. Meghan, I think I'm actually falling for him."

I slid my palm beneath my bangs against my forehead and looked down at the grass. "Say *psych* right now."

"I will not." Jill swirled her glass before sipping the last of her drink.

My eyes drifted to Abigail, who was leaning through the sliding glass door talking to the guys now. Did Jill know about Xander's close relationship with her? "What about Abigail?" I asked, returning my gaze toward Jill.

"She seems really sweet," Jill said, combing her fingers through her wavy, blonde hair. "He talks about her sometimes. I think they've known each other since preschool. I'm not worried about her, if that's what you're hinting at."

She might not have been worried, but I was. It almost made my stomach hurt, because my best friend was going to find out the hard way that Xander was in love with someone else. Despite her optimism, I had a bad feeling this was going to crush her. But I would be there to pick up the pieces, just like she was for me when things fell apart with Chase.

chapter thirty-one
chase

The last hand of the night ended with Mason raking in the final pot—a respectable $82 in cash. "How many Squishmallows can that buy for Finley?" Owen teased, clinking his beer bottle against Mason's. We'd kept the stakes pretty low, with bets small enough to keep things fun but just enough to feel competitive. I ended the night down twelve bucks—not bad, considering I spent most of the first half pretending I remembered the rules.

Socializing with new groups of people had always been a little difficult for me, but those guys made it pretty easy. The conversation flowed effortlessly, along with the beer, making me glad Meghan encouraged me to come.

Eventually, the two parties merged, and we joined the women outside beneath the patio lights. Owen started a fire in the pit as I slid next to Meghan on the sectional. She scooted closer to Jill to make room, and I tried to ignore the creepy way Jill wiggled her eyes at me, almost sloshing her drink out of her glass as she scooted. She seemed a little wobbly.

"Someone's going to be hung over for their morning broadcast," I observed.

Jill lowered her glass, and in her booming news anchor voice, she slurred, "Good morning, Woodvale. Today we're going to keep things *very* quiet and turn down the lights as this news anchor lays her head down on the desk. Back to you, Bernard." She ended her monologue with a real hiccup, and everyone laughed.

On the other side of the patio, Mason leaned down to kiss Kendall on the lips, saying, "Hey, princess. Guess who just won eighty-two bucks?"

She widened her eyes and shot him a look. "Mason. You just kissed me in front of *literally* all the reporters in town."

"Fuck," Mason laughed. "At least the school year's almost over."

"You guys are really bad at keeping your relationship a secret," Owen laughed, stoking the fire.

Meghan smiled, tipping her glass toward Kendall. "You're safe with us. Nobody here's breaking that story."

I slid my arm along the back of the seat behind Meghan, close enough to touch her, but I didn't. I wasn't sure if she wanted that kind of attention in front of everyone, and the last thing I wanted to do was make her uncomfortable.

On her other side, Jill let out an annoyed sigh. "We have to run all our stories past our CEO now, anyway. Silas is controlling everything we report, so that probably wouldn't meet his approval."

"Ah, Silas Brown," Owen muttered, taking the seat next to Sarah on the swinging loveseat across from us. He looked into her eyes. "Our favorite person." His tone was dripping in sarcasm.

"Stop," Sarah whispered, her eyes widening. "That's their boss."

"Girl, spill the tea," Jillian said, hugging the pillow on her lap. "Why do *you* guys hate him?"

Sarah and Owen exchanged a look. After a moment, Sarah let out a sigh. "This is off the record, right?" We all nodded. "Okay, first of all, that man has bad breath."

Meghan almost choked on her drink next to me, and everyone else erupted into laughter. Even Xander was smiling.

"I've had to work closely with him a lot throughout the relocation," Sarah continued, staring at the fire, "and I'm not sure about him. It's obvious he's a self-serving narcissist who barely has a grasp on reality." She was pretty spot-on.

Owen cleared his throat. "Yeah, not to mention the fact he tried to use his generosity as leverage—"

"Bribery," Sarah interrupted.

"—*bribery* to get a spot as a guest on my podcast."

I couldn't imagine what someone like Silas Brown could bring to the table in a STEM-themed podcast. Xander seemed just as confused. "What? You didn't tell me about this."

With his arm draped over his wife's shoulders, Owen took a swig of his beer. "He cornered Sarah with this whole 'I scratched your back, now you scratch mine' approach. Tried to get her to change my mind about it."

Sarah shuddered. "He stood so close…"

"Yeah, all of that tracks," Xander said, leaning forward in his seat. "Silas uses his position of power to persuade people. It's kind of his whole schtick. And now he's literally controlling the news—manipulating what we produce." He motioned to the rest of the news crew sitting there. "He's preventing us from telling the truth."

"None of that sounds ethical," Owen said. "Borderline illegal, even."

"At the very least, we know we can't trust our local news anymore." Mason looked up at us as he spoke. "Not that it's any of your guys' fault."

"Xander, you should report on this," Sarah said, tucking her hair behind her ear. "Expose this guy and show Woodvale who he truly is."

Xander shook his head without even giving her suggestion any thought. "Hell no. I've pissed off plenty of politicians and city officials in my day, but none of them were the guy signing my paychecks. No thank you."

As the conversation continued, with Sarah venting about her many run-ins with Silas in the halls of our building, I noticed Meghan had gone quiet. She stared at the flames in the fire pit, twisting her pendant necklace against her chest. Thinking she might be lost in a daydream about her mom, I hesitantly lowered my hand to her shoulder.

She turned toward me, took a deep breath, and said, "Maybe I should write an exposé on Silas."

Around us, the conversation died down. "What'd you say?" Jill asked.

Meghan faced her. "The people in this town deserve to know what's really going on. I'm going to compile all of his sketchy dealings in one big, fat exposé."

"Are you sure?" Xander gave her a skeptical stare. "You didn't handle the negative feedback on your Lenny article very well. The fallout from this will be huge."

He wasn't wrong, but I could tell from Meghan's tone she meant what she said. "Yeah, I think I really want to do this. What do I have to lose? He's determined to make sure the paper keeps going downhill, anyway."

"Could you get fired for doing that?" Kendall asked.

"She very well could," Xander answered, still staring at Meghan. "He won't hesitate to come after you. You'll have to be very careful in your wording. It's a lot to take on alone."

Meghan nodded like she understood. "I know."

I glanced from Xander to Jill to Meghan, setting my beer on the ground between my feet. "What if you don't do it alone?" She turned to look at me, and I rushed out the next words before I had a chance to change my mind. "What if you add my name to the byline? Then you won't be taking the fall alone."

Her eyes locked onto mine. "You'd be willing to do that?"

I nodded, holding her gaze. "You go down, I go down with you," I said, echoing what we'd told each other that day we kissed by the waterfall. The corners of her lips turned upward in a smile.

Xander leaned forward, resting his elbows on his knees. "I've already got a ton of research on Silas's involvement with Weston that you could use. You can throw my name on there, too. If you want."

"Well hell," Jill said, slapping Meghan's knee. "Don't leave me out of the group project. I want to help with this."

With the four of us forming an alliance to take a public stand against our CEO, it was still a huge risk. But together, we had a real chance of making a change. There was strength in numbers, after all. An exposé written by most of the reporting staff would carry more weight than it would if it came from just one person.

"He can't fire you all, right?" Owen asked, motioning across the patio toward us.

Meghan pulled out her phone. "I'm FaceTiming Graham."

"I was going to suggest you leave him out of this, but okay," Xander muttered, settling back into the cushions again.

"We have to have his support, or he won't let us print it," Meghan said just as Graham answered the FaceTime call. As Jill leaned over Meghan's shoulder so they'd both appear on the screen, the man let out a long, melodramatic grunt.

"Ah, jeez. Sorry, ladies, I don't have bail money." He wanted to appear grumpy, but I could see his smile over Meghan's shoulder.

Ignoring his joke, Meghan got right down to business, explaining everything we knew about what Silas had been up to. As she spoke, Xander walked around the fire to squeeze between her and Jill, detailing some of what he knew about John Weston.

I even took the phone for a minute, sharing what Sean had witnessed outside the comic bookstore. "You don't know anything about him wanting to downsize us, do you?"

"No, I don't," Graham said, and though he could have been lying, his shock sounded genuine. He repeatedly ran his hand along his stubble as he listened to Meghan describe the exposé she planned to write, adding our names to the byline for protection.

"But," she said, making sure she had his full attention, "we can't do it without your approval."

Graham let out a low whistle, shaking his head in disbelief. "Meghan, you've got some serious balls."

Jillian leaned over Xander's lap to look at the screen, her grin wide. "Ovaries, Graham. They're called ovaries."

Meghan didn't miss a beat. "So, do I have your support or not?"

Graham let out a sigh, pulling away from the phone to yell at someone over his shoulder. "Sorry, it's my weekend with the kids, and my son's playing Fortnite—let me go out to the deck."

The screen wobbled as Graham stood, the sound of a sliding door whooshing open in the background. As we waited, Meghan exchanged a glance with me, and then Xander.

We were all quiet as Graham settled into what looked like an outdoor chair. Finally, he stared into the camera again, saying, "You guys, this is insane."

"He couldn't fire us all, could he?" I asked, leaning against Meghan's side.

"He absolutely could," Graham said flatly. "Silas has the power to clean house if he wants to. He could start fresh with all new reporters. Pay them a hell of a lot less, too."

"And just what would the community think about that?" Meghan locked her eyes on the screen. "If he fires Jillian fucking Taylor?" She shot a glance at Jill, who gave her hair a dramatic flip and pretended to inspect her nails.

"There would be an uproar," Sarah interjected.

Graham frowned. He knew just as well as we did that Silas was the one who needed to go. He shook his head, but it wasn't a no. "It's so risky for me. I've got child support. I'm trying to buy a new house right now. I've got—"

"Womp, womp," Xander said, leaning over to appear on the screen. "And I have a motorcycle payment." It made the entire group laugh. Jill shook her head at him, mouthing something inaudible.

"Come on, Graham," Meghan urged. "Do the right thing."

He pinched the bridge of his nose for a moment and cursed under his breath. And then, adjusting his position in his deck chair, he moved his phone closer to his face. His eyes seemed to darken as he said, "Fine. Do it. Light the damn match. And add me to the byline."

Meghan clapped her hand over her mouth and Jill squealed, but Graham quickly spoke again before anyone had the chance to interrupt.

"But we have to go about it the right way. I'll have my personal lawyer review the story, and my buddy up at the *Star* could look at it, too. And if it's solid, we'll put it above the fold. How soon can you put this together?"

"With everyone's help?" Meghan glanced up at me. "Give me one week."

Xander and I exchanged a nod over Meghan's head.

"Alright. Let's shoot for publication next Friday, guys," Graham said, blowing out a long, melodramatic sigh. "And that's when we'll all meet our demise."

"We're all in this together," Jill sang out, making Graham shake his head.

"Wow, Jillian," he said, blinking a few times. "You should bless the town with that singing voice of yours on the morning news."

"Maybe I will," she said, leaning over Xander's lap again so she'd appear on the screen. "I'll do it just for you, Graham."

"I'm counting on it."

"Alright, bye now," Xander said, his hand shooting up to end the call.

The energy on the patio shifted the second Meghan put her phone down. A collective cheer went up, including those who'd been quietly watching this conversation unfold. Sarah rubbed her arms, flashing Meghan a grin. "That gave me goosebumps. I feel like we just witnessed something historical."

"I'm both scared *and* excited for you guys," Kendall said, glancing from Meghan to Jill.

I watched Meghan grin down at her lap and take a few deep breaths. She looked even more beautiful than usual under the soft, golden glow of the patio lights above. There was something different about the way she carried herself, too—a quiet kind of confidence that hadn't been there before.

I knew, without a doubt, this was the woman I wanted to be with forever. It was going to take some time and effort to get it right, but she was worth every bit of it.

She caught me staring, shooting me a sweet, sly grin. And, rolling her eyes in surrender, she leaned over and kissed me right there in the center of that chattering group. It was just a quick, light, kiss, but that tiny display of affection told me she, too, believed this was going to work.

chapter thirty-two

meghan

By Tuesday afternoon, the list of people willing to add their names to the byline of this exposé had grown. Byron was the easiest to persuade—he was happy to be a part of something. I thought I saw just a hint of something sinister in his eyes when he scowled and said, "I don't like that man."

Devonte was a little more hesitant, being the person in the newsroom least affected by Silas's assholery. He just wanted to show up, write his sports reports, and go home. He even said that. But when Xander reminded him Silas was a Cowboys fan, Devonte glanced at his Philadelphia Eagles mousepad and tensed up. "Okay, but I hope I don't regret this."

Chase and Jillian also discussed the plan with their producer, Marco, who was immediately on board. Marco even came upstairs to talk to me, sharing some insight he had on Silas pushing some stories while killing others. "And I'm sure you're aware, but Noah Sherman will be officially announcing his bid for mayor tomorrow morning," Marco said, "and guess who already made a sizable donation to his campaign?"

I didn't have to guess. "That sounds like election interference." If Silas wasn't stopped, next year could get messy.

Marco nodded. "It's unethical at best, dangerous at most. The donation is public record, so that should give you a little ammunition. Don't *call* it interference—just imply it," he warned before he left.

Xander wheeled his broken chair into my cubicle to read what I'd written so far. It was a messy draft, but he nodded as he skimmed the document on my screen. "Is it okay so far?" I asked.

Xander licked his lips, rereading some parts in silence. His hesitation made me feel sick to my stomach. "It's getting there," he said, his pointer finger hovering over the screen. "Add the word 'alleged' here. Might save your ass. All our asses."

I typed the word quickly, giving him a grateful nod for pointing out my oversight.

He stood up to leave, pushing his chair toward the opening of my cubicle. Just before he turned the corner, he paused to look at me and say, "It's good, Meghan. You're definitely the right person to write this."

Compliments from Xander were rare, so it was all I could do not to spring to my feet and hug him. I resisted, however, knowing he'd only push me away. "Thank you." I swallowed. "And hey, come back here for a second."

Xander reluctantly walked his chair back over to me and sat down. "What?"

I stared at his face. "What are you doing with Jill?"

His lips twitched as if trying to suppress a grin. "What do you mean?"

"You know exactly what I mean." I folded my arms across my chest. "What are you doing?"

He leaned back in his chair and shrugged. "Just having fun."

"That's what I'm worried about." I kept my voice low. "I'm worried you're going to end up breaking her heart."

Xander gave me a look that was almost too casual. "What if she breaks mine?"

The way he said it made me pause. I scanned his face, trying to read him, but his expression gave nothing away. "What about Abigail?"

His posture stiffened. "Abigail's… seeing someone. A woman."

"Oh. Is she…?"

"She's bi." He gave a small, lopsided grin. "So yeah, that pretty much doubles the competition. I can't compete with all these angelic women walking around with their soft lips and long hair and the way they… smell."

"Are you *trying* to compete with them, Xan?"

"No," he answered quickly, his folded fist covering his mouth as he leaned on my desk. But I wasn't convinced. There was a flicker of something in his expression—resentment, maybe. Did Abigail turn him down? It felt like she had, and now he was rebounding with Jill. "I like Jill. I really do."

I raised an eyebrow. "What do you like about her? And don't say her boobs."

Xander rolled his eyes. "She's cute. She's intelligent. I like her laugh. Her tenacity. She's like… a little Energizer bunny."

A slow grin spread across his face, and I narrowed my eyes at him. "If you're about to make this sexual, stop right there."

"You asked," he said with a smirk. "I'd interrogate you about what you're doing with the ghostbuster, but I don't think I want the answers."

"Good, 'cause I don't have any," I said, turning my chair back to my computer screen. I needed to get back to work. Xander returned to his own cubicle, letting me write in silence.

But thoughts of Chase kept me from concentrating on anything else. He'd been pretty busy helping Sean pull everything together for the Comic Con, which was only a few days away. It seemed like everything was going wrong, from a delayed shipment of VIP badges to one of their art vendors getting rightfully canceled for saying some pretty problematic stuff online. People were calling for Sean and Chase to uninvite the artist from the convention, which they eventually did, but it was a whole mess.

When I picked up my phone to text him, there was already a notification from him there, waiting for me.

Chase: Come over for dinner tonight. I want to cook for you, like I used to.

I bit my thumbnail, grinning at my phone. Out of the two of us, Chase was always the better cook. Not that I was bad, it was just that he loved experimenting in the kitchen, trying to impress me with new techniques he picked up from the Food Network. It usually worked.

Meghan: I'll have to think about it.

Chase: Reread that last message, babes. I wasn't asking you, I was telling you. See you at 6.

Babes? That was new, and I liked it—almost as much as I liked this subtle display of possessiveness. He knew exactly how to handle me when I tried playing games. I had to cover my mouth to muffle the way I giggled as I tapped a reply. Damn that man.

I gave in, setting a reminder to grab a bottle of wine on my way to his apartment. And then I pushed my phone away to give this Silas story my full attention again.

Paragraph by paragraph, I went through the draft, rearranging sentences and tightening the flow, but no matter how much I fiddled with it, the story still felt incomplete. I sighed, slumping back in my chair. Xander said it was good, but he'd also said, *"It's getting there."* That was the feedback I couldn't quite shake.

As I stared at the blinking cursor, I worried all the information I'd gathered wasn't enough. Most of my evidence was just hearsay or speculation, when what I needed was a strong piece of evidence that would leave Silas no room to manipulate or discredit it.

I needed a smoking gun.

chapter thirty-three

chase

"What do you have cookin' up there?"

When I came downstairs into The Comics Vault on Tuesday morning, Erika was at the back of the store, assembling swag bags for the convention. The Woodvale Comic Con logo was printed in white on black bags, and she filled them with stickers, keychains, and exclusive trading cards.

I strolled up beside her with my hands in the pockets of my jeans. "California chicken focaccia flatbreads," I said, "and stuffed mushrooms. For Meghan." I glanced at the Batman clock on the wall—she'd be here any minute.

Erika turned to me with bugged-out eyes. "Look at you," she exclaimed, taking in my appearance, "coming down here smelling all fresh with your damp hair and your button-up shirt and the smell of good food wafting down the stairs? Someone's getting laid tonight."

Sean looked up from the box he was cutting open at the front of the store. "We're baby-free tonight, so I hope we're *all* getting laid. Right?"

Erika looked at her husband with mock disgust. "Fat chance. Bending over this table is making my back hurt."

"That's what back rubs are for," Sean called out.

"Uh huh, I've heard that one before," she said with a grin, rolling her eyes. She turned to me. "Do you know what back rubs lead to, Chase?"

I adjusted my glasses. "Babies?"

"Exactly. Back rubs lead to babies."

"I'll keep that in mind," I answered, looking up just in time to see Meghan approaching the door of the shop. The bells above her head jingled as she stepped inside wearing a black dress and carrying a bottle of white wine.

"Hi," she said, taking a few nervous steps forward, as though she felt out of place. Erika and Sean greeted her, but I stood back and swallowed, too mesmerized by the sight of her in that dress she was wearing to speak. It was nothing fancy, just a simple, short dress that flared out a little at her hips, but the way it fit her made my chest feel tight.

And she was here for *me*.

"Wow," she said, looking around the shop as she tucked her wavy hair behind her ears, holding the wine bottle casually at her side. "It's changed a lot in here since I last saw it."

Erika grinned, violently shaking a fresh empty sack to open it. "Yeah, we've put a lot of work into it."

I stepped forward, finally finding my voice. "The Ms. Pacman game was my idea," I said, nodding toward the arcade game up by the kids' section. Meghan glanced at it, then at me, her eyes traveling slowly from my shoes to my face. Not wanting her to compliment me first, I quickly said, "You look incredible."

"Thanks," she said, giving her dress a casual glance before returning her gaze to me. "You clean up pretty nice yourself."

"Aw, you two are sickeningly cute," Erika said, shaking her head. Sean asked her if she thought he was sickeningly cute, too, and she told him to drop the *cute* part. The two of them kept bickering, barely noticing the way I took Meghan by the hand and led her toward the doorway leading to the stairs. She uttered a quick goodbye before we disappeared around the corner, making our way up to my apartment. The second the door swung open and she stepped inside, she paused to clutch her stomach and laugh.

"Oh my God, Chase," she said, eyeing the Venom cardboard cutout, "why is he wearing a Hawaiian lei?"

"Because he's in summer mode, obviously." I glanced at the timer on the stove just as it hit ten seconds.

Meghan shook her head, coming all the way in and spinning slowly as she took in the room. Her eyes drifted toward the large windows facing Main Street, and she pressed her hands to the glass. "Oh my gosh, I love the view," she whispered, and it made me grin, knowing what I was about to show her.

"Glad you like it," I said, grabbing a pair of oven mitts. I pulled the flatbreads out of the oven and nodded toward the lidded ceramic dish on the counter. "Grab that, will you? Follow me."

She eyed the dish curiously but picked it up without question. "Where are we going?"

"You'll see," I teased, leading her back out into the hallway. But instead of heading downstairs, I opened another door to a second set of stairs leading up.

When we reached the top, I pulled open the final door and held it open for her to step out onto the roof. Meghan gasped as the cool evening air hit us, glancing around in awe at the scene. I had a table set for us, complete with a bucket of ice to keep our cucumber and tomato salad cool. I couldn't take credit for the lights strung up above—Sean did this very thing for Erika when they had to cancel their babymoon. One day I'd tell Meghan I'd stolen this idea from him, but for now, I was enjoying the way she spun around in awe.

She set the container of stuffed mushrooms on the table to walk toward the ledge, taking in the sight of the sprawling metropolis of Woodvale, from the bakery that used to be a bank to the clothing boutique that also used to be a bank. "You're so getting into my panties tonight," Meghan said, turning back around with a grin.

And she hadn't even tried my food yet. With the sun dipping low in the sky, we took our places at the little table and enjoyed each other's company while we ate and sipped our wine. She vented about Silas, and I told her everything Sean and I were working on in the final days leading up to the Woodvale Comic Con. In every quiet pause, we exchanged this knowing grin like we were asking ourselves, *"Are we really doing this right now?"*

We had cheesecake bites for dessert, just something I'd picked up from the frozen foods section. Meghan didn't seem to mind that they weren't fully thawed yet. She picked one up and drifted into silence, staring at the sunset behind the buildings. I caught that faraway look she often wore when she was deep in thought.

I tapped my fingers on the arm of my chair. "What do you think downtown Woodvale looked like when Fannie and Evelyn were alive?" This whole Silas thing had put our project about them on the back burner. If we couldn't work on it, though, at least we could talk about it.

"Well. There was a wooden boardwalk connecting all the storefronts back then," she said, "so the townspeople's shoes wouldn't get muddy—Main Street was still a dirt road. It wasn't paved until the turn of the century."

Of course she knew that. As soon as she stopped talking, she let out an embarrassed chuckle and tucked her hair behind her ears.

"Sorry, I've just… written about the history of this town a lot."

"I know. And don't apologize for the things you're passionate about. It's one of the things I love the most about you." *Fuck, did I just say* love? We were *so* not there yet. She smiled sweetly and looked down at the table without saying a word. But her silence lingered, like something was on her mind.

"Is something wrong?"

Meghan let out a heavy sigh, staring at the cheesecake bite she held between her thumb and pointer finger. "*That's* the kind of stuff I write about. My quirky little historical articles… that's where I thrive. This whole Silas thing—maybe I'm in over my head."

I scooted my chair back slightly and patted my thigh. "Come here."

She hesitated for a second, but she quickly finished the last bite of her cheesecake and walked around to my side of the table. As she slid backward onto my lap, her weight settled perfectly against me. I wrapped my arms around her waist, resting my chin on her shoulder.

"You're not in over your head," I murmured against her skin. "You've got this. You're doing something important, and you're not doing it alone. We're all in this with you."

She leaned into me, her body relaxing a little. "I just… it feels so big. I'm worried it's not going to have the impact we're all hoping for. It's missing something."

I pulled some of her hair away from her neck. "Silas can't keep getting away with his shady behavior, Meg. Publishing this article might be our only chance at saving the network from a complete downfall. It's going to be impactful enough. Trust me."

Meghan settled against my shoulder with an exhale. I hoped my words meant something to her. She at least seemed more relaxed, interlocking her fingers with mine and staring down at our hands. I lightly brushed my lips against her neck, inhaling the floral scent of her perfume. She shivered, a smile stretching across her face. "Don't, you know what that does to me."

I nuzzled my lips just below her ear, because I knew what *that* did to her, too. Her body shifted, turning on my lap so she could kiss me properly. I kissed her back, slow at first, but once she tugged on my bottom lip with her teeth, all bets were off.

One of my hands slid around her body, cupping her breast through her dress. She arched into me as my lips trailed down her neck again. I dropped one hand between her thighs, teasing her with slow, circular strokes against her skin.

Meghan faced me, pressing her forehead right against mine just as my thumb grazed the hem of her panties. "Chase..." Her voice was barely a whisper as I swiped my thumb over her panties again, this time brushing over her clit. She squirmed, her hips moving instinctively, pressing harder into me, and I could feel her getting wet beneath the fabric.

"I wonder if any of the people in the taller buildings can see us," I whispered. We were in total view of the office building on the other side of the street. It was late enough that everyone had probably gone home for the day, but what if they hadn't?

Meghan attempted to suppress a grin as she shifted her hips, making the front of my jeans tighten. "We'll have to be discreet."

"Then it's a good thing you wore a dress," I said, yanking it out of my way with one hand while pressing my other palm flat against the damp fabric of her panties. I draped her dress back over my hand to hide what I was doing. I rubbed her through the fabric, listening to her breathing speed up, before slipping my fingers beneath the waistline of her panties. The satisfied sound she made when my fingers reached her silky folds was a sound I wanted to hear her make again and again. I slid two fingers through her slick heat, teasing her with slow, deliberate strokes, just enough to pull another breathy moan from her lips.

Meghan's eyes drifted shut as I circled her clit with the perfect amount of pressure, coaxing more soft, desperate noises out of her. When I sunk two fingers inside of her, she cried out, arching her back even more than before. "You like me sinking my fingers deep inside you while we sit out here in the open, don't you? Anyone could see us…"

I curled my fingers, hitting just the right spot to make her squirm. And the more she wiggled on my lap, the harder my dick pressed against her ass. I thought she was close to coming when her eyes shot open and she said, "Take your dick out."

I sucked in a sharp breath as she lifted her body up just enough to slip her panties off. I had no choice but to obey. I fumbled with my jeans to free myself and teased her entrance with my tip. "Don't be shy," I whispered. "Sit back down."

Meghan lowered herself onto me, letting her skirt drape around us to conceal the act. With a breathy moan, she began to move, moving slowly at first, her hips rolling in rhythm with mine. I cupped one of her breasts over her dress, easily finding the hard peak of her nipple, teasing it with my thumb. My other hand slid lower, and I began rubbing her clit with two fingers in slow, teasing circles.

"God, Chase," she breathed, reaching one arm behind my neck to tug on my hair. "I love the way you ruin me."

That was all the encouragement I needed. "Yeah?" I worked her clit faster as she rode me, bucking my hips to help her. "I want to see you completely unravel," I told her. The sound of her soft gasps turned desperate as her head fell back onto my shoulder. Meghan's entire body shuddered as she came, her walls squeezing around me in a way that almost undid me right there.

I groaned, gripping her thigh as she rocked through the aftershocks. And with one more thrust, I followed, the tension finally snapping as I spilled inside of her.

Her head still rested against my shoulder with her eyes closed as she tried to catch her breath. "Fuck, Meghan," I whispered, pressing my lips to her sweaty forehead as I wrapped one arm around her waist. "That escalated pretty quickly, didn't it?"

She opened her eyes to stare into mine, giving me a lazy, satisfied grin. "We barely made it through dessert." God, she looked beautiful just like this.

I held her for another moment before we had to come back to reality. With a little awkward laughter, we cleaned ourselves up the best we could. I walked her downstairs to the bathroom, pointing out the clean washcloths on the shelf.

A few minutes later, as I was putting away our leftovers, Meghan emerged from the bathroom with a copy of the *Woodvale Times* in her hands. "Where'd you get this?"

I leaned onto my arms on the island and raised one eyebrow at her. "I kind of... have them delivered?" With a smile, I added, "I pay a fee, a pimply kid brings them to my doorstep—it's a whole thing. Maybe you've heard of it?"

That earned me a cute giggle out of her. "I'm just surprised," she said, settling onto my couch as she opened the paper on the coffee table. "It's funny, I rarely look at the-"

Meghan stopped suddenly, her gaze locked on the open newspaper in front of her. Curious, I walked around the island into the living area to get a better look at what she saw, suspecting a glaring typo that made it to print or something. However, she was staring at a big, quarter-page ad for the laundromat John Weston owned. "What's wrong?" I asked.

"I'm so stupid."

"Well, I disagree. Again, what's wrong?"

Meghan looked up from the paper, her eyes wide, like the pieces were clicking into place. "Why haven't I thought to talk to the ads department? If anyone would have concrete evidence of Silas's favoritism, it's them."

I winced as I turned on the lamp to brighten up the dark room. "Yeah, they would, but good luck getting them to share it with you."

"Don't need it," she said, sitting up a little straighter as she closed the paper. She watched me move around the coffee table to sit next to her. "I can be very persuasive."

"I know," I said, leaning back with my hands in my pockets. I gave her a crooked grin. "I mean, look at us. I let you wear me down for the second time. I guess anything's possible."

She lowered her chin to glare at me. "I wore *you* down?"

"Yup. At least, that's what I'm going to tell everyone when they ask how we ended up back together." I maintained eye contact with her, testing her reaction. However, she didn't even flinch at the notion of us being "back together." But she *did* smile.

chapter thirty-four

meghan

Our ads department merged with WWTV's when Silas bought us out. He crammed them all into an open-plan workspace near the news studio on the first floor. It was the place where deals were made, ad spots were sold, and contracts were typed. If there were any traceable receipts of Silas's favoritism, it would be down there in the ads department.

As I made my way down the stairs the following morning, I silently prayed I'd be able to meet with Quentin, an ad salesman I had drinks with one time last summer. He was a decent guy, but he clearly had issues with me being taller than him, seeing as he mentioned it no less than three times on our one date. I didn't feel like wasting my time with someone who might feel threatened by me wearing heels, so we left it at that. But since then, we'd been cordial, even friendly, and he still viewed all of my Instagram stories. Every last one.

That gave me some pull, didn't it?

Unfortunately, when I walked into the drab ads office, Quentin was nowhere around. In fact, there was only one person working: Tiffany Brent, a middle-aged woman I'd had a few conversations with during my time working at the paper. "Are you looking for someone?" Tiffany asked, peering at me over her glasses as I hesitated at the front of the office.

"Is Quentin working today?"

"He works remote now, hon. We're a skeleton crew nowadays. Is there something I can help you with?" Tiffany had kind eyes and a warm smile, but I didn't know her well enough to ask any favors. Did I?

I imagined what Xander might do in this situation. He would come up with a sneaky way to get Tiffany to share the info on Weston's account—maybe even lie. If the evidence Xander found was damning enough, his method for obtaining it often didn't matter. He toed the line carefully to avoid legal repercussions, a skill he mastered up in Chicago.

But because I had very little experience in skirting that ethically gray area Xander lived in, I decided an honest, direct approach was my best bet. Even as I approached Tiffany's desk, I doubted myself, but this was all I had.

"Actually, Tiffany, there might be something you can help me with."

"Oh?" She folded her hands on her desk. "And what's that?"

I looked her in the eyes, hoping that would help me gain her trust. "I'm looking into John Weston's relationship with the network. Specifically, if there's anything unusual about his ad account."

There was a momentary pause and the subtlest, almost-imperceivable flicker of surprise in Tiffany's eyes that let me know I was on the right track. "Unusual... how?"

"I just need to know if there's anything that stands out in his contract."

Tiffany stared up at me and blinked a few times. "And what's this for?"

I had only a few seconds to decide how honest I wanted to be with her. I could dance around the truth, keep it vague— but something told me that Tiffany would see right through that. I took another step closer to her desk, lowering my voice just enough to signal the seriousness of the situation. "I'm working on a big story. An exposé, actually. I'm looking into Silas and how he's been favoring certain clients while manipulating what we cover."

Tiffany chewed on her bottom lip as she listened to me, rubbing her fingers along the lanyard around her neck. "That sounds… incredibly risky. John Weston has more power in this town than anyone," she said. "More than Silas. More than the mayor, even."

"Exactly," I said, resting my hands on the corner of her desk. "And through Silas, he's controlling the news."

"He might be," Tiffany said, glancing at the door to the hall like someone else could walk in, "but none of us would have a job if it weren't for Weston. If we lose his ad account, we're finished. The amount he's paying us… it's astronomical."

Red flag after red flag. "I'm sure it is." I inhaled, looking at the framed photo of three little girls in dress-up clothes on Tiffany's desk. "But on the other hand, exposing Silas's corruption might be the only way for all of us to *keep* our jobs. Anyone here can see that man is running this place into the ground, right?"

Tiffany didn't speak. She stared at me, holding the diamond heart pendant of her necklace between her fingers and running it back and forth along the chain. Ha, I knew that move. And I knew what it meant, too—she was anxious.

"If I could peek at Weston's contract it might give me some answers," I said, glancing at the green filing cabinet along the wall.

"If I do share it with you, it can't come back on me," she warned. "I don't want my name anywhere in that exposé."

"It won't be," I said firmly. "Your name stays out of it. I won't say how I got the information."

She hesitated as if trying to read me. The tables had turned, and now Tiffany needed to feel like she could trust me.

"Listen," I said, trying to level with her, "I know what it's like to feel stuck between doing what's safe and doing what's right. But if we don't stop Silas now, it's only going to get worse—for all of us."

After a few seconds, Tiffany nodded, wheeling her desk chair around with a reluctant sigh. She walked over to the green filing cabinet I'd just been eyeing and pulled a key out of a little white basket on top. I watched her bend over to unlock the bottom drawer, pulling out a thick manilla folder. "All of our contracts with Weston for the past fiscal year," she said, coming back to her seat. "The one on top is what you need to see."

She opened the folder and pulled out the contract on top—a few pages stapled together. My heart sped up as she flipped to the last page and flattened it against the desk. Her eyes scanned the paper until she found what she was looking for.

"Here," she said, turning the paper around so I could see it. She pointed at a clause. "This is a new clause. And for the record, it's not just Weston's account. We're adding this to many of our new clients' contracts, even the new barber shop."

I pulled the paper closer to me to read the clause in question: *"Any unfavorable or critical coverage of Weston Properties may result in immediate withdrawal of advertising funds without notice."*

Bingo.

My hands began to shake. This was it—I was holding actual, concrete evidence that Silas was handing Weston the power to manipulate the news. This proved that our loyalty was to our wealthiest ad clients, not the truth. Our reporting wasn't just biased, it was being bought and sold.

And it had to be stopped.

"Can you make a copy of this for me?" I asked, trying to sound calmer than I was.

"You're sure I won't be implicated?"

"You have my word, Tiffany. I promise."

Tiffany gave a small nod, got up from her chair, and walked to the copier in the corner. The copy she made was still warm when she handed it to me. I thanked her—honestly, I wanted to *hug* her—and hurried back upstairs to my cubicle, smoking gun in hand.

chapter thirty-five

chase

We were all experiencing the calm just before the storm on Friday morning. There was a different energy in the studio, at least amongst the people who knew about the exposé that was likely being delivered to people's doorsteps right as Jill and Bernard wrapped up their morning report. Meghan timed the online publication for 8:00 a.m., and when that time came across my phone, a knot formed in my stomach. For her. For all of us.

"That's it for today, folks. Thank you for starting your day with us!" Jill's voice carried across the studio to my desk, where I was rushing through some quick trims and edits of video clips. "I hope everyone gets out there and enjoys this warm weekend. Maybe you'll see me at the Woodvale Comic Con?"

I'd be heading to the convention center as soon as I wrapped up here. Sean and I had a busy day ahead of us—we'd be working with our volunteers and vendors to get everything set up for the next day. That was why I was hurrying through my work, prepping files and waiting for them to upload. I'd already returned a few emails and reviewed our segment line-up for Monday. It was miraculous, really, how much I could accomplish in a short amount of time when I was in a hurry to get out.

I was just getting all of my things packed up and put away when my phone lit up with a text from Meghan.

Meghan: It's live. I'm so afraid I've just made everything worse for all of us. I feel like I might throw up.

Immediately, I dropped my bag on my desk chair and headed toward the studio doors. Jill must have sensed my urgency, because she looked up from her papers at the news desk and called out, "Where's the fire?"

I turned around with my hands in my pockets. "Meghan's having a slight panic attack up there. I'm going to go make sure she's okay."

"Wait for me, then." She removed her lapel mic and spun in her chair to get up from the desk. We walked out of the studio together, both of us keeping our eyes peeled for Silas, like he might already be on a rampage in this building somewhere.

We ran into Sarah in the hallway, carrying a coffee thermos as she greeted some late-arriving kids. Her eyes widened when she saw us. "Is today the day?"

"It's published," I answered.

"Oh gosh." She peered over her shoulder like she, too, feared Silas was lurking around. Owen had agreed to talk to Meghan for the exposé, detailing the way Silas tried to twist Sarah's arm into letting him have a spot on the podcast. That was just another example of how the man used his power to manipulate people. It was understandable why Sarah would be nervous like us. "I hope it all works out."

"It will," Jill said, holding her head up high.

When we got to the newspaper newsroom, it was exactly what I feared. Meghan was slumped over her desk, her head buried in her arms, with her published article up on her laptop screen. There was our headline: *The News You Deserve: How Power and Profits Have Corrupted Our Coverage.*

Xander was sitting just outside of her cubicle scrolling on his phone, and Graham was pacing with a cordless phone in his hand. "Oh, sweetie," Jill said, taking in the sight of her best friend. "You should be feeling on top of the world right now."

"She's cycled through about ten mood swings in the last twenty minutes," Xander muttered. "Don't worry, the confidence will return."

Meghan lifted her head to look at me, her face red from the position she'd been sitting in. "If something bad happens to the company and we all lose our jobs, it's all my fault."

I squatted beside her, placing my hand on her thigh. "Hey. Did you force any of us to put our names on that byline?"

She shook her head.

"Exactly. We let you write it because you're the one with the talent, but we're all in on this." I gave her leg a squeeze. "For us to know what he's doing to this network and silently watch it happen would have been the bigger risk."

Meghan took a deep breath and nodded. "I know. I know you're right."

The newsroom phone rang, making us all jump. Graham walked away to answer it. "Phone's been ringing off the hook all morning," Xander said.

I nodded, rising to my feet again. "Anything from Silas yet?"

"Nope. He's MIA."

"Good. I hope he's in hiding like a scared little boy," Jill said. "Like the terrorist he is."

Xander grinned. "Jesus, Jill."

"Do you think people have read it yet?" Meghan lifted her head to look at her computer screen. "I wonder how they're reacting."

"I shared it to the Concerned Citizens of Woodvale Group from my fake troll account," Xander said. "The comments are rolling in already."

I watched Xander scroll through Facebook comments on his phone. "You have a troll account?"

"I enjoy getting the people riled up."

Meghan twirled around in her chair to face him. "Is that how you've been racking up more views on your stories this whole time?"

Xander pulled his phone away from his face and blinked. There was her answer.

"You sneaky little bastard," Meghan said.

"Nobody told me I couldn't." Xander shrugged.

"I'm telling Graham."

"Who gets credit for the exposé in your little competition?" I nodded my head toward Meghan. "She does, right?"

"Graham said it doesn't count," Xander said, glancing at Meghan, "since both of our names are on the byline."

Just then, Graham came up behind us, stretching his arm out to hand Meghan the phone. "Will you take calls for a little bit?"

She looked up at him with panicked eyes. "Where are you going?"

Graham took a slow, deep breath and put his hands in pockets. "They want me to come downstairs for an emergency meeting with the entire board."

"Oh shit," I blurted.

"Yeah," he said. "Oh God, I can feel my heart beating in my butthole."

Ignoring that weird statement, I reached out to touch his arm. "Hey. Stand your ground in there." I swallowed, knowing plenty about Graham's history of kissing Silas's ass, based on what Meghan had told me. "Make sure no one here gets thrown under the bus."

"That's not going to happen." He looked me in the eyes, and I knew he was telling the truth. Dropping his gaze to Meghan, he added, "If one person takes the fall over this, I'll make sure it's me."

He and Meghan exchanged a nod, and then he was on his way, leaving the four of us there to sigh and exchange looks. I felt my phone buzz in my pocket and pulled it out to see a message from Sean. He'd sent a photo of the exhibit hall starting to come together and wanted to know when I'd get there to help.

"I need to go," I said, putting my hand on Meghan's back. I hated that I had to leave when she was stressing out like this. "Sean and I have to set up. It's going to be a long day."

"Okay, good luck," she said, giving me a smile that didn't seem too forced. "I guess I probably won't see you until tomorrow, then."

I panicked. I had nothing but Comic Con duties from dawn until well past dark the next day. Had I agreed to cover an assignment with Meghan and forgotten it? "What's tomorrow?"

She licked her lips, her smile getting wider. "I'm coming to your convention, silly."

"Oh." My mouth fell open. "You—I—tickets are sixty bucks at the door. Text me when you get there, and I'll-"

"I already have a ticket," she said, ruining my plan to get her in for free. I couldn't hide my shock. "I've been getting your email blasts with the event schedule and everything."

I laughed. "Okay, then I guess I'll see you there." I leaned down to kiss her on the temple, which she turned into a kiss on the lips with a quick tilt of her head. I touched the side of her face with one hand. "Good luck today. Keep me updated."

"I will."

Before I left, I glanced from Xander to Jill. "You guys got this?" I nodded toward Meghan, knowing they'd both understand.

"We'll keep your girlfriend from spiraling, Chase," Jill assured me. The inclusion of the word *girlfriend* set my heart on fire. If Meghan's best friend was saying that, it must be true.

I glanced at Xander, who rolled his eyes with a reluctant, "I'm not going anywhere."

She was in good hands.

**

When I arrived, the convention center was already buzzing with pre-event chaos, with the massive exhibit hall coming together bit by bit. Vendors wheeled in crates of merch, a team assembled a stage, and volunteers set up tables and chairs in between lines of gaff tape on the floor. There was still so much that needed to be done, it was hard to know where to start. One of our vendors was disgruntled about being placed too far from an outlet, despite not paying extra for access to electricity. I did my best to track down an extension cord and got busy taping it to the floor to prevent guests from tripping over it.

I shuffled backward on the floor, bending over the cord, when my butt suddenly made contact with something—or someone. "Oh shit, I'm sorry," I said as I whirled around.

And there was Ethan Killian.

He let out a deep laugh, removing his sunglasses. "That was actually my fault—I wasn't paying attention." My brain short-circuited for a few seconds. Ethan looked even cooler in person, wearing a brown leather jacket over a faded Counting Crows T-shirt. He shot me that unmistakable roguish grin he was known for and said, "Ethan Killian."

Oops, I hadn't noticed he was holding out his hand for me to shake. "Oh, uh—hi. I'm—?" Did I just forget my name? It took a couple seconds for it to come to me as we shook hands. "Chase. I'm one of the guys in charge. I think you've mostly been in communication with my… other guy."

Ethan tucked his sunglasses into the collar of his shirt, grinning at the way I stumbled over my words. I ran my hand through my hair, doing my best to calm myself down, but my heart was pounding in my chest. I glanced around, wondering if Sean was aware Ethan was here already. "I'm sorry," Ethan said, sticking his hands in his pockets. "I'm not trying to thwart your set-up plans here. I just checked into my hotel this morning and decided to head out and explore your town. And that took all of… forty-five minutes. There's not a lot out there."

"Sorry," I said, like Woodvale's dullness was my fault.

Ethan chuckled. "It's okay. Anyway, I just thought I'd take a gander at where you'll have me set up tomorrow, is that okay?"

Fuck. We hadn't even begun assembling his autograph-signing area yet. No backdrop, no table and chair, no queue ropes—all of that was still sitting in a U-Haul in the parking lot.

"Actually," I said, looking over my shoulder. "It's going to be right around this area. I'm sorry, we don't have that set up yet."

"Hey, it's cool," he said, likely sensing my nervousness. The way he studied my face only elevated my anxiety, though—what was he trying to figure out? "I drove past the haunted Banyon Manor."

My brain stalled again. "What?"

"It doesn't look so ominous in the daytime, does it?"

"I'm sorry, what? How do you—?"

"Oh, I watched quite a few of your videos before I agreed to come. Had to find out a little bit about the people in charge, you know? Your YouTube channel was the first thing that popped up. Fascinating stuff."

I had to hold myself back from repeating "what" for a third time. "You think the videos are... fascinating?"

"Oh yeah, of course," Ethan said, "I mean, you're a talented storyteller. The way you weave the history of the locations you investigate into present-day myths about the ghosts that supposedly haunt them? It's compelling as hell." He grinned with a playful twinkle in his eye, like he knew this compliment could potentially change my life. He might have even been bullshitting me just to make my day, but I didn't care. Ethan Killian, beloved sci-fi icon, was a fan of *me*.

"Wow, thank you," I said, shifting on my feet. "Most people watch our videos for Sean. He's the main draw."

Ethan's brows furrowed. "Yeah, he's definitely entertaining. I'm more of a history buff though, so I get really into the storytelling aspect." He clapped me on the shoulder. "Just don't tell me this convention hall is haunted, or I might not show up tomorrow, alright?"

I laughed. "I think you're good."

He stood next to me for a moment and looked around the space, taking in all the volunteers setting up tables and hanging decorations. He gave a satisfied nod and started to turn toward the exit.

"Could I get a selfie?" I blurted. My cheeks felt warm, but I had to ask it. Who knew if I'd remember to get a picture with him in the midst of all the chaos the following day? He agreed, putting his arm around my shoulder as I pulled my phone out. In my first attempt to snap the selfie, I had the camera facing the wrong way like some kind of idiot. Ethan was patient with me, though, even suggesting we "take a silly one," in which he gave me bunny ears.

That was going to be framed on my wall for the rest of eternity.

"Thank you," I said, shaking his hand again. I glanced around for Sean, but he was at the far end of the room up on the stage, talking to the sound people. Before I could suggest that Ethan should introduce himself to Sean, he waved at me and ducked out of the exit.

Did that actually just happen?

I opened my photos app and scrolled.

Yeah, that just happened. Immediately, I texted the "silly" selfie to Xander, wanting to make him jealous. He'd probably get his own selfie with Ethan during his interview the next day, but I still had to gloat.

Xander: Holy shit. What's he like in person? Was he cool?

Chase: So fucking cool.

Xander: I knew it.

Chase: Any updates on the Silas situation??

Xander: Nothing.

Xander: Actually, Graham just walked back in with a shit-eating grin. Talk later

chapter thirty-six

meghan

"Gather 'round. Big news. Hurry up."

I felt like I might throw up as Xander, Byron, Devonte, and I made our way to the front of the newsroom, where Graham stood at the head of the conference table rubbing his chin. But he was smiling, and that was a good sign.

He'd been downstairs for almost three hours, with no word from anyone about what was happening in that meeting. Jill told us they drew the shades in the conference room, leaving us all in the dark. All day, we fielded online comments and phone calls from people wanting to know what was going to happen to the news network, but we didn't have any answers to give.

But maybe we would now. Graham watched us all take our seats, his raised eyebrows creating creases on his forehead like he was in a state of shock. "What did you find out, Graham?" I asked, pulling up my chair. "Is anyone losing their job?"

He held his palms together in front of his mouth and took a deep breath. With a slow exhale, he lowered his hands and said, "Silas Brown has been placed on administrative leave."

My jaw dropped. Across from me Xander let out a low whistle, running a hand through his hair. "Holy shit." I gripped the edge of the table, my heartbeat pulsing through my ears. My head spun with questions, but I was momentarily unable to speak. I decided to just let Graham explain.

"He's being investigated by the board of directors." Graham leaned onto the table, putting all of his weight on his hands, and looked into my eyes. "Meghan, you kicked the hornet's nest with your exposé. Everything you wrote—it's all just the tip of the iceberg."

"What do you mean?"

"There's a lot I can't repeat, and even more that I don't know. But I will say this—the board already had Silas under a magnifying glass. Some of them were willing to sweep his shady behavior under the rug, but your article forced them to address it." He paused, clearing his throat, and stood up a little straighter. "What I can tell you is that when they looked deeper into Silas's dealings with Weston, they uncovered some… misappropriation of funds."

"Embezzlement?" Xander questioned.

Devonte clicked his tongue. "Sounds like textbook embezzlement to me."

Graham looked down at the table. "I don't want to use that term. But money has been shifted around in a way that doesn't totally make sense. Some funds have disappeared altogether."

"Are you saying this could lead to an arrest?" I asked.

"I don't know. Too early to tell."

Xander glanced from me back to Graham. "What do we do now?"

"The only thing we can do is wait for them to dig through the mess and decide if it's enough to take Silas down. As far as our reporting on this goes, we will have to wait a few days until we know more. And in the meantime, do *not* take any calls from anyone associated with John Weston."

"Does this mean I'm off the hook with my assignment?" Byron asked. "I was supposed to interview that Weston fellow this afternoon…"

"Yeah, cancel that," Graham said, and everyone at the table could sense Byron's relief as he exhaled. "Everyone can just carry on like they did before Silas was involved, as far as I'm concerned. But speaking of that…"

He stood up a little straighter and angled his body toward the chart on the chalkboard, where Xander was still clearly in the lead. Both of our names were on this Silas article, so despite its virality, neither of us got credit.

"Does anyone remember what today is?"

I looked at the date on the newspaper sitting at the center of the table. May 8th. Why did that ring a bell? Was it Graham's birthday?

Finally, I realized our contest was over.

Xander had officially won, and in that moment, I didn't even care. He was staring back at me like this realization hit him at the very same time, his eyes widening just slightly. "Have fun in New York, Xan."

Graham scratched the side of his head with a nervous sigh. "I, uh… I actually did get a confetti cannon, just to annoy you guys, but it sort of doesn't feel right. I left it in my car."

"Thank you for that," Xander said, staring down at the table.

Everyone was quiet for a moment. Graham turned away from us with his hands in the back of his pockets and paced a little bit, like he was anxious about something. When he turned back around, he rubbed his nose and said, "Okay, don't hate me for this, guys, but…"

Xander and I exchanged a glance. We were probably going to hate him for this, weren't we? "Spill it, Graham," I demanded. "What'd you do?"

"I… might have actually had tickets for the ECJ conference for the both of you this entire time."

I blinked, struggling to process Graham's words. "Tell me you're joking."

He held up both of his hands in defense. "Hear me out, okay? I thought it'd be the best way to push you two. Get a little fire going."

"I interviewed a goddamn *bird.*" Xander crossed his arms with a scowl, and suddenly, this wasn't as serious. I shook my head, but I couldn't prevent myself from smiling.

"You sneaky, manipulative, little asshole." Even as I insulted him, Graham smiled back with twinkling eyes, making me glad I had a boss I could say these things to without any repercussions whatsoever. "Tell me I don't have to share a hotel room with you guys?"

"No, no, you'll get your own room. We'll discuss this all further when it gets closer. Anyway, guys," Graham took a deep breath and shook his head in disbelief. "That's all I have. Good work, Meghan. We all owe you a lot right now."

He gave me a little congratulatory nod before leaving the newsroom. Byron and Devonte returned to their cubicles, but Xander and I stayed glued to our seats for a little longer. The newsroom felt oddly quiet. Too quiet.

"Are you upset I'm going to the conference with you?" I asked Xander.

He glanced up without moving his head. "No. You belong there." And with that, he knocked on the table a couple of times and stood up. I could have hugged him right then, and truth be told, I *really* wanted to, but I knew he would just push me away. I sat there and smiled instead, with the knowledge that I'd earned two rare compliments from Xander Pierce in one week.

I stayed put just a little longer, letting that moment linger before grabbing my phone and heading outside. I had two pieces of important news to share with Chase, and I couldn't wait a second longer.

Kendall had her class on the freshly mowed school lawn, playing a raucous game of Duck Duck Goose. She looked up and waved at me as I walked past. Just as I waved back, a girl with long, brown hair tagged Kendall with a triumphant, "Goose!" and she shot to her feet. Their giggles echoed off the side of the building as they ran around the circle.

I smiled at the sight but kept moving until I reached my car. Once inside, I sank into the driver's seat, exhaling as I tapped Chase's name. He answered on the second ring.

"Hey," I said. "You sitting down?"

"Oh boy," he replied, his voice wary. "Do I need to be?"

I cut right to the chase. "Silas is on administrative leave," I told him. "He's under investigation, and I think my reporting just scratched the surface of his corruption. He's out."

Chase clicked his tongue. "Damn. That's a relief. Glad he won't be looming around my desk anymore."

I couldn't help but laugh, even though I still felt uneasy. "At least he liked you."

"I didn't *want* that asshole to like me. And I definitely didn't like what he was doing to everyone else. The way he talked to you and Jill… it was appalling."

"I know." I relaxed against my seat. "I just feel weird, you know? I'm relieved, but I'm also anxious about what comes next."

Chase's voice softened. "Whatever happens, you did what needed to be done. You should be proud of yourself."

His words settled over me like a warm blanket, but before I could respond, he added something that stopped me in my tracks.

"And Meghan… you know your mom and dad are smiling down on you so hard right now."

I sucked in a breath, the words hitting me square in the chest. I hadn't realized how much I needed to hear that until that very moment. A lump rose in my throat, making it impossible to speak for a moment. A memory flashed through my mind, a vision of myself running through the front door of my childhood home to tell my parents I made the fourth-grade spell bowl team. The night before, they each ran through the list of words with me, both of them assuring me I'd do just fine, despite my inability to remember how many Cs were in the word *necessary*.

"I think a celebration is *necessary*, don't you?" my dad asked my mom after school that day. The three of us went to Applebee's for supper, where they bragged about me to our server.

A burst of laughter from Kendall's class over on the lawn made the memory dissolve, leaving a dull ache in my chest. Tears streamed down my face, and I couldn't hold back my loud, shaky breaths. "Oh Meghan," Chase said, his voice gentle but strained. "I'm sorry. I didn't mean to bring you down."

"No," I managed, holding back another sob as I rubbed my pendant between my fingers. "I'm glad you mentioned them. I needed that reminder that they're still with me—somehow."

Chase cleared his throat. "They're constantly cheering you on from the other side. You have so many people in your corner, Meg, both here and in the afterlife." He paused for a moment, listening to me take another deep breath. "Hell, even Fannie and Evelyn are probably proud of you for taking Silas down, although perhaps a little disappointed you didn't handle it with poison..."

I laughed through my tears. In just the span of a few minutes, Chase had given me exactly what I needed: he'd reminded me that my parents were still with me in spirit, with words I so desperately needed to hear. And then he put a smile back on my face just when I thought I might crumble from the weight of my grief.

With him, I knew I'd be okay.

chapter thirty-seven

chase

Sixty vendors, four panel discussions, and one C-list celebrity attracted three thousand attendees to the inaugural Woodvale Comic Con. We were only halfway through the day when Sean and I found each other at the center of the exhibit hall to simultaneously declare we'd be making this an annual event. Besides a couple of minor snags, the convention was an enormous success.

People came out in droves to meet Ethan Killian, of course, but he wasn't the only draw. Artists stopped me and told me it had been their most successful vendor fair of their lifetime. Families walked around in matching costumes, including Erika, Sean, and Dimitri—two Ghostbusters and the cutest Stay Puft Marshmallow I'd ever seen.

Like Erika and Sean, I was wearing a Ghostbusters costume, but I'd shipped the outfit to my mom in Michigan so she could sew on a very important detail: an Egon nametag.

Meghan was going to love that. I'd hoped I could show her the costume before I had to go on stage for Owen's live podcast recording in one of the presentation rooms, but I couldn't find her in the crowd. I knew she was there somewhere, because my last text from her said she was on her way, but I'd have to track her down later. It was time to chat with Owen.

I was used to speaking in front of a camera, sometimes in front of a crowd, but that room was filled with a hundred and fifty people. They were all here for Owen, of course, but I felt the pressure to be a good podcast guest for him. Now that Sean was giving up paranormal investigating, I couldn't rely on his funny commentary to lighten the mood. Somehow, I had to make ghost hunting sound exciting while also appealing to the science nerds. Just before we went on, Owen slapped my back and said, "Let's go get 'em, tiger," like a cool, older brother would, and it made my nervousness melt away. Oddly enough, the fact he was cosplaying as Han Solo made him even easier to talk to.

On stage, we dove into the tools I used to detect paranormal activity, and he asked a lot of questions about the video equipment we used. When he asked if I'd uncovered anything particularly fascinating lately, I shared a little bit about the sigils Meghan and I had discovered. "I don't want to give too much away, but we have some new info on the Woodvale Witch we'll be revealing on our blog, *Woodvale Whispers,* pretty soon."

Did I just promote our blog to Owen's thousands of listeners? I worried it might annoy him—like I was using his platform to get more views on our website—but he wanted to know more about it. "Well now you've got me intrigued," Owen said, "and for those of you unfamiliar, the tale of the Woodvale Witch is one of Southern Indiana's oldest and creepiest local legends."

Owen went on to give a little background on the lore behind Evelyn, and I interjected to add some key details every so often. As I opened my mouth to tell him how many people attended Evelyn's public execution, my gaze drifted to the crowd—and that's when I saw Meghan.

Wedged between Xander and Jillian in the press area just in front of the stage, she was staring back up at me with the cutest smirk.

Because she was dressed like Wednesday Addams.

With her hair in two braids, she wore a black dress with a white collar complete with black tights and black boots. I could tell she was fighting the smile, doing her best to pull Wednesday's signature deadpan stare, but it wasn't working.

After a few seconds, I turned back to Owen, trying to remember what we were just talking about. "I'm sorry, I lost my train of thought there."

Owen chuckled, clearly amused by my sudden distraction. "It's okay, it's hard not to be distracted by all the cosplayers in this room. I can see at least three Jokers from where I'm sitting, and it's a little unsettling."

He wasn't wrong about that.

We wrapped up the interview, and Owen told his listeners—and our live audience—to check out the show notes for links to my blog and YouTube channel. I felt a buzz of excitement flowing through me as Owen and I stood up and shook hands. Thanks to him, the relaunch of *Woodvale Whispers* was already off to a great start. "Thank you, man," I said.

"No, thank you—this was a blast," Owen said, completing the firm handshake. He squinted toward the crowd filtering out the doors into the hall. "Now I have to figure out which of these Princess Leias is my wife."

I laughed as I hopped off the platform, making a beeline toward Meghan. She was mid-sentence with Jill, but I grabbed her by the waist anyway to pull her toward me. "Look at you," I whispered, tugging her body against mine to plant a kiss on her lips. She giggled into my mouth, putting her hands on my waist. "Is it weird that I find this really, really sexy?"

"That was kind of the point, Egon," she said, eyeing my nametag with a grin.

I pulled back from her so I could look her up and down. "Where and when did you get this costume?"

"Costume?" She looked down at her dress, flaring it out with her hands. "I already owned everything you see. This is no costume."

Of course it wasn't. I kissed her forehead, watching Xander and Jillian make their way across the hall to the cosplay dance. Jill was either dressed like April O'Neil from the *Teenage Mutant Ninja Turtles* or she'd just decided she was really into yellow pantsuits. I took Meghan by the hand, leading her out of the room. "I hope a lot of people turned out for the dance," I said, glancing at my watch. "It's been underway for about forty-five minutes."

When we got to the banquet room, however, it was like being transported back to my middle school Valentine's Day dance. Hordes of people clustered awkwardly along the walls, sipping their drinks or pretending to text. The dance floor was empty, despite the DJ's efforts to get everyone to throw their hands up. Only one sad guy in an inflatable T-rex costume tried, but the state of things was pretty pathetic. "This is painful," I whispered to Meghan, sidling up beside Xander and Jill at the back of the room. They were talking to Mason and Kendall, who were dressed like Thor and Barbie. That made sense. "Where's your kid?" Xander asked them.

"She got bored, and we had her grandpa come pick her up," Mason said, "so we could have a wild, kid-free night." He eyed the empty dance floor and inhaled. "Obviously."

Abigail approached from the other side, decked out in an impressive Poison Ivy cosplay. I caught Xander eyeing her bare legs before quickly shifting his gaze to Jill. "Wow, Xan," Abigail said, "I'm disappointed in you."

I swallowed, fearing she was about to call him out for ogling her body, but she grinned.

"You're the only one of us who didn't dress up."

"Because you all are nerds," he said, shaking his head. "I'm not one of you."

Meghan laughed, rolling her eyes as she interlocked her fingers with mine. "Bullshit. Did you or did you not bring your *Starlight* DVD for Ethan Killian to sign?"

"Shut up."

"We just need to get you some fairy ears and bat wings," Abigail said, giving Xander a playful shove that made Jill scoot closer to him and take his hand.

"Never say that combination of words to me ever again," Xander deadpanned just as Graham, of all people, wandered up.

"What the hell are you doing here?" Meghan blurted.

"Thanks for that warm welcome, Meghan. I have hobbies and interests, too, believe it or not." He dangled a swag bag in the air, scanning the row of misfits in front of him. "Damn it, I knew I should have dressed up like the rest of you. I would have at least worn my Sherlock hat."

"Aww," Jillian said, just as Xander mumbled, "Christ."

Graham shook his head, adjusting the bag on his wrist. "I have some news for you guys," he said, locking his eyes on Meghan's as those of us who worked for the news instinctively inched closer. Graham glanced over his shoulder like he might be overheard, turning around to announce, "Silas fled."

"What do you mean?" I asked.

"Left town. Skedaddled. Ran away with his tail tucked between his legs."

Meghan's mouth dropped open. "But why?"

"Because he knows what's coming," Graham said, "and he probably has more to hide than we even realize. It's not looking good for him."

"What's this mean for all of us?" Xander asked, glancing at Jill. "I mean, who's taking his place? For all we know, it could be someone even worse."

Graham stared back at Xander, a smug grin spreading from ear to ear. "Well, this might not be what you guys want to hear, but they've asked me to step in as the interim CEO until they—"

"No, that's good!" Meghan blurted. The rest of us nodded in agreement. Graham could be a kiss-ass, but he had our backs when we needed him most. He understood us a hell of a lot more than the men on the board, especially in his *Doctor Who* t-shirt.

He blinked in surprise. "You guys really think I should agree to it?"

"Yeah, but will you still be our editor?" Xander asked.

Graham took a deep breath. "I have to choose a temporary editor," he said, glancing from Meghan to Xander. "It would be just for the summer, or until they get things sorted out on top."

"Oh," Xander and Meghan said in unison, turning to each other. Were we about to witness a showdown? Xander glanced at the floor before turning to Graham. Nudging Meghan with his elbow, he said, "She should probably take that role. She's more suited for it."

Graham gave Xander a couple of slow blinks. "I know, that's why I was about to ask her and not you," he said. I had to suck on my bottom lip so I wouldn't laugh. "Meghan, what do you say? It's going to increase your workload, but you'll get a temporary raise."

I silently prayed Meghan would have enough confidence in herself and her abilities to say yes. She drew her eyebrows closer together, giving this some consideration. "Editor?"

"Temporarily. But you'll still be able to add that to your resume."

Meghan glanced at me, as if needing some kind of encouragement, but I kept my expression neutral. This had to be her decision. I bowed my head and stared at the floor, catching her adjusting her bangs in my peripheral vision. "Editor," she repeated. "I mean, I do already know how to put the layout together…"

"And I'll still be in the building when you have questions," Graham pointed out. "Are you in, or are you going to let the dingus next to you do it?" He nodded at Xander.

"I'll do it," she said, and my hand shot to her back in a sort of congratulatory hold. Meghan was so hot when she was confident. She'd earned this, and she fucking knew it. We all knew it. When she looked up at me, I saw happy tears forming in the corners of her eyes as I leaned down to kiss her on the temple.

"That's my girl," I whispered in her ear, making her bite her lip.

When I looked up, I spotted Sean making his way across the barren dance floor, shaking his head beneath the DJ's strobe lights. "This is sad," he said when he reached us.

"Why did we think a *dance* would be a good way to close out a Comic Con?" I pressed my palm to my forehead. "These are the kinds of people who skipped their high school prom to stay home and play *Dungeons and Dragons*."

"I told the DJ to play the *Guardians* soundtrack," Sean said, backing against the wall so he could look out at the room, "but it's not helping."

"Someone just has to start dancing, and others will jump in," Jill said, uncrossing her arms. And then she grinned at Meghan, yanking her away from me to drag her to the dance floor. I couldn't help but laugh at the way Jill forced Meghan to dance, twirling her to the rhythm of "Come and Get Your Love." Seconds later, Abigail, Sarah, and Kendall joined, and the five women bumped hips and pulled some of the lamest dance moves I'd ever witnessed. One of Sarah's space buns was coming loose, but she didn't seem to care—or notice.

Owen scooted closer to fill the gap. "Why are we with these dorky women?"

At that very second, Jill twerked against Meghan, who covered her face with both hands and backed away.

"That's why," Xander answered, trying not to smile as Jill waved for him to join her. He shook his head, mouthing a firm "no." Sarah was a bit more persuasive, though, coming over to pull Owen to the dance floor with both hands. It wasn't long before the rest of the guys, myself included, were awkwardly forming a circle around the women. Erika tapped Sean on the shoulder, and the two of them started dancing, with their chubby Stay Puft Marshmallow squished happily between their chests.

"I think it's working, "Graham pointed out a couple minutes later, nodding at the way a lot of other people were coming to the dance floor. Ewoks, Trekkies, two Spider-men pointing at each other—the amount of nerds brave enough to come to the dance floor increased by the minute.

The song faded into "O-o-h Child" by The Five Stairsteps, its tempo keeping the crowd moving while slowing just enough to compel me to put my hands on Meghan's waist and pull her close. "I can't believe I'm sleeping with the editor of the *Woodvale Times* tonight," I murmured in her ear.

"I'm pretty sure that transition doesn't happen until next week, so I'll let Graham know he's got a hot date tonight."

I chuckled against her cheek, inhaling the spicy, floral scent of her perfume. "I'm choosing to only focus on the words 'hot date' from that sentence."

Meghan brought her mouth to my ear. "You should tell me some sexy line Egon said in *Ghostbusters.*"

Pulling back so I could see her face better, I raised an eyebrow at her. "You… you've watched that movie, right?"

Meghan threw her head back and laughed, and I wrapped my arms around her a little tighter. Just as I leaned in, preparing to thank her for giving me a second chance, she surprised me with a kiss, cramming her tongue in my mouth with her hands on either side of my face.

"What was that for?" I breathed against her lips.

With her palms still pressed against my cheeks, Meghan focused on my eyes. "I love you," she said.

My heart could've burst right out of that stupid Ghostbusters jumpsuit. My hands flexed on her waist as I pulled her flush against me again, like she might slip away if I didn't hold on tight. Meghan loved me again. She *loved* me.

Her sudden declaration had me at a complete loss for words. Of course I loved her too, but I was too stunned to form the words right away. "Really? That's so cool," I laughed out.

Meghan giggled so hard she snorted. I hadn't heard *that* sound in ages. When she tilted her head back to laugh even harder, I kissed her on the neck.

"I *never* stopped loving you, Meg." I rested my forehead against hers, breathing her in. Our friends danced like idiots around us, but we stayed locked into our own little world for a moment longer. Nothing felt better than holding Meghan in my arms, and this time around, I'd never let her go.

Woodvale Whispers

Echoes of Forbidden Love:
The Secret Affair of the Woodvale Witch

For 170 years, the story of Evelyn Stewart has cast a dark shadow over Woodvale's history. Known to most as the infamous "Woodvale Witch," Evelyn was sentenced to death in 1846 for poisoning her husband. On that fateful day, over 10,000 spectators gathered outside the old courthouse to witness Indiana's last public hanging, hoping for a glimpse of something sinister. Many claimed to hear Evelyn singing hymns and chanting incoherently as she was led to the gallows, fueling the rumors that she was, indeed, a witch.

Evelyn lived deep in what is now Ackerman Woods, and, as the story goes, her spirit has wandered there ever since, trapped between this world and the next. Over the years, many people have witnessed a pale figure gliding silently among the trees, her long dress flowing behind her. Some even reported hearing Evelyn's mournful moan echoing through the park at dusk.

However, her spirit is not alone.

We've uncovered a second spirit haunting Ackerman Woods. Those brave enough to walk the trails after dark may also encounter the ghost of Fannie Decker, a local chicken farmer who lived just beyond the woods in the mid-1800s. Fannie and Evelyn would often meet by the waterfall, enjoying fresh vegetables from Fannie's garden or drinking brandy made from Evelyn's apple trees.

Wondering how we know all of this? We recently acquired a journal belonging to Fannie Decker herself. Within the pages of this journal, Fannie expresses a fondness for Evelyn that expands beyond platonic friendship. The two women were entangled in a passionate, clandestine romance, a kind of love forbidden in their time.

"The fire in the hearth matches the warmth of my loins. For both, I have Evvy to thank." Fannie's diary includes several mentions of Evelyn, whom she lovingly nicknamed Evvy. The two created a secret form of communication using symbols, enabling them to declare their love without being discovered.

In the journal, Fannie describes the poisonous foxglove planted in her garden—the very flowers that were ground into Jacob Stewart's tea, leading to his death. Could the women have conspired together? Was their plan to get Jacob out of the way so they could finally be together? Evelyn never implicated Fannie during her trial, choosing instead to take her secrets to the grave. Fannie met her own demise a few short years later, taken by the deadly blizzard of 1849. Their forbidden love remained buried in the shadows of Woodvale's history… until now.

With special permission from the parks department, we devoted ourselves to spending a full night in the woods, *Blair Witch* style. (Parks director Nolan Campbell wants us to remind our readers that camping in this section of the park is not typically permitted.) We pitched our tent in the exact spot where Evelyn's hut once stood, well beyond the marked trails that wind through the park.

Unfortunately, we didn't even make it until sunrise.

As you'll be able to hear in the video (attached), we awoke to a piercing, feminine-sounding shriek at 3:33 a.m. About thirty seconds later, we were able to capture a second scream on video. (Please ignore the sound of Meghan exclaiming, "Chase, I'm going to piss my pants.") After consulting with a local wildlife expert, we're aware it's possible the sound may have come from a bobcat in search of a mate. In fact, this is a detail your two bloggers disagree on. While Meghan leans toward logic and would prefers a scientific explanation, Chase insists the sound was Fannie Decker's voice echoing through time, crying out as she learned of her beloved's death sentence.

We'll let you give it a listen and decide for yourself. Is Ackerman Woods really haunted by the spirits of Evelyn Stewart and Fannie Decker, forever bound by love and tragedy? Or could the mysterious apparitions and sounds be explained by science?

One thing is certain—Woodvale's history is full of secrets, and Fannie & Evelyn's love affair is only the beginning of our exploration. We're determined to uncover more stories like theirs with this relaunch of *Woodvale Whispers*. We hope you're just as excited as we are to see where this journey takes us!

-Meghan & Chase

Acknowledgements

I first need to thank my husband, Clint, whose unwavering support while I was grieving the death of my father kept me going. You are all the best parts of Chase, Mason, and Owen combined. Thank you for reminding me that the love we read about in romance books can truly exist.

I want to thank the real-life Woodvale Smut Sluts: Haley, Anne, Salwa, Krista, Taneil, Marcilyn, Corinna, Elizabeth, Thomas, and Katie. Your belief in my work means the world to me. I love that I've been able to share my unfiltered thoughts and unedited drafts with y'all, and you're still here.

Megan—insert the Josh Peck "Megan!" meme here. Just kidding! Thank you for going through this draft with your em dash axe. (I couldn't let you take them all!) You truly are the best.

Huge shout-out to Lyssa for once again nailing it with the cover illustration. You captured Chase and Meghan perfectly.

Thank you to my family and friends who constantly cheer me on. You're the ones I turn to first when I have a book-related announcement. I would never have felt like I could do *any* of this without you guys.

I want to thank my beta/early readers for every morsel of feedback and unhinged comment left for me in the Google Doc. I live for your "AAAAAAAHHHHH!" reactions.

And lastly, I want to thank my readers and fans of the Woodvale series. I'm so glad you're here! Your enthusiastic DMs are the reason I keep writing.